MELANIE J FIRTH trained  inger,
and now teaches Perforr ıdary
school in South Yorkshire of all
things pink, fluffy, glittery nated
her since a very young age in the
dry stone wall of her back garden. Melanie describes herself as
a 'Spiritual Junkie' – addicted to all things magical and holistic.
As well as writing, she loves to spend her time watching her
beloved football team, Sheffield Wednesday, and being a Mummy
to her daughter and pets.

THE FAERY TALE OF

Rosie Quartz

MELANIE J FIRTH

SilverWood

Published in 2014 by SilverWood Books

SilverWood Books Ltd
30 Queen Charlotte Street, Bristol, BS1 4HJ
www.silverwoodbooks.co.uk

ISBN 978-1-78132-192-8 (paperback)
ISBN 978-1-78132-193-5 (ebook)

British Library Cataloguing in Publication Data
A CIP catalogue record for this book is available from the British Library

Set in Sabon by SilverWood Books
Printed on responsibly sourced paper

This book is dedicated to my beautiful Mum,
a true Faery Queen, who taught me always to follow
my heart and believe in my dreams.
I love you xxx

Contents

	Gratitude	8
	A Note on Faeries	11
1	The Runaway Cow	13
2	Guy Flower	26
3	Soggy Jeans	39
4	The Thirteenth of April	57
5	Helena Spotswood	69
6	Making Contact	83
7	The Last Snowflake	96
8	Spring in the Step	111
9	The Faery Ring	124
10	Homecoming	135
11	At the Agate Abode	144
12	The Fortune Teller	156
13	In the Quartz Palace	164
14	Dear Diary	173
15	Truth Tongue	189
16	Dear Diary Part II	201
17	Taken	212
18	The Faery Fancy Dress Ball	219
19	Jam Jars	231
20	In Search of Sulphur	242
21	Michael Depth	250
22	The Return?	259

Gratitude

This beautiful universe with its ever-serving Law of Attraction brought me the opportunity to share these stories and for that I am eternally grateful.

In addition, there are so many people who make my disco ball shine!

Glitter filled wishes and sparkly pink lip-gloss kisses to:

My cute as a button daughter who fills every room with sunlight. (And my furry daughters who mainly just fill every room with pet hair but are cherished all the same.)

My precious parents (obvs!) whose constant love, help, support and devotion enables me to do all the things and be all the things I could ever imagine wanting to be.

My totes amaze family; Nannan, Uncles, Aunties, Sisters, Brothers and Cousins whose team I feel so proud to be a part of. Thank you for everything you do for me.

My mucho fabuloso friends who make me giggle and smile. Promise we'll continue to shop, share secrets, eat, drink and be merry together for the rest of our days.

Catherine and Leanne for the real life cow, washing line and river experiences – the hilarious memory of which gave me the inspiration to pick up a pen and write the first line.

Helen, Emily and the whole Silverwood team who have worked tirelessly on my behalf and treated my book with ultimate care and respect. I am blessed to have found such wonderful people to share this new journey with. Agnes, my editor, who ironed out my naivety and has made me look far cleverer than I actually am. Ali, for the cover design of my dreams. It's a perfect representation of The Faery Tales and everything they stand for.

My three truly divine celebrity muses; Zac Efron, Samuel Preston and Christian Cooke, whose beautiful faces gave me an image on which to pin my three principal male characters in this story.

And You, who taught me about the first flutter of excitement and the first kiss. Oh to be that young again! Enjoy it, girls.

Finally thank you to the faeries for allowing me a glimpse of their world. And to you the readers for holding this book in your hands and realising that this is a tale you simply cannot afford to miss…

*The word 'faery' is French in origin and began to replace the
Old English word 'elf' during the Tudor period.*

*It is derived from the Latin term 'fatum' meaning
destiny or enchantment.*

*Throughout the years, faeries have been forgotten,
downtrodden and misrepresented. Especially in books.
They are not a figment of the human imagination.
In fact, I was lucky enough to meet one
and to learn of the Land they inhabit.*

So now I have a tale to tell…

1

The Runaway Cow

There is a lane that winds to the left and winds to the right, and if you were to walk the snaking track by foot, as many people often do on a sunny day, you would soon be out of breath, for the lane winds up and up towards the top of an extremely steep hill. There are a lot of hills in Steeple Village, but this one is probably the highest. Although cars occasionally bob and trundle upon the uneven cracks and loose stones of the lane, it is largely neglected by vehicles, since it leads to nothing but a great many fields. Tractors, of course, are easy to spy, if you are so inclined to take particular notice of them. Fields tend to equal farmers, and farmers drive tractors – the hum of which can generally be heard, if not at hand, then somewhere in the distance. The biggest mistake people often make on the lane is to attempt a family outing with bikes and picnics. I tried it myself once, and can tell you I never shall again. But like me, folk making this error are usually from out of town. The villagers of Steeple know better than to pedal the land rise, let alone under the weight of pork pies or pots of jam.

The three girls had found the lane as most people often do. They had been slightly bored during the long school holidays, and set off wandering with no particular place to be or point to prove. They were not in search of a great adventure. On the contrary, they were enjoying the sublime stillness and comforting quiet that countryside brings. They linked arms as they climbed, the way twelve-year-old girls do, and purposely tried to keep their steps in time with one another – an enjoyable, unspoken game. There was an irony, however, to their present preference for silence, since only half an hour previously they were banging the hell out of a set of drums in Sally's garage. Billie had turned up the amp so loud on her shiny, red electric guitar that the cobwebbed windows had rattled in their panes. Rosie had underestimated the power of her own new microphone and all three had cowered with hands over ears when the reverb screeched. As anticipated, Sally's mum appeared at the garage door, looking very angry; a tea towel and soapy casserole dish in her hand. She didn't need to say a word. They'd been warned enough times. They could only rehearse in here under very strict conditions. It looked like the wannabe rock stars had just pushed their limits.

"I'm ready for some fresh air anyway," said Sally, guiltily placing her drum sticks upon her dad's fridge of bottled beers. "The heat's sending me dizzy and we're not getting very far. The chorus sucks. We have to write some better lyrics. Maybe a walk will inspire us."

"Or a chocolate chip ice cream from the shop," added Billie, unhooking a rainbow coloured strap from around her neck. "Sorry, Mrs Nuttall. We'll get out of your hair for a while. It's really good of you to let us base our band here. You won't regret it when we're famous and mentioning you in live interviews."

"I'll be wanting more than a mention for putting up with that racket!" Mrs Nuttall called as they slipped past her into the hot garden. "A new car would be nice – or a thatched bungalow – or just a million pounds…" But she was smiling now, back to drying the dishes as they slipped out of sight.

The Steeple village shop, which doubles as a post office, is curiously small, with a sign on its yellow wooden door requesting that no more than four people enter at any one time. The shop sits amid a row of equally tiny terraced houses, all with a tangled sheet of ivy hiding their natural stone walls.

Sally peeped inside and a tin bell tinkled above her head,

alerting the shopkeeper of custom. Luckily it was empty, and the girls were able to make their way straight over to the ice cream counter by the till. Rosie was ready to hand her coins over for a double rum and raisin cone, but she screamed, and snatched back her hand.

"Oh my God! Oh my God! What is it, Rosie?" Billie and Sally jumped up and down on the spot, arms flapping, their own nerves shot by the sudden outburst from their friend.

"Something…something just brushed past my legs!" Everyone present, including the lady shopkeeper, looked down at Rosie's legs which were slightly pink from the recent weeks of sunshine, and poked out of the hem of a short summer skirt. Her scrunched socks and shiny white trainers were about all else there was to see.

"It was furry! Eew!"

"Yes, well, cats usually are dear," said the rather short, round lady in a patronising tone, still holding out her stubby fingers across the counter for the ice cream money. She tutted. "It'll have been Spooky on her way back in through the cat flap. Look, there she goes into the stock cupboard in search of her lunch. She's in luck 'cos I've just put it out. Great white ball of fluff! Did I say, that's 95p please?"

"Oh yuk! I'm going to be sick." Coughing and spluttering like *she* was a cat dislodging a hairball, Rosie shoved her cone into Billie's hands and made a dash through the door, tinkling the bell again in her wake.

"Err…sorry about that," Billie said, taking it upon herself to pay the rounded and now reddening shopkeeper from her own purse. "She's allergic to cats – terrified of them. Makes her go all funny if one touches her. Have a nice day."

Back out in the village square, Rosie was fanning herself with a wad of post-it notes from her handbag. She leant against a set of iron railings which protected some battered Medieval stocks. They were considered a tourist attraction and drew many people to the ornate gates of the Steeple churchyard. Rosie, however, had little consideration for them right now.

"Are you okay, Rose?" said Sally, offering her friend a sour sweet from her open pack. "Wow, you freaked. What is it with you and cats anyway?"

"Do you get a rash or something?" said Billie.

"I just hate them, alright? Come on, let's get out of this square."

And that was when they set off up the lane, Rosie soon forgetting about the cat. The ice creams and sweets from the shop ran out and each girl, though united by friendship, became lost in her own thoughts. Rosie suspected the other two were immersed in imagined melodies and potential lyrics for their band. A pleasant picture they made, strolling side by side. Elderly couples walking in high spirits and hiking boots smiled fondly at them as they passed. Rosie caught sight of their reflection in the muddy water of a horse's drinking trough and giggled at the image. They looked just like a staircase, sweeping along in decreasing size order. Admiringly she surveyed her two companions.

Billie Featherstone was the tallest, in fact strikingly tall for her twelve years. She had long black hair, the intensity of coal, and on more than one occasion had been mistaken for a much older girl. Her mother's side of the family had come from China and although that was now several generations behind, the Oriental beauty could still be traced in her skin tone and eyes. Billie's appearance did little, however, to dictate her manner. Of all the girls in Steeple, she was the renowned tomboy. Billie just wasn't complete without metal toe riggers and a baseball cap tilted back to front. She liked the Goth style and most of her black, slashed clothing was emblazoned with skulls or angry album titles. Vampires, she said, were the coolest thing on the planet, and Sally and Rosie had to use all their skills to keep her from turning every song they wrote into a gory bloodbath. Amazingly, in respect of Billie's raw individuality, people (especially boys) loved her. Not even a long metal-spiked trench coat on a hot summer's day could hide her beauty and charm. People naturally warmed to Billie. She could tease and wind you up in a strangely enjoyable way. She was easy to be around. She empowered others with her own confidence. Although Sally and Rosie were her best and closest friends, they were certainly not the only ones.

Sally Nuttall, on the other hand, was quite timid and shy with anyone she did not know so well. Opposite to Billie in every way, tiny Sally feared the days of her growing an extra half inch would never come. With sugar-brown pigtails and long eyelashes, she was adorably cute, in a porcelain doll fashion. Impeccably polite and sweet-natured, she was just the kind of girl your parents would want you to hang out with, as Mrs Quartz, Rosie's mum, had stated on numerous occasions when Sally had been round for tea.

And in the middle was Rosie. *And I'm just me*, she thought, as the sun burned even warmer down the back of her neck. *Middle height, middle looks – just unremarkable old me.*

But I shall tell you what the innocent and clouded mind of Rosie Quartz had missed out. For a start, picture this. She had hair which tumbled to her waist in waves the colour of powdery, yellow, seaside sand. She had cheeks which shone as warm, pink and rosy as her namesake suggested, and eyes which twinkled silvery-blue like stars on a clear night. She had a beautiful and powerful singing voice, which had initially inspired the girls to start up their quest for rock band super stardom when they'd met at Steeple High School a year ago. She was kind and generous and loving and trusting – all of the things we know to be endearing in a young lady. Yes indeed, Rosie Quartz was anything but unremarkable. And yet, as she reached the top of the lane, and all three friends breathed a sigh of relief at the hill's decline, she still had a long way to go before she would find out just how special a girl she really was.

"It's just green fields for miles and miles," said Billie, adjusting her cross-bones cap after clearing a rickety, moss-eaten stile with her long legs.

"Yellow fields," corrected Sally with a bright smile. "Look at the buttercups!" She bent down and picked one, twirling it around between her thumb and finger. "Let's see if you like butter!" She thrust the flower beneath Billie's chin, who knocked it away irritably.

"Okay then, it's just green *and yellow* fields for miles and miles," said Billie, "with dots of black and white if you want to count the cows as well."

"It's just beautiful, that's what it is!" cried Rosie. "The perfect place to write our music. Come on, let's find a spot to sit and feel inspired. Meditate amid the moos!"

Sally laughed and grasped at more buttercup stems as she skipped, already intent on making a chain.

Twenty minutes later they were propped up on their elbows, lying flat amid sweet smelling grass, now strewn not only with buttercup weeds, but also florescent pink post-it notes which they had stuck around them. Cows munched lazily, but paid little attention to their fair-weather visitors. Thin bands of cloud moved slowly above, like a careless conveyer belt in the corn-flower sky. Funny faces and mythical monsters formed hidden pictures among the white patterns. *A witch on a broomstick. A bucket and spade.* There was a whole other story up there if you took the time to read its pages.

"I could just drink a pint of ice cold milk," said Rosie, momentarily looking up from her scrawl on the paper.

"Milk! Ugh! More like ice-filled lemonade! How can milk be refreshing on a hot day?" Billie eyed the nearest cow suspiciously.

"I like milk."

"Well, the supply's there on tap if you fancy getting it. Just help yourself." Billie pointed and waved. The sudden movement of her arm made the cow lift its head. Nonplussed, it blinked and went back to grazing.

Rosie laughed. "No thanks. I like milk, but not that much."

Sally had been humming throughout their conversation, a pile of buttercup bracelets and anklets now deserted at her side. "What about this, girls?" She repeated the tune, this time tapping out an additional drum beat with a twig on a loose rock.

"Yeah, I like it," said Rosie, sitting up cross-legged in attention, "and it sort of goes with what I've just written." She grabbed a post-it note and began to sing.

Don't you know I've always thought of you?
It started long before I met you.
I've spent my childhood scouring clouds for you.
I guess it's something that I just had to do,
'Cos I never could stop thinking of you.

There was a silence in which the first breeze of the afternoon lifted the fringes of the girls' hair, refreshingly cool and welcome against their foreheads.

"What does it mean?" asked Billie after a while. "Who is it about?"

"It's about nobody," Rosie shrugged. "That's the point. I haven't met them yet."

"But how can you be thinking of them if you haven't met them?"

"Duh!" Sally said, aiming the long twig she had used for drumming at Billie's head like an arrow. "Stop being so literal. It's 'art' Billie! Isn't it obvious? The song's about 'The One.' You know. That special guy who you hope exists somewhere, and you know you'll meet someday when you're older, but you just don't know when or where."

"Oh per-lease!" said Billie, pretending to push her fingers down her throat. "Since when did we become all sad and sloppy? We're a *rock* band!"

Sally got to her feet, brushing grass and decapitated buttercups from her denim skirt as she stood. "We're a *band*," she said. "We're supposed to be writing about things that mean something and matter to us."

"Exactly," Billie stood too, accentuating the sudden difference in size between the pair, "and the last time I checked, boys were certainly NOT at the top of our priority list!"

Rosie sat giggling at the argument she had unwittingly caused. Shy, retiring Sally had a wonderful way of putting all that timidity behind her when Billie purposely wound her up.

"It's easy for you to say that. Boys throw themselves at you. You're a boy magnet. You've a million boyfriends."

"Oh, I wouldn't go that far," said Billie, but her cheeky smirk belied the truth of the matter. "Just thousands." They all laughed. "All I'm saying is that when we're selling records, we want to please our paying public. And believe me, vampires seeking suckable blood is the only way forward."

Rosie was the only one left sitting on the ground when the sudden noise put an abrupt end to the conversation.

"What...?"

It started as a rumble, like approaching thunder, but the sun, ever persistent in blinding their eyes, logically spelled out the fact that such a change in weather was quite impossible. Then it sounded like a struggling car engine, a tractor maybe, or someone revving against a locked handbrake. Perhaps it was an electric saw, someone at work in their tool shed, and yet it would have to be some saw for the noise to travel so far. The nearest houses were way back down in Steeple Square. Had they left the guitar amp on, kicking out reverb and sending Sally's mum crazy? No. In fact, as the rumble grew increasingly closer to the girls, it sounded remarkably like a...

"COW!!!"

The animal was charging towards them. A newly burned track of upturned soil lay like a trampled carpet in its wake. Unlike the docile beasts which had shared the field with Rosie, Sally and Billie just moments ago, this cow was not black and white splattered, but a light brown shade – and angry. VERY ANGRY. Running faster than the legs of a cow could feasibly carry her, the animal tripped and stumbled with every step, skimming grass and buttercups in all directions. This did little however to detract the speed at which she ambled on towards the girls, and littler still to dilute her apparent annoyance and distress at something hot in her pursuit.

Sally screamed. "Oh my God! We're going to die!"

"Move it!" shouted Billie. "It's coming straight at us!"

Grasping as many of the precious sticky post-it notes as she could find and simultaneously stuffing them into her open handbag, Rosie rolled sideways and swiftly launched herself off the ground, like a choreographed Kung-Fu super-move. Her friends were now a good ten yards in front of her, their only priority to exit the buttercup field.

"Hey, wait up! Don't leave me!" Arms flapping above her head, handbag swinging, Rosie sprinted.

"Where's…it…come from?" panted Sally, her little voice broken into painful gasps as they ran.

"From another farm, I guess." Billie's long legs served her well, and she had to keep slowing down to wait on the others. "It obviously doesn't belong round this field. Something's upset it. It's flipping mental!"

"And now it's taking it out on us!" cried Rosie, daring to steal a look over her shoulder. Worryingly, the cow had shown no sign of letting up. In fact she seemed closer and angrier than before. A strangled moo echoed in her throat, a low and fierce sound which presumably portrayed violent threat in dairy language.

"Just get to the stile!" shouted Billie. "It can't get over there, then we'll be safe."

At that moment another sound pierced the countryside. Birds poured from trees, flapping their wings hysterically. Dogs in distant locations began barking ferociously. It was a gun shot. Loud and clear and in very close range. Shock and terror froze the three girls in their tracks, pinned to the spot by a sudden dread of something far worse even than a mad cow. Luckily, the cow also halted and the impact sent her off balance, her own big behind barging into her front legs. Her knees buckled and she fell to the floor. Men's voices were approaching. Their muffled, precise words were unclear, but the sharp tone suggested supreme rage.

"They're going to shoot her!" said Rosie, suddenly quite concerned for the animal, who now looked lost and helpless in a heap on the ruined grass. "No wonder she's going crazy. Oh, the poor, darling, little thing!"

"Little? Where are you looking?" snapped Billie. "And they're probably shooting it because it's already gone crazy in the first place. Let's get out of here before they accidentally shoot us instead. Or, wait a minute, I'm sorry, were you just stopping to get that milk you wanted?"

The sarcasm was wasted. Rosie had already turned round and was making her way towards the trembling beast. As she drew level, she could see it had thick white foam oozing from its quivering mouth. The large brown eyes rolled in the deep sockets. Giant flanks rose up and down in huge mechanical movements as the cow struggled to find her breath.

"There, there, steady girl. What do they call you? Doris, maybe? No one's going to hurt you. Look at you, Doris. Poor thing. You're frightened to death." Tentatively Rosie reached out a hand.

"Doris is it now? Okay, let's get this straight," Billie was chirruping under her breath, "I have a friend who's terrified of fluffy white pussy cats, but quite openly prepared to dice with death when confronted with a mental killer cow. Okay, that's fine, just so I know."

And then the second gun shot went off, destroying any calmness previously restored. Doris reared her head, emitting that awful strangulated moan. Kicking out her hind legs, she sprang to her hoofed feet and knocked Rosie backwards. Sally screamed, and Doris headed once again straight at her. Billie veered sideways out of danger to lift Rosie. The men's voices were clearer now.

"*Don't run!* Stand still. You're making her worse by running. The sudden movement scares her!"

"Ha! Who are they kidding?" spat Billie in the direction of the voices. "It's easy to say 'don't run' with a rifle in your hand. That thing's bonkers. Come on. We're nearly at the stile."

If the girls had thought the wooden stile was their safety net, they were mistaken. Clearing it one-handed with the easy confidence of children used to the vault box in gym lessons at school, they all breathed a sigh of relief as their feet hit the lane on the other side. Although Doris had no intention of following via the same route, she had no cause for hesitation, since seconds later she came plundering through the hedgerow, stabbed, scratched and dazed. Sharp, thorny branches stuck out of her torn sides, making her resemble something more like a giant hedgehog than a cow, but once again she rose from another fall and continued her rampage. The only way now was down. Down the winding lane by which they had come.

Terrified, Rosie was sure that any minute she would lose her footing and come crashing to the bumpy ground. Sharp stones and paving cracks played havoc with the grip on her trainers, and as the hill sloped almost vertical before her, the legs she'd once trusted now picked up speed without her brain's say so. They were out of control, running faster than she could handle, till they felt like jelly and not part of her body at all. Tears streamed down her face, as she pictured her own tragic death. Doris, whether purposely or not, responsible for trampling her head into the broken rocks, before surging forward to take her friends.

"OH...HELP! HELP!" she screamed.

Sally and Billie were nowhere to be seen now. In front or behind? She wasn't sure. Everything had blurred out of order in her burning head, the only thing clear was her fight for survival. Another gun shot, and the cow roared behind her. Had it fallen? Was Doris dead? Suddenly the idea didn't seem as sad as it had a moment earlier. Killing the cow could be the only answer to saving her own soul. Still, she didn't risk looking back to find out. Rosie kept on moving, her eyes tight shut and stinging.

The next time she opened them, there were houses around her. They were large detached houses with bright shiny windows and sparkling sandy driveways. Or at least some of them were. Looking up, Rosie realised there were many houses incomplete, some without roof tiles. Bare wooden frames exposed to the sun like a skeleton of dinosaur bones. Sheets of blue plastic hanging limply from them like the last remains of rotting skin. Small JCB diggers sat in the square gardens, which were currently clumped soil patches marked out with temporary tape. Red and blue flags bearing the golden crest of a company logo sagged in the lack of wind, from a set of portaloos and office cabins. She must have veered off track and run into the brand new Steeple housing estate. She'd heard her dad saying the other day how he'd love to move into this new development patch, even though it was only a ten minute walk from where they lived now. Steeple Willows, it was going to be called. Very pretty name, her mum had said.

"Oh Daniel, can we go and look round the showroom, please?"

"No point, Debs. It'd only get your hopes up. We just can't afford those prices. They're going for an absolute bomb. Mainly high-flying business sorts from out of town moving in. Makes you sick, doesn't it? An old writer like me doesn't stand a chance of putting their foot inside one, any more than does a workman in muddy boots once they're carpeted in cream!"

Daniel Quartz wrote history textbooks aimed at secondary school students. Rosie often got very embarrassed when teachers distributed them at her own school, and everyone turned to ask if her dad had told her all the answers.

Doris the cow having been temporarily forgotten, Rosie was suddenly rocketed to her senses when another gun shot sounded in the distance, and breaking into a canter on the horizon was the now familiar brown, bulky form. Rosie instantly remembered her lost and separated friends.

"BILLIE! SALLY! Where are you?"

Hearing Rosie's voice, Doris darted towards her. Rosie pushed a wheelbarrow of cement mixture onto its side and ploughed through the plastic tape like she'd just come first across a finish line. There was a tall, grey wheelie bin beside the wall of one of the houses. Too tired to run anymore, and her heels sore with blisters, Rosie flung herself down behind the bin. She tucked her knees to her chest just in time before Doris came careering past and headed on up the new estate. Those houses further up where people had already moved in began to twitch with opening windows and doors. Families had heard the gun shots and naturally wanted to know what on earth was going on.

Rosie sighed and swept her long, tangled hair back from her face. She was safe. The danger was ahead of her, and it seemed pretty unlikely that Doris would turn back with the gun-wielding farmers hot on her track. Rosie's heart was still beating fast, rattling frantically inside her ribcage like a trapped bird. She could feel pain all over her body. But for the first time since Doris's dramatic appearance, Rosie managed a bemused smile. Oh, the absurdity of it all! The only thing now was to find her friends. Shoulders stiff and aching, she winced slightly as she rolled the wheelie bin away from her. And then she saw the washing line.

This, you may think, is a strange place to stop. A chapter of a story never ended with a cliffhanger about a washing line.

But trust me, I know best.

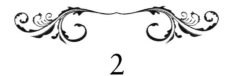

2

Guy Flower

It was not an empty washing line, as one would expect to find in the garden of a half-built house – neither neatly coiled nor cellophane-wrapped. It was a washing line full of clothing. Clothes dripping dry in the sunshine. There were mainly striped football shirts and multi-coloured sports socks, but also a couple of hand-knitted cardigans and a pair of blue jeans. Rosie panicked all over again. She had thought the house empty. The washing line obviously meant that somebody was already living here. Lifting her eyes skyward, she saw that unlike the buildings either side, these red bricks had been patted and pasted into position some time ago and dotted around the exterior were windows with tie-back curtains.

Wiping beads of sweat from her forehead, Rosie pondered. How strange that people were living amid the shells of the unfinished properties! Her father had been right when he'd said folk were desperate to get in. And no sooner had she thought this, than a pair of purple carpet-slippered feet came walking out of the front door. They passed the wheelie bin, oblivious of company, and continued up the path. Anxiously, Rosie watched a lady carry a round wicker basket over to the washing line and begin to add a new load of pegged socks to the rest. They were long and twisted from the wash, hanging like creepers from exotic jungle trees. The woman's back was turned as she continued her task and Rosie quickly weighed up her options. A: *Remain perfectly still till she'd gone, or* B: *Make a sudden calculated dash from her hiding place and take off down the road.* Silently cursing herself for having got into yet another predicament, Rosie remembered the peculiar amount of running she'd already partaken in, and settled for gently rolling the wheelie bin back towards the wall so that it sheltered her from sight. There was nothing now to do but wait and pray that the lady didn't see her as she went back into the house. The imagined embarrassment of being spotted was almost unbearable. Not only was she trespassing in someone's garden, but she was doing so in a strange crouched fashion behind their rubbish bags! The woman was bound to think Rosie had been about to steal one of the football shirts from off the line. Everyone knows how expensive they are nowadays! Or worse, she could be accused of taking a pee. Oh, the shame of it!

Rosie watched the lady run her palm across the cardigans and apparently decide they were dry. She unclipped them and popped them into the wicker basket, tightening her blonde ponytail with her free hand, before heading back to the front door. Rosie just had time to assess that the lady was strikingly pretty with a kind face, probably around the same age as her own mother. As she drew level however, Rosie sincerely doubted she'd remain quite so kindly in appearance if she found a twelve-year-old girl stowed between her used teabags and shredded electric bills. She squeezed her eyes tight shut and sunk her head deep into her shoulders, hoping, like an emu, that obstructing her own vision would render her invisible. But as mums have an unbelievably infuriating knack of doing, the lady must have noticed that the wheelie bin was not entirely positioned where it should be. It was jutting out just too far, not snug enough against the brick wall. Tucking the basket under one arm, she grasped the bin handle and forcefully shoved it back right into Rosie's shins. Try as she might to keep quiet, it was no use. Rosie screamed in pain. The lady screamed in fear, and threw the basket high up into the air. The contents came crashing down, a cream woollen poncho landing like a veil on Rosie's head. The veil was not however as transparent as a bride's, and Rosie sat trembling, knees still tucked to her chin, in a world of darkness. She liked it this way.

She would have preferred to sit like this with the poncho on her head forever. Anything was better than confrontation. Maybe the woman would call the police? Suddenly Rosie saw the advantages of having let the runaway cow chase her for a few more miles. And where were Billie and Sally when you needed them? Were either of them facing the most embarrassing situation of their lives right now?

"Goodness me, you gave me one heck of a scare there, love. Here, let me help you up." The lady pulled her clothes from Rosie's head and offered an outstretched hand.

Knowing from the heat in her cheeks that her face must be bright red, Rosie averted her gaze as she took the help and was pulled to her wobbly feet. The lady's skin was smooth and soft, like she'd used silky hand lotion. In fact everything about this woman seemed to be telling Rosie that she wasn't a person to fear. Still, the only logical intention was to get out of here and fast. Quickly, she snatched back her hand, mumbled something that was supposed to sound like, "Thank you", and turned to go.

"Hey, wait a minute young lady. You're hurt. There are scratches all over your legs. And that's a pretty bad cut on your elbow. It looks deep. You ought to get that cleaned up. How far away do you live?"

Rosie instinctively turned her elbow to see the damage and surveyed her red swollen legs. She looked like she'd been dragged through a hedgerow backwards. And then she remembered, she more or less had! Like a small child screaming dramatically many minutes after actually encountering an accident, Rosie felt a delayed reaction of pain kick in once she'd been made aware of it. She felt a sharp stinging sensation seep through her body. A vague memory of catching her arm on some barbed wire fencing flashed through her brain. It made her dizzy and she stumbled into the lady.

"I'm Jemma," she said quickly, supporting Rosie around the waist and holding her steady. "Jemma Flower. I promise you can trust me. Come inside. You look like you need a cold drink and a comfy chair. Goodness knows what you've been up to? You can clean yourself up if you come in the house, and then use the phone to call your parents. Come on, slowly now. Here, take my hand."

Of course it was not the best idea to enter a complete stranger's house at will. I'm sure that's what you're thinking right now, and I would have said the same. But Rosie felt far too weak to argue. Maybe it was the intense heat, or just the strange turn of events which had finally caught up with her – and Jemma Flower certainly didn't seem the type of person to kidnap innocent children, nor was Steeple Village a renowned hide-out for villainous sorts. Oh alright, *no one ever does, nowhere ever is,* I hear you say, but Mrs Flower happened to smell very nice, like peaches in syrup, and Rosie was sure that child-catchers would never take the time to spray pretty perfume before they pounced on their prey.

What had started out as a seemingly bad dream, now merged into an almost pleasant one. Rosie found herself sitting in a beautiful living room, tastefully decorated in shades of scarlet and brown. Paintings showing farm and woodland scenes hung in elaborate gold frames. Previously used candles, burnt low in their fancy wrought iron holders, stood either side of the huge Victorian fire surround. The curtain drapes were a thick and luxurious velvet, which hung to the floor like a framed proscenium arch at the theatre. Peering out of the sunlit window, Rosie half expected to see Shakespearean players acting out the final moments of Hamlet's death. Instead, a tortoiseshell cat leapt up onto the sill and began to preen itself. Shuddering, Rosie quickly turned away and continued to take in her surroundings. A grandfather clock. A standing lamp. Tall mahogany bookshelves lined the walls, but instead of containing countless volumes of classical books, like the ones her dad had at home, these displayed an adorable array of collectible porcelain ornaments. They were faeries, each involved in a different task. Some were frozen in a skipping motion, a basket of hyacinths collected on their arm. Some rode on the back of a speckled sparrow, legs outstretched mid-flight. Some played catch with acorn shells, the expression on their painted faces clearly displaying the immense joy in this game. Some simply lay sleeping beneath bluebell hoods, whilst curious bumblebees looked down. They were divine. In fact, everything about this house was just so. Her mother would love it. Rosie pictured later replaying this scene to her over buttered toast and bedtime TV. It would do little to dilute Debra Quartz's desire to see the Steeple Willows showroom. Rosie smiled at the thought, and actually felt herself begin to relax.

Jemma Flower walked into the room with a washing-up bowl full of soapy water and a large football shirt over her arm. She placed the bowl on a towel at Rosie's feet.

"I love your ornaments," Rosie offered shyly, trying hard to take her first step towards forging a friendship with this woman who had been so nice to her. "The faeries. They're gorgeous."

"You do? Oh, thank you." Jemma bent down, adjusting her fitted skirt as she gently helped Rosie out of her trainers and socks. "Here, put your feet in the water. It'll sting at first, but you need to clean those cuts. The faeries, I make myself. Believe it or not, I've earned quite a good living out of it." She laughed, as though guilty of this proclamation.

"You made them yourself? Oh gosh, how clever! How on earth do you do that?" Rosie looked again at the shelves in disbelief.

"Well, I create them. The manufacturer mass produces them now. They bought the rights to my designs. They sell quite well in jewellers and department stores. Everyone likes faeries. I started off just showing them at a stall in our local craft fair, and then it kind of took off." She stood back up and added as an after-thought, "Which is good, or we'd never have been able to afford to move here when my husband left."

Rosie quickly glanced at Jemma's left hand, which she noticed was completely free from jewellery. She had immaculately French manicured nails, but no wedding ring. Rosie sensed a change in the atmosphere. Without really understanding why, she frowned and said, "I'm sorry."

"Oh, no need. It's all worked out for the best now. As when

anyone leaves, it takes some getting used to at first, but you eventually come round. You have to. And we like it here. Steeple's a lovely village. My mother and father live in the square, which is why we chose it. Guy's a little nervous about having to start a new school, but I'm sure he'll be fine. He'll have forgotten all about it after the first week." Jemma laughed, heartily this time. "Guy's certainly not the kind of boy who struggles fitting in. Anyway, enough about me and my troubles. You haven't told me yet young lady, just what you were doing in our garden, and how you got all these cuts and bruises. Which reminds me! Here, take this t-shirt of Guy's. It'll bury you, but you seem to have torn your own vest down the front, and you could do with protecting your modesty on the way back home." A frown crossed her face. "Has someone hurt you? Do I need to call the police?"

"A moment back, I felt sure you'd be calling the police. Only, I thought it would be to arrest me for trespassing. I thought you'd think I was trying to steal your football shirts from your washing line."

As she spoke the words, Rosie realised that the shirts weren't of course Jemma's, but her son's, and ironically now she was handing her one over anyway. She pulled the delightfully fresh blue and white striped material over her head and as she emerged, Rosie noticed for the first time that besides those showing scenic landscapes, there were other pictures on the living room walls. Photographs – of a boy. She leaned forward to get a closer look, but the shadows cast by the sun's late afternoon retreat rendered the face invisible. Rosie sensed Jemma was staring at her in anticipation of a greater response to her previous question. She shifted her weight in the chair and wondered where to start.

"Did you hear the gun shots earlier?"

"Gun shots?" Jemma looked horrified.

"Yeah, farmer's guns. They were after the cow."

"The what?"

Rosie actually laughed at the expression on Jemma's face, liking this woman more by the second. "It all seems so funny now from the safety of your lovely house." And Rosie told her the full story, of her friends and their rock band in the making, of the walk up the steepest, longest lane, and of deadly Doris and the frightening near-escape. Stopping for breath at the end of her monologue, Rosie wondered if she had actually given a little too much detail. Why wasn't her own mother so easy to talk too?

"We ought to put the TV on, or the local radio station," Jemma was saying excitedly. "This cow has got to have made the news. I can't believe we didn't hear the gun shots, but then again I had just told Guy to turn his music down. It was like Wembley Stadium in here."

"This is Steeple Village," Rosie said. "We never make the news." But she was distracted. If she'd just heard right, then Jemma had indicated that her son was at home right now, lurking somewhere within these walls. Suddenly Rosie didn't feel quite so comfortable anymore. It had been far cosier, chatting idly with only Jemma and her porcelain faeries as an audience. As if in anticipation of intrusion, Rosie pulled her soaking feet out of the bowl and frantically began to towel her legs dry. She winced in pain where her elbow still stung, although it had now been bandaged with antiseptic.

"How old did you say you were, Rosie?"

"Err, twelve. I'll be in Year Eight when we go back to school after the summer."

"Oh wow, that's just great. You'll be in the same year as my son. Maybe you two could get to know each other beforehand, then Guy'll have a friend before he even starts at Steeple High. Let me call him downstairs, although he'll probably have his eyes glued to a football computer game. I think he's currently managing Chelsea in his own little world. GUY! GUY!"

"Err, wait, no. It's okay. I'm sure he won't want to be disturbed. Don't bother him!" Rosie was close to tugging on the cropped sleeve of Jemma Flower's blouse in protest. This couldn't happen. She would die of embarrassment. "I...I have to be going. My friends will be wondering where I am. They've probably been to my parents and they'll be really worried."

"Guy, come downstairs, there's someone I want you to meet!"

Although she'd never had a boyfriend, or even just a friend that was a boy, Rosie knew enough about the twelve-year-old male species, to have ascertained that they were mean and selfish and moody and intolerably cruel to girls. He would undoubtedly make her life misery for invading the privacy of his home, let alone having the further audacity to sit on his sofa in his favourite team shirt. He would hate his mother for forcing him to shake hands with her and catch "girl's disease". Him and his future school friends would laugh and poke fun at her in the corridors, once he'd relayed her unfortunate plight to them in graphic detail. In this instant and intense dislike she'd already built up for Guy Flower, Rosie desperately hoped that he'd be a scrawny, spotty, frog-face with taped glasses. Somehow though, she just knew there was no chance of that being the case.

"Hi, sweetheart. This is Rosie Quartz. She lives just down the road. She'll be in the same year as you when you start at Steeple High. Thought you'd want to gossip. She can fill you in on some inside information before you start; which teachers give the most detentions, which kids to avoid sitting next to, that kind of thing."

Rosie had heard his footsteps coming down the stairs. Rooted to the spot, she firmly refused to turn around.

"Hi, Rosie. Nice to meet you."

The voice was not at all what she'd expected. It was soft, with a genuinely curious tone. Still facing the opposite wall, Rosie conspicuously tried to straighten her hair with her fingertips. She smoothed her fringe down sideways and adjusted the baggy vacuum of the shirt round her belly. Suddenly for some unexplainable reason, it seemed to really matter what she looked like. And sadly, she realised, spirits falling, her appearance must be far from perfect right now.

"Rosie, are you alright?" Jemma was looking at her.

"Mm, yeah, sure."

"Good, then I'll leave you kids to talk. Maybe Guy'll walk you home, Rosie, so you don't have to limp alone. Also, he can protect you from that mad cow if it makes another appearance."

33

Guy laughed. It was a lovely, warm-hearted sound. "Did you say a mad cow?"

"Rosie will tell you all about it. I have some more washing to sort before we lose this sunshine for the day. Take care, girl. It was nice to meet you, and stay out of trouble if you can." Jemma had gone.

Now Rosie Quartz would tell you I'm sure, that when she turned around (for she did of course turn around – eventually) that it was one of those precious and priceless moments that for various reasons you remember crystal clearly and replay continuously over in your mind forever. Seeing Guy Flower for the first time was so extraordinarily special, because Guy himself was clearly so extraordinarily special. He did not slip easily into any category that Rosie, Sally and Billie had invented for boys at school. In fact, he was about as different to the other boys Rosie knew as broccoli stalks and chocolate cake. The overriding factor was quite simply that this boy was gorgeous. GORGEOUS! She had never, ever seen anyone or anything like him before. She knew, of course, that cute boys did exist. On CD covers maybe, on TV screens, in movie scenes, and spread across the pages of magazines with staples through their middle. But here in Steeple Village, here in the real world, surely it was impossible? A miracle?

Guy had rather a lot of straight floppy hair which hung in streaks of brown and yellow across his tanned, slightly freckled face. When he smiled he had perfect teeth, whiter than the fresh page of a new exercise book. He was chewing gum and Rosie kept catching a flash of it, like a stray sock spiralling behind the glass of a washing machine door. Guy leaned casually to one side, observing his visitor with bemused interest from beneath the long fringe. His eyes were large, animated and hazel brown, his grin lopsided.

Rosie had forgotten how to breathe. *In. Out. Inhale. Exhale.* Come on now Rosie, that was it. That was the way. Was it possible that this strange boy had her under some kind of spell? Was he a wizard, hiding a wand in his jeans pocket? Should she run? Instead, for the second time in minutes, she noted how intoxicating the scented blue and white shirt smelled upon her.

"So you go to Steeple High, yeah? I have to confess I'm a little nervous about the change. I was dead settled at my old school. I've given Mum a real hard time about moving me, but I guess she had no choice. What with Dad and all... So you're twelve too, yeah? Cool. You can be my first acquired ally."

Rosie could tell he was trying really hard to make conversation, and also being touchingly honest. She knew she just had to stop acting like a stuffing-filled rag doll. She had all the personality of a rock right now. Remembering Billie and her overwhelming confidence, Rosie tried hard to muster an image of what her brash friend would do in this situation. Surprisingly the trick worked. Rosie smiled back at Guy and soon began to tell him all about school life in Steeple.

"...and never forget your homework for Mr Anderson. He'll have you do double next time, and that's as well as missing break for the lecture on lack of respect.

"...Simon Leak's not to be messed with. I saw him shove Jack Baxter into the wall last term, and Jack's pretty tough himself. Leak should have been expelled long before now, but I reckon even the Head's scared of him.

"...and you never need to sit struggling with history work," she added at the end of her thorough biography of any teachers or students worth discussing. "My dad writes the books. *Progression in Secondary History by Daniel Quartz*. I have all the answers scribbled on the inside cover of my lever arch file."

"So you'd sell them to me for a small fee?"

"Oh, no fee! I'd give you anything anyway!"

Detecting a little over-generosity in her eager exclamation, Rosie dropped her head embarrassed and feigned interest in the floral pattern of the carpet.

Guy also looked slightly sheepish and averting his eyes shyly muttered, "Thanks."

As if to ease the tension, or at least change the subject, George Orwell came padding softly into the room and began to circle

Rosie's feet, pressing his proud body against her bare legs. George Orwell was the long-haired tortoiseshell cat she'd seen out on the windowsill earlier. Knowing this was not the moment to shriek and jump hysterically on the spot, Rosie took control of herself by breathing deeply, and began to edge her way backwards to the other side of the room. Orwell inquisitively followed.

"He likes you," grinned Guy.

"Yeah, well, I'm not quite so keen on him." Rosie tripped over a low magazine rack, but righted herself quickly enough to hope it went unnoticed.

"This is Mr Orwell, named after the author. *Pleased to meet you Rosie*, he's saying in cat language. *Delighted to make your acquaintance.*" Guy watched her squirm with faint amusement in his eyes. "Are you allergic to cats or something?"

"Maybe. Well, I'm not sure. I just don't like them. They creep me out. They're just so sneaky – and pouncy – and prowly." As if to confirm this, George Orwell, bored with his inquisition, pounced and prowled out of the room from whence he came.

"You're weird," said Guy, "but I like you. Come on, Rosie Quartz, let me walk you home." He held out his arm and Rosie took it straight away. Hesitation had done her no favours so far this afternoon.

As they walked, Rosie was contained by a raging vanity, where she wished that everyone she knew could see her right now. Strolling along on the arm of Guy Flower! Maybe she looked ridiculous in the football shirt which was umpteen sizes too big, but solely because it was his, she felt as glamorous as a blushing bride on her way down the aisle. What would Sally and Billie say when she told them? They'd absolutely flip! Prompted by the image of her friends, Rosie remembered the song she'd started earlier today. The lyrics to Sally's tune. A new series of words formed in her mind.

Don't you know I've always needed you?
Could it be maybe you need me too?
My only dream was to be here with you.

Just when it seemed the dream could never come true,
You were smiling and I recognised you.

Much sooner than she'd have liked, Rosie realised that they'd reached Steeple Chase, where she lived. They stopped beneath a lamp post and she gazed resentfully at the stain-glassed door of her house. Like a giant candle flame which some higher being had just extinguished, the sun was now gone.

"Well, here we are. Thanks so much Guy. It was really good of you to walk me home." She fingered the hem of the shirt around her knees, long enough to be a dress, and prepared to pull it off.

"Keep the shirt," he said. "You can give it me back at school. It's only two weeks away now."

Rosie beamed unashamedly. "Thanks". Did this mean he was setting up a situation whereby they'd inevitably have to communicate again? She'd heard about this kind of complicated riddle called the dating game. Billie was an expert.

"Bye then."

"Bye."

For a moment they stood there awkwardly, facing each other in the street. Then Guy took her hand and inched closer. The simple action was as thrilling as plunging from a deadly drop on a sky-high roller coaster at a theme park. Rosie felt her stomach had been left behind at the starting line and she was crying out to be saved. Guy's lips were hovering precariously close to her own. She could feel his breath against her throat, smell the peppermint of his gum. Her own jaw was locked tight from the previous impact of the roller coaster ride. She could sue for whiplash. She trembled. He was going to kiss her. The world had stopped…and then before they made contact, he broke away.

Guy shifted his weight from either foot and looked around him. He was embarrassed. "Yeah, well…right, yeah…I best get going…see you around, Rosie…I mean, see you at school, yeah…alright. Bye."

Somehow it didn't matter that he was walking away out of sight. It didn't matter that he hadn't actually kissed her. The intention had been enough. The magic had been there. It had been the most wonderful moment of her life. As she skipped airily up her garden path, Rosie felt she was being carried by an invisible force. Lifted by imaginary wings. So, this was what they meant when they said love had you walking on clouds.

Whether down to her dreamy reverie, or the misty glaze in her eyes, or the stupid smile glued to her face, Rosie opened her house door and failed to notice the commotion at the bottom of her garden.

There were some upturned terracotta plant pots there. Various sizes, cracked and chipped. They had been that way for a long time and were covered in thick velvety moss and tangled weeds. The soil was damp and crawling with insects. Stone boulders shielded this neglected patch from the otherwise carefully tended smooth lawn. But the dustpan and brush which had been left out on one large jagged rock, since Debra Quartz had half-heartedly attempted to clear up down there, came crashing down onto the path. Presently the brush shuffled along the path a bit further, and then it had second thoughts and changed direction, heading back to where it had come from. Flipping itself upright, the brush catapulted through the air and landed back on the rock. Here it seized movement. All was quiet. Except somewhere in the distance a cow was heard mooing.

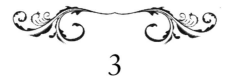

3

Soggy Jeans

Every time the Nuttall family had undergone a carpet change in their home, chopped scraps of the old offending nylon were scattered across the stone flags of the garage floor. It had become a sort of ceremony over the years, and now the various textures and patterns were jostled together, overlapped like one gigantic tessellated rug.

Rosie was picking loose threads from a rectangular cutting of gold-leaf print, causing a bald patch, while she waited for Billie to retune her guitar. All three girls sat cross-legged, perched on their own carpet pieces like frogs fly-fishing from lily pads. The garage door had been hoisted up to the ceiling. It was hotter today than it had been yesterday and the slightest breeze was a welcome relief.

Sally swatted a large bee which had idly floated in and was now buzzing persistently about her head. "Shoo! Shoo!" She prodded it with one of her wooden drumsticks. The insect bravely withstood a couple of jabs before sensing defeat and vanishing into the vast sky.

"So, you say you know he was going to kiss you, but he didn't kiss you? Well, how can you be sure he was going to, if actually he didn't? And if he wanted to, then surely he would have?" Billie voiced her mock confusion without looking up, as her fingers worked the pegs at the top of her instrument. She hit a series of chords, which jarred awkwardly in the fresh air acoustics. Frowning at the trembling strings, she shook her head and continued twisting.

"Maybe he got nervous or embarrassed?" offered Sally, absentmindedly coiling one of her brown pigtails around the drumstick like a heated hair roller.

"That's exactly what happened!" Rosie was thankful of this accurate interpretation. "He took my hands...he leaned towards me...*I could smell his gum for goodness sake*...and then we both kind of moved away."

"Well if he was really as cute as you say he was, why didn't *you* make the move to kiss him?" Finally resigned to the fact that the band were getting nowhere musically yet again this afternoon, Billie set her guitar down beside her and smiled wickedly at her friend.

Rosie knew she was purposely winding her up, but couldn't help taking the bait. "I didn't want to kiss him!" she shouted, and then added more shyly, "I wouldn't have known what to do."

"So you meet the boy of your dreams, you tell us he was perfect in every way, and then you just let him walk right out of your life without a second glance?"

"Well, technically speaking, he isn't out of her life, is he?" Sally jumped to her tiny bare feet. Her hair sprang loose from the forgotten drumstick, which dropped and rolled off to nestle beneath a disused microwave. Having often been on the other end of Billie's ruthless provoking, she knew only too well how Rosie was feeling, and tried hard to fight her corner. "If he really is starting at Steeple High in September, she'll see him then. Maybe the kiss will be a sort of delayed reaction and she'll fall straight into his arms the moment they meet!"

"Or maybe she'll fall straight *through* him because really he's a ghost – a figment of her crazy imagination!"

That did it. Furiously, Rosie marched straight over to Billie and slung a plastic carrier bag into her lap. It was as though someone had just held a lighter to a stack of bonfire wood. She burst into flames of an emotion which she'd bottled for the past twenty-four hours. "Well if I only imagined him, then what do you call this?"

Billie upturned the bag and examined the contents, smiling. "Your brother's football shirt?"

"You know I don't have a brother!"

"Your football shirt?"

"You know I don't like football!"

"Oh Rosie, you're so funny when you're mad." Billie stood up and hugged her friend, squashing her angry red face against her chest. She manoeuvred her into a playful headlock and ruffled the top of her blonde hair. "You're smitten, aren't you? Hey, if the mystery Mr Flower is this special, I might not be able to let you keep him for yourself. What do you say, Sally? Best friends share everything, right?" Releasing Rosie, she screwed the shirt into a tight ball and tossed it underarm to Sally, who caught it with both hands, laughing.

"Right."

The two girls began to throw it back and forth between each other, while Rosie darted desperately at them, an unwilling piggy-in-the-middle victim, her arms flailing madly in the air. "Give it back! Hey, pass it here!"

"Are you going to be carrying this thing around all the time then? Like a prized shiny trophy or something?" Billie stopped the game to hold the shirt against herself, admiring the colours in an imaginary mirror. She stuck out her tongue, pulled her ears, and tried to train her eyes to her own nose.

Giggling, Sally barged past and grabbed the fabric from Billie's hands. Easily it slid on over her own clothes, drowning her tiny frame even more than it had Rosie's. She tucked a fashionable knot in the side of it to create a ruche at her hip, and began to parade up and down, pouting her lips, as though on a catwalk. Sally wiggled her bum as she travelled across a strip of red cast-off, which could have passed for the Oscar carpet. Even Rosie had to laugh, despite still protesting for the safe return of Guy's t-shirt.

"Give it back. I don't what it stretching or getting dirty!"

"Stretching? Who are you kidding? It's like a marquee on her!"

"I just need to give it back to Guy in one piece, okay?"

Tired of expending too much energy in this heat wave anyway, Billie propped herself against an old decorating bench, and Sally fidgeted back out of the enormous stripy folds.

"You know, I do reckon you're right, Rose. He only asked you to keep hold of that thing, so you'd be forced to seek him out at school. It's a guaranteed ice breaker! Clever move, I say. This kid knows his stuff. But aren't you gunna feel kinda dim trotting round corridors with that plastic bag, just on the off-chance? I mean, suppose he's not even in any of our classes? Steeple High's a big place."

Rosie looked genuinely horrified at Billie's remark. She pressed her hands to her cheeks, as if to stop her head from splitting in two. "Not in our classes? No!…No!…I couldn't bear it!"

Sally and Billie exchanged glances, clearly concerned for their friend's sanity.

"I mean, you don't know what I've been going through. You don't know how hard it's been just getting through one day. I could hardly sleep last night. Tossing and turning and hearing him over and over again in my head. It's like I'm going insane. And that's not it! I can't eat. I've lost my appetite. I can't concentrate. My attention span is at an all time low. And to think I have two more whole weeks of this torture. And then on top of this, you're speculating that Guy may not even be there in our form room first registration back. I'll switch. I swear. I'll switch to wherever he is!"

Not really sure what else to do at the end of this uncharacteristic outburst, Billie and Sally sat still for a moment, before breaking into a tremendous round of applause. Mrs Nuttall's inquisitive head appeared at the adjoining kitchen window to see what all the fuss was about. She rolled her eyes and went back to her chores.

Feeling slightly better that she'd managed to get all of these new and very strange emotions off her chest, Rosie managed a weak smile at the reaction of her companions. Cheeks burning, she tucked Guy's t-shirt safely back into the carrier bag.

"You know, if you're really loved up that bad, you don't have to wait two weeks to go and see him." Billie swung her legs from aboard the decorating table, an idea forming in her pensive face.

"What do you mean?"

"Well, who says school's got to be your only meeting ground? You know where he lives now, don't you? Let's go round and call on him!"

"No!...No!...I mean, that's crazy! I couldn't...Could I?"

"Of course we could." Billie grabbed at the carrier and dangled it before Rosie's face like a freshly-caught fish. "We have the trophy, don't we? You have the perfect excuse of returning it. We can all go and drop it in. Besides, I'm dying to meet him! Aren't you Sal?"

Sally shrugged. "Well, yes, but I think I'd be a bit embarrassed. We're strangers. What if he thinks we're being weird?"

"Sally, you are weird. But we'll say we just let you hang out with us because we feel sorry for you."

Sally punched Billie in the arm, but the three girls jumped to their feet as though they'd reached a collective decision.

At that moment, Mr Nuttall's car pulled up in the drive. The sun's rays bounced off the silver bonnet as he sprung out two-footed with a cheery wave. Tucked beneath his smart, shirt-sleeved-arm was a newspaper, neatly folded, and as he entered the garage, he tossed the car keys to Sally in order to manoeuvre the paper into both hands. With a flick of his wrists, he rolled it out and held the front page aloft as though reading from a royal scroll. To emphasise this role-play he pursed his lips and made the squashed, exuberant sound of a trumpet fanfare. The three girls eyed him with impatience, but Simon Nuttall was clearly enjoying his brief dramatic act. Clearing his throat, he bellowed out the headline, which drew his wife to the kitchen window again.

"MAD COW ON THE MOO-VE STRIKES FEAR IN STEEPLE LOCALS!"

Ears pricked up at that point and the girls went from indulging the man's poor humour to raising themselves up on tiptoe to squint a view of the accompanying picture. They could just make out the hefty back end of Doris clearing what looked like the wall of the village post office.

"Give it here Dad, give it here," Sally squawked, waving her small hands like fluttering butterflies in the air around him as Mr

Nuttall happily trailed the paper out of her reach.

"Patience, patience, Sally my girl," her father reprimanded, now rolling his bait into a make-shift cricket bat to swipe Sally's hands away. "My initial disbelief of your tall tale yesterday at least affords me the first indulgence of the proof in writing."

"How do you work that one out?" said Billie, forgetting her manners. It had been very difficult assuring all adults concerned that yesterday's encounters really had occurred exactly the way they said. Sometimes it was very infuriating being twelve. Old folk expected you to make things up. Okay, so most of us who are or have ever been children know that generally that assumption is valid, but that is small consolation when you actually need them to believe you.

> Villagers were in for a shock yesterday as a 520lb dairy cow ploughed through streets, sidewalks, gardens, allotments and driveways. Public safety was placed in severe jeopardy and the calamity lasted a total of four hours before order was finally restored.

Mr Nuttall lowered his read. "It's not that I thought you were lying to me, girls," he continued in a softer tone, "It's just that I find it far more reassuring seeing the facts in black and white and backed by the words of others. For example, here's Mrs Strudel from the post office, who says she'd never been so frightened in her whole life:

> 'I had just pulled down the shutters for the afternoon,' she said, 'and was watering my potted geraniums out front when I heard the most almighty cacophony. I thought a wretched travelling circus was passing through. My prize Persian cat Spooky was hissing at the door frame, riveted in shock. If you ask me, the whole thing is in extremely bad taste. There was a time something of this nature would be unheard of in a quiet village like Steeple. Bullets fired through the air and dangerous beasts cavorting around the streets! How

an innocent bystander was not killed, I'll never know. Those farmers want to count themselves extremely lucky that no one was seriously hurt. It's just a good job they murdered that cow before it had one of us first!'

There was a prominent silence before Sally muttered, "Murdered? So...so they did kill her in the end then? Oh Doris, the poor thing."

Even Billie hung her head out of a queer respect for the doomed creature.

"Does it say anything else, Dad?"

The cow had escaped from a barn in nearby Lock Marshland, before making her plummet across numerous fields towards Steeple. Farmers had tried to corner her at regular intervals which had alarmed the animal and turned her mad with rage. Farmer Thornton from Lock Marshland Dairy said that putting the animal out of its misery was the kindest thing to do, not to mention the safest for the passing public. 'We had called a veterinary surgeon to the scene and were well equipped to handle this emergency,' he said. 'There was absolutely no chance of any villager being harmed during the use of our rifles.'

Rosie, stealing a quick glance at the large dark scab on her elbow, begged to differ.

"I've put you some potato salad out, Simon," called Mrs Nuttall, who had stood by, only half listening, the other half electrically whisking some fresh dessert cream in a plastic bowl.

"Cheers Amanda. I'll just get out of these work clothes." He tossed the paper onto a swaying stack of others previously discarded upon the decorating bench, and disappeared into the house.

"Sally dear, will you be wanting any dinner yet?"

"No, Mum. We're off out for a bit."

The three girls left the garage in a mutual daze of silent reflection.

They walked that way for a while until each had pondered long enough to bring her mind back to the task at hand. Having temporarily forgotten the purpose of their outing, Rosie at once felt her stomach turn and there was an odd sickly feeling in her throat. Hazy, halo-coloured images of Guy Flower swam before her eyes, like perfect reflections in angelic whirlpools; but these visions only served to weaken her resolve to call on him today. Why should he want to see her? What were the chances he'd understand? It had been a bad idea from the start, and now it seemed even worse. Maybe Billie was right. Maybe she had distorted their parting moments into how she wanted the memory to read. Maybe Guy had never given her any foundation for all this hope. Had she, in her euphoria, misread the signs?

As they rounded a familiar corner, the clean red bricks of the new houses rose into view. Every Steeple Willows driveway sparkled with the diamond-like dust of a beach as you stroll barefoot on a foreign holiday. The red and blue flags drooped on their posts, but the JCB had gone from the first garden to the right. Considering she had been running from the clutches of a mindnumbing scenario the last time she was here it was surprising how many small details Rosie had stored and replayed in her brain.

"It's that one over there. Number seventeen. That's where I ran to get away from Doris."

"Come on then, what are we waiting for?" Billie popped some gum and strode on with determined purpose.

Once level with the house, Rosie stood still and gazed at the scarlet tie-back curtains. She thought of Jemma Flower busying herself inside with colour coded washing piles or spraying her wrists with flowery perfume. This made her smile. Maybe Jemma at least – if not Guy – would be pleased to see her again so soon. Tip-toeing on the scuffed rubber of her pink trainers, she scurried to catch up with her friends who had edged down the garden path.

Three girls in decreasing size order stood staring in at the Flower's living room window.

"Go on then, Rose. Knock on the door."

"I…I…Listen, I don't really know if I can."

"Course you can. It's no conundrum. Just tap the glass."

"But what if he answers?"

Sally had been quiet but spoke for the first time. "Isn't that the whole point? We want him to answer, don't we?"

"Well, yeah, but…"

"Oh for goodness sake you two, I'll knock!" Billie lunged forward but Rosie caught the back of her long black trench coat and halted her.

"No! Billie, wait. This doesn't seem right."

"I don't understand, Rosie. Why is it so difficult? You even have us with you as moral support this time. How on earth did you manage before?"

"Before was different. I got in via the wheelie bin. And somehow I don't think that'll work a second time around."

Sally looked bored now, kicking the glistening white stones which trimmed the edges of the tidy lawn, and Rosie remembered that the girls needn't have made this journey, but had just to humour her.

"No Billie, you're right. I've got to be brave." On that note, Rosie came face to face with the golden letterbox and the shiny numbers one and seven neatly screwed above the leaded glass pane. She had very nearly taken action when a sudden movement within caught her eye. A shadow had been cast by a person entering the hallway beyond the door.

"Oh my God, he's there! Quick! Run!"

Befuddled by the sudden shrieked instructions, Billie and Sally spun and swayed, then followed their friend's quick flight back up the path and on past the house, leaving any chance of Guy-collision far behind.

Six identical doorways down, the new estate came to an abrupt halt. Here a rough-constructed fence hung loosely together with a handful of nails and some uncoiling barbed wire. This temporary measure marked the end of all current building work.

I must tell you, however, that this very fence is still standing today – I only know because I walked past last Tuesday – so it can't actually have been that bad a job. But before the Steeple Willows houses were built, the land here was nothing but an open stretch of woodland. Here villagers walked their dogs and children played hide and seek. Indeed it was pleasant enough, though not particularly useful for someone needing a place to live, unless you happened to be a squirrel or a badger. Since there was an abundance of greenery in Steeple and the surrounding areas, the talk of building was never considered too great a sacrilege to locals. Steeple Willows had emerged with little fuss.

Rosie, Billie and Sally stopped at the fence. Beyond this ragged marker the light changed and the sun struggled to illuminate areas wild and un-groomed. Tree roots thick with moss threw sinister shadows across a potentially negotiable footpath. Maybe in future years the building will extend, as it often does, and the estate will stretch further. But for now, and at the time the girls had run from the Flower residence, the view from the fence was still obscured with high brambles and angry-looking stinging nettles.

Rosie took control of her quickening breath. Tiny dancing dots caught her eye, flickering in the long grass ahead. Spiders, no doubt. Woodlice and centipedes and other such nasty specimens. All going about their creepy crawly business. She sighed. Horrible as it was, there was unfortunately no alternative. It was forward or nothing. The girls couldn't go back past the house again now. There was a chance that Guy had seen her in the first place and what a freak he'd think she was, constantly hovering at his perimeters. At least by carrying on over the fence, she could claim that their passing was complete coincidence as they scoured the woods in search of Sally's lost poodle. Sally, of course, had not got a dog, but that was entirely beside the point.

Riled, but otherwise obedient, Billie and Sally squeezed through sharp-toothed gaps and ducked wooden planks which crumbled some more at the disturbance. On the other side there was much tugging and peeling of loose clothing, which had to be prized free from the spokes of wire. It was only on retrieval of her baggy sleeve that Billie released her tirade.

"What the hell did we do that for? And what in heaven's name are we doing now? If he comes out and sees us in here, it'll look even worse – stark raving mad!"

"I might have worked up more courage in a bit. I just need time to think about what I'm actually going to say." Rosie turned and defiantly waded further into the knee-high grass.

"Give me strength!" Raising her hands, Billie directed her frustrations skyward, but quickly snapped her attention back to the ground as she tripped on a rock face.

"This is dangerous," Sally offered timidly. "That fence is there because the builders have washed their hands of this place."

Low branches curled on all sides like encroaching fingernails. Sticky weeds caught on their clothing hems and snapped at their legs, and the girls slowly moved forwards as if fighting through toffee. Each time a hidden obstacle cost them their footing they would reach out for the support of a gnarled bark, only to find their palm left damp with slime-green residue. Elbows, cheeks and pink trainers grew muddy, smeared with nature's grime like Red Indian war paint. Warily, Rosie continued to survey the undershoe activity, picking up her heels like a gymkhana pony.

"I've never minded bugs at a distance, like in books or on the TV, but the thought of them inside my socks is not particularly comforting."

"Ugh! Why? What have you seen?" Sally, particularly squeamish, danced on the spot, trying in vain to catch her knees up beneath her chin.

"I don't know, but the grass is alive. Probably beetles and worms and what-not."

"Oh heavens, I have to turn back! Worms make me heave. The way they die and then put themselves back together is worse than any zombie movie I ever saw."

"Pack it in, Sally," Billie said. "There's not even anything there."

"I'm sorry, but *yes* there *is*," challenged Rosie. "In the grass. See it moving? They're having their own little party down there."

"Rosie must have x-ray eyes. Like those night cameras on the nature programmes. Plus, don't forget it was her idea to come round here. Just chill out Sally."

Suddenly the mad, dancing Sally let out a scream, but it wasn't from the insects. She'd been nettled.

"Ohhhhhh! It kills! It kills! That's it! I'm going home."

"Oh for goodness sake, get a dock leaf or something. This is your fault, Rosie. Go and find her one."

Rosie felt her temper rising as her friends continued to moan and press the responsibility of all unpleasantness on her. But since she was almost entirely to blame for their journey into darkness, she felt obliged to hold her tongue, at least until they found a way safe out into the open.

"What am I looking for?" she called back over her shoulder as she edged off their current trail and deeper into the trees.

"A dock leaf," Billie shouted back.

"Yeah, I know, but how can I tell which leaves are dock leaves? What are their characteristics?"

"I don't know. They're green and pointy."

"Okay. So that's just about everything around here."

"Quite big. Rough texture. Oh bloody hell, I don't know!"

Sally's screams formed the backdrop of their debate.

Rosie reached down to a clump of something which vaguely resembled her memory of a nettle-sting-soother and dug with her thumb and forefinger to grasp the root. Startled by a movement she quickly relinquished her grasp and jumped away from the occupied leaf. She'd initially failed to notice there was something on it. What was that? Just a butterfly? Now *that* she didn't mind. At least they were pretty to look at. But no. It couldn't be a butterfly. She'd never seen a transparent butterfly before. Like glass. The colour of clear running water. And the wings were so huge.

"Billie. Sally. Come and look at this."

"Is it a dock leaf?"

"Well, yes and no. Come and look what's on it. It's the strangest thing I've ever seen."

"Just bring the dock leaf for God's sake, Rosie. Sally's chomping at the bit here."

"It's like a butterfly, but it's not. Its wings are vibrating so fast."

"OK, Attenborough, it's a dragonfly then." Billie called impatiently from the other side of the trees.

"No." Rosie hesitated and then shrugged her shoulders. "Never mind." Batting the creature away with the back of her hand, she watched it rise into the sky until the bright white light emanating from it merged with the treetops out of sight. She grabbed the leaf and nettled herself in the process.

"OUCH!"

Nursing their red speckled knuckles, Sally and Rosie gingerly trudged on in the tracks forged by Billie's heavy soles. It occurred to Rosie that they should have worked in this logical way all along, but only now did Billie's boots seem possessed with a determined purpose to find an alternative route out of here.

"Hey!" Billie stopped and pointed ahead. "This clearing comes out around the back of the houses. If we count six up, that should be Guy's." Indeed it was. The three girls surveyed the scene in wonder, their spirits lifted at the sight of normality, like a dehydrated hallucination at the height of some Sahara desert hike.

The upstairs window had blue and white striped curtains and on the windowsill stood a neat row of shiny bronze football trophies.

"That must be his bedroom," Rosie whispered, suddenly scared to be heard.

Unseen to them before, the girls now noticed a thin stream rising from the ground. It had taken leave from beneath a stack of smooth, perfectly oval boulders, hiding the source since their entrance at the fence. Although a mere trickle at first, the stream quickly jumped into life. It opened out and converted to a considerable width, which forced the girls on the opposite side of the bank from the line of houses and back garden fences. The ground here took a dip downhill making the water rush on at a fair pace before it hit a gathering of jagged rocks and produced a frantic whirlpool of foam. As the water carved its journey through layers of dislodged stone, a melodic gurgling like the murmurs of a newborn baby, filled the air. It was cooler here by the rushing water and an enormous sense of wellbeing rose up in the three of them. Without thinking, both Rosie and Sally simultaneously let their dock leaf bandages unravel and float to the floor.

Billie scooted to the edge of the bank. She pushed at the sludgy ground with her steel capped toes to test it for a firm hold. "There's a tall tree here. If I climbed it, I bet I could see right into his bedroom. If he's in there I could see what he looks like – get a look at him without him even knowing – which I'm presuming is what you'd prefer now, little Miss Blushing Rose?" After a sarcastic glance at Rosie she pushed the tree's trunk with both hands and nodded satisfactorily to herself, as if the fact that it hadn't budged confirmed her theory.

Rosie felt invisible fingers pinch her in the stomach. Just the sight of his stripy curtains had done it again. Those feelings back on boil, cooking with gas once more. She grinned. "Do you know what, that's ingenious Billie. The best idea you've had all day! We'll both climb. Then I get my fix but I don't actually have to confront him. I can totally indulge myself but avoid any awkward embarrassment. Brilliant, Featherstone!"

Billie placed her right foot firmly on the trunk and steadied herself. With both arms stretched out above her head she could almost reach the first branch, and so only needed a small kick-off with her left foot to catapult her grasp to the waiting shelf. Holding on tight, she swung there for a few moments before raising her knees to her belly, and then used the strength in her elbows to lift her feet over the branch. Pleased with herself, she swung her legs in a sitting position and gestured for Rosie to copy her. Tinted by the euphoria of a chance to glimpse Guy, Rosie completed the same task with little thought of how she'd got there. She caught her wrist and felt it sting, but it didn't matter. She was up. Laughing gleefully at their double perch, the girls embraced and laughed out loud.

"Come on, Sal. Are you coming? It's great up here."

Shielding her eyes as she squinted upwards, Sally didn't look convinced. "Are you sure that tree can hold the pair of you at the same time? It doesn't look that strong to me. I think I'll just stay with my feet on the ground. Besides," she added, reaching for the plastic carrier which Rosie had tossed to the ground, "someone needs to protect Guy's t-shirt from wild animals." She hugged the bag to her chest. "You can relay the action to me from there. I trust your descriptive skills Billie."

"Come on then, Rose. We need to get up further if we're to see properly. I'd say another three branches and we'll be level height with his window."

Ever the tomboy, Billie rose easily and as she climbed each consecutive branch, turned to grasp Rosie's hand and pull her up after her. A couple of times Rosie lost grip on the damp moss and her heart stopped as she felt her feet plummet, but then she'd sigh a great relief as they caught on the safety of a lower branch.

"Whoa! We're quite high now Bill!"

Billie had claimed the safest seat on the topmost sturdy branch and Rosie pressed herself firmly against the security of the trunk with her feet on the branch below. Having achieved their goal they stopped and held their breath, watching the window intently, like an animal patiently dissecting its prey. As they watched a shape moved inside.

"That's him! He's there!" Rosie wiggled in excitement and leant over Billie to point at the window frame.

"Move out then girl, I want a better look. I'm finally going to get to see if this dude's as gorgeous as you say." Straddling the branch awkwardly now, like riding a seaside donkey, Billie budged forwards, holding herself steady in front with imaginary reins. Rosie adopted the same position, mirroring her friend's action close behind. The branch was fairly long and stretched out horizontally over the river. "If I can just get nearer…"

"Watch it Bill," Sally warned from below. "The branch gets pretty thin out there. It won't hold your weight."

The thinning branch began to reverberate and sway like elastic. The weight of both girls made it dip and the entire tree leant to one side. Sally screamed.

Rosie saw the swirling brown water beneath her suddenly rise very close – girl and element face to face.

"Oh my God! Oh my God!" From the bank Sally waved the t-shirt of Guy's wildly above her head like an emergency flag, as though this desperate motion may somehow miraculously bring someone to their rescue.

In order to keep hold of the branch, Rosie clung in a koala bear position upside down with her knees and hands scrabbling for grip around the bark.

"Flip yourself upright, Rose," Billie was forcefully commanding. "You're bringing the branch down you div!"

"I can't budge. If I move a muscle I'll…"

But Rosie never finished her sentence. The combination of tree slime and nervous sweat on her palms was too much. Losing all abrasion in her life-lines, Rosie's fingers splayed and with a satisfying SPLASH the stream claimed her. For a moment she was gone, and then not quite as elegant as the Lady of the Lake or as glamorous as a bikini clad Bond girl, Rosie emerged from the foam, righting herself in the water which came to her knees. Plastered round her calves, her jeans felt heavy and her sodden trainers wobbled on the stony and fast moving surface.

The reaction from her friends was not quite what she had envisaged. Looking up for sympathy, her ears were filled with uncontrollable snorts and squeals. They were in absolute hysterics. Sally grabbed her stomach as though so much laughter was ripping it apart. "Oh stop it! It hurts! It hurts so much! The pain! I haven't laughed this much since…since…since never! Hahaha! Ohhhhhh!"

Billie had to lay her cheek against the branch to stop her huge chuckles from rocking her into the water too. "You're drenched! Oh, Rose, your hair, it's soaking! And you've got twigs in it! Hahaha!"

"Oh well, you two just stay there, why don't you? Go on, have a good laugh. Don't bother trying to help me out or anything!"

Sally tucked Guy's t-shirt under her arm and reached out with her free hand. Steadily she edged toward the tip of the bank.

The ground squelched into trainer-sole patterns where she trod. "Sorry, Rose. Come here. Take my hand. I'll pull you up."

Annoyed but with no alternative, Rosie unpicked the pasted folds of dark denim from around her knees and waded forwards. Shakily she clasped Sally's little fingers in her own.

"Ooo don't touch her hands," called Billie. "She's all stinky and slimy. She'll turn you into a swamp monster!"

That did it. Bursting into a fit of laughter once more, Sally lost her footing on the muddy edge and slid forwards. Slow to anticipate this sudden action, Rosie fell backwards still linked to Sally and the pair of them came crashing into the stream. Billie let out a howl from the tree. "Haa! Hahaha! Oh my!"

The water which reached Rosie's knees was almost waist height on poor Sally, and unlike Billie swaying in the tree above, she didn't find the whole debacle quite so funny anymore. Glancing round in fear, she noticed the blue and white football shirt floating away downstream.

"You idiot!" Rosie screamed, catching sight of it at the same time. "Quick! Do something!" But it was Rosie herself who had to lunge forwards and catch onto the washing instruction label before it was too late. She lifted it, mud-splattered, into the air. "Oh lord. It's ruined."

Such a peculiar amount of noise outside his bedroom window forced Guy to abandon his team winning on the computer screen and look out into the woods. Twisting the handle he pushed open the glass and gasped at the sight. The first thing he saw was a girl in a tree. The second thing he saw were two girls in the stream, one knee deep in water and the other almost drowning. Frozen in surprise, it took Guy a while to truly focus and steal a second glance at the blonde girl with a leaf stuck to her cheek.

"Rosie? Rosie Quartz?"

Rosie stared back at the boy of her dreams in panic stricken horror.

Billie cut in quickly to terminate the awkward silence, her chirpiness totally juxtaposed to the tension. "Well hello, Guy Flower. Wow! You really are as cute as Rosie said!"

Guy looked in confusion at the girl hovering creepily close to his bedroom window, and then, switching his attention back to Rosie, asked, "What on earth are you doing?"

"Err, err…"

Again, Billie spoke. "I'm Billie. Billie Featherstone. And the other girl down there is Sally. We're pleased to meet you, handsome." She batted her dark eyelashes and outstretched an arm from the tree. The change in her body shape upset the balance and the branch leaned again, thrusting Billie and her hand out closer towards Guy. Startled, Guy jumped further back into his bedroom. His face was cast in shadow, but he continued to address Rosie.

"What are you doing in the stream?"

Mustering what she hoped looked like a smile, Rosie lifted the handful of saturated material from her side. She held it up in the air and watched it dripping. "Returning your football shirt."

As Guy frowned, Rosie's fake smile began to fade, and like every scrap of her carefully applied make-up, melted away downstream.

4

The Thirteenth of April

An abandoned crisp packet danced on a rare breeze filtering low through the gaps in the trees. A ballerina, it pirouetted in flight, and the foil, which once had guaranteed freshness to the consumer, now shone fiercely in sun rays cutting through the leafy roof like a knife. Following briefly the bend in the stream, the journey was short-lived. With no further wind in its sail, the litter took rest by a clump of stinging nettles in the woodland surrounding Guy Flower's house. Here, the movement Rosie had astutely spied in the tangled grass continued to flicker and play. Not spiders as Rosie had suspected. Nor beetles, woodlice or dragonflies. These insects were of course at hand: if you turned over a loose rock or boulder you would find them there, but they were not responsible for the constant motion.

The rocking dandelion, which swayed on its stem to and fro, was a potential suspect. After all, the breeze had stopped. *Ba-bum. Ba-bum. Ba-bum.* This fluffy yellow weed had a definite rhythm. And it bent just so from a weight upon its bed; from the person lying on it. His green cap was stuffed beneath his neck for comfort and one leg was propped up on the other raised knee. He spat on his hand and used the glistening moisture to clean his scuffed leather shoes. He noticed, as he folded his muscular, tattooed arms across his bare chest, that his skin was grass stained and mud splattered. Even the leaf-patterned waistcoat which hung open, torn and buttonless, was of questionable colour, though it too should have been green. Having a constant deep brown tan he could get away without visiting "The Baths" for weeks at a time. But grudgingly he realised that a thorough wash was long due. Not today though. The air was so still and precious. It was far too heavenly just lying here and gazing up at the chinks of light in the green gauze far ahead. He was tired. He'd been working out for a good hour. Pulling his toned body up and down, dangling from the rusted spout of an old watering can to build the strength in his arms. The "Can" was a regular hangout for this pursuit, his private gym where, blissfully, his little sisters knew not to disturb him.

There was silence. Not even noisy humans could be heard, and his mind was free to roam through the stack of immediate issues which currently occupied the in-tray of his brain. Occasionally, a particularly bright slice of sun sought him out and he was forced to scrunch up his hazel eyes. The heat on his shaved head was a pleasure, and a smile of contentment rested on his handsome face in the heat. At seventeen years of age, the young man could have had a full head of wavy brown hair if he'd wanted it. But he didn't. Keeping the stubble at bay with the razor edge of a rose thorn was a daily ritual his sisters kindly endured for him. The things he had come here to dwell on were not problems as such, but being the wise and thoughtful fellow his Elders had come to know, he liked to be sure he had the right notion before making any final decisions. He shifted position on the dandelion. The many glinting gold earrings which lined the lobes of his ears, some looped, some studded, began to chafe his skin if he rested on them for too long.

"Moss? Moss? Are you here?"

An unwelcome metallic clang sounded on the nearby watering can, indicating that someone had squeezed through the gap between its base and the rock which held it in place. Moss groaned. His youngest sister's voice pierced the air like an arrow from a hunter's bow. A perfect aim which prized him from his peaceful solitude.

"Moss Agate, can you hear me? I know this is where you go, so don't pretend you're not here. Where are you hiding, Moss? I need you to come out at once!"

Moss propelled his body into a forward roll and tumbled from his dandelion bed with ease, landing two-footed on the soil below. His sister jumped back, startled by the sudden appearance from above. She had expected him to put up more of a fight, knowing how he hated intrusion in his private realm.

Not wanting to give her guilt away, Fire ran her fingers through her short, flame-red hair and straightened the tooth-jagged edge of her orange, mini-skirt. "You're late. We've been looking for you. They refuse to start until you're there, and we said the hour of four, remember?" She placed her hands on her hips and rolled her eyes in annoyance.

"We said the hour of five. I scratched it onto my rucksack with coal. Look!" Moss held up a bag made from chopped, woven elm leaves which he'd deposited at the foot of the dandelion stem. Sure enough, a messy number five glistened black on the fold of an outer pocket.

"Well we changed it to four, and if you'd been home and not hiding out here where no one can ever find you, then you'd have known The Council had altered it when everybody else did." Fire pursed her lips together and held him in her stare

"Hey, no harm done. You found me out and now I'm all yours. Come on, little Sis, lead the way." Moss slung his rucksack over one shoulder and placed a free arm around his sibling. Her scowl softened and together they lifted their heels and kicked off from the ground. Their silhouettes rose as a pair through the branches till they were nothing more than a brilliant white, merging with the sunlight.

Three dishevelled girls, all in varying degrees of distress and untidiness, sat exhausted in the beautiful living room. Rosie shivered and drew her tartan blanket closer. She squeezed numb toes together and surveyed her pale feet, regretting that she hadn't got round to painting her nails this morning. Her once pink trainers stood by the door on a folded sheet of *The Steeple Print*, the same local newspaper Mr Nuttall had read from earlier today. Now black and unbearably odorous, they would have to be thrown away. Maybe Billie would piggyback her home. Having avoided the water, Billie was the least shaken, and sat with her legs pulled cosily beneath her in the fireside armchair, as though she had lived here all her life. Whistling the funeral march for some bizarre reason known only to her eccentric self, Billie ran her fingers through her long black hair and raked out several bits of tree, which had attached themselves in the great climb. She held her baseball cap like a soup bowl and placed each offending leaf in its depth.

"Nice house," she murmured. "So how much are these going for, then? No, don't tell me – I should mind my own business. Are your parents rich?"

Rosie cringed, but luckily Guy was in the kitchen and if he had heard, he pretended not to have.

"His dad left, remember?" Rosie hissed under her breath, lifting her leg to kick Billie's chair from her own spot on the settee.

"Whoops!" Billie clasped her hand to her mouth apologetically, but soon lost interest as she lifted a copy of *Country Arts & Crafts* from the magazine rack and began flicking through its glossy pages. "Ooo – 'How to make the perfect scrap book' – I keep meaning to get round to displaying my Harajuku prints."

Sally had been crying and her eyes were red and swollen. She had a blanket like Rosie's and was trying her best to hide her face in a fleecy corner. Her clothes underneath were saturated.

"Are you alright, Sal?" Rosie gave her leg a gentle squeeze across the gap between them on the three-seater.

Sally nodded and sniffed. Rosie knew how she felt. It was beyond her how Billie could act so carefree and self-confident in the face of complete catastrophe. She glanced at the football shirt drying on the radiator. This had to be the most embarrassing event of her life.

Guy walked into the room with a tray of tea things. There were four chunky mugs with multi-coloured polka dots on them, emitting steam, and filled with what looked like bubbly hot chocolate. There was also a side plate of biscuits in wrappers and frost-speckled Viennese Whirls. Billie whooped and applauded his entry.

"Here, girls. I'm not very handy in the kitchen, it may taste suspect. Mum's out though, so I'm afraid it's all I can rustle. At least it'll warm you up. Don't want you getting pneumonia. Do you reckon you can catch your death in the summer?"

Guy grinned as he slid the tray and its contents onto the low wooden coffee table. Like a hawk, Rosie followed his every move out of the corner of her eye. He linked his arms behind his head to stretch and the hem of his crisp white t-shirt lifted to reveal a flat, brown belly. Nauseous with desire, she snapped her eyes shut and pretended not to have noticed.

Pushing the brown and yellow stands of his long fringe away from his face, Guy pointed down at the gap between Rosie and Sally. "Can I squeeze between you there? A Flower between two dripping thorns!"

"Sure, of course you can. I mean, it's your room – your house. We're so sorry to intrude...again!" Rosie shifted closer to the soft sofa arm to create a larger gap for Guy.

"Yeah, about that...are you gunna make a habit of dropping by here unannounced in ludicrously bizarre situations, Rosie Quartz?"

She had been awaiting this reprimand – preparing herself for a tirade of anger – so she completely missed the jovial humour which played in his tone.

"I'm sorry. I am so sorry. I really can't apologise enough for this. But I swear it's a total coincidence. We...I mean *I*...had absolutely no idea that those woods backed onto your house. We approached from the opposite side. It was my Nanna's silver chain, you see. In the river. *Yes!* And I'd be in such trouble if I were to lose it..."

Billie laughed out loud and tossed the open magazine back into the mahogany rack to reach for her mug. "And of course, she just happened to have your shirt on her in case the woods did actually back onto your house after all!"

Rosie shot her a look to kill, but Guy laughed along and much

61

to her immeasurable surprise, leaned back into the cushions and extended his arm around her neck. As he did so the hem of his t-shirt rose again, and Rosie felt her whole body swell with warmth at the effect of this blissful contact.

Billie raised her black eyebrows, clearly impressed, and even Sally managed a small smile in appreciation of this open show of affection.

"So, Mr Flower, you're starting Steeple High in September?" Billie wiped chocolate froth from her mouth with the back of her hand as she asked.

"Yep."

"Well, you can totally rely on us to show you around. Steeple's like quick sand. You need to know where to step and how to tread in order to survive. But we three have it sussed. Stick with us and you can't go wrong."

Rosie groaned yet again at her friend's invasive manner, but Guy was nodding his head. "Rosie's already given me the low-down, but thanks, I appreciate it."

"I wonder what form group you'll be in? You're the same age as us, yeah, so you'll be starting Year Eight when we go back?"

"I'm nearly thirteen," Guy said.

Billie let out a friendly tut. "We're all *nearly* thirteen, Guy. I'm *nearly* sixteen if you give or take a few years. But I bet I'm nearer thirteen than you! I'm the oldest in our year group. Thirteen at the end of September."

"Gutted." Guy had entered into the spirit of the fight and had moved his arm from around Rosie to lean across the coffee table towards his opponent. "You win." He shook hands with Billie over the tea tray. His grip was firm. Instantly impressed, the tomboy in Billie noted that he wasn't afraid to hide his strength just because she was a girl. She liked him. "So when is your birthday, Guy?"

"Oh, I'm a long way off. Teenage-dom lurks far away in a distant future called April. The thirteenth. Unlucky for some, huh?"

Silence hit the room and hung there intense while the grandfather clock ticked away several passing seconds. "The thirteenth of April," Rosie whispered. She clung to the words like they were expensive on her tongue. "That's my birthday too. We were born on the same day."

The magic of the moment was broken by Billie howling. "Woo-hoo, there you go! That's it now then. Destiny calls. The powers that be knock upon your door. You know what they say about two non-related people born on the same day, don't you?"

"What?" Sally, intrigued, had peeled her tiny body free of the tartan fleece. The custard-centred wafer she'd been nibbling on had brought her back to a more relaxed zone of wellbeing. Just as Guy had said it would.

Rosie and Guy exchanged suspicious glances as an over-dramatic Billie donned a mystical face of superstition. Rosie wouldn't have been surprised if she'd suddenly pulled a pack of tarot cards from her back pocket and fanned them out on the coffee table in a Celtic spread. Billie's Mum, Dahlia Featherstone, could read palms and tea leaves. So she said. But Rosie of course thought it rubbish, and scoffed when Billie claimed to have inherited her mother's psychic talent.

"They say you are sealed for all time. Destined to be together. A love that cannot be broken. It's fate. No matter how hard you or others may fight against this bond, it is never to be severed. Two hearts beating together forever." The way she spoke the words was strange, like they didn't belong to her, echoing from another place in time. Guy reached for Rosie's hand and squeezed it tight.

Sally reached for another biscuit. "Or it just means you get to share the same party and have a doubly cool time."

"That as well," Billie chuckled, and sounded like herself again. "Good point, Sal. We can have a great joint shindig for the pair of them."

"A double party, now that sounds more like fun." Guy rubbed his chin in contemplation.

"Well, don't you forget it. Rosie, Sally and I will hold you to that Mr Flower. The thirteenth of April…"

At that moment the front door was heard to open and the sound of carrier bags rustled onto the hallway mat. Car keys jangled as they were replaced on a wall hook and the soft sound of humming floated down the corridor. Rosie recognised the smell of Jemma's perfume before she had even entered the room.

"Sweetheart, I'm home. Could you come and give me a hand with this shopping, please?"

"Sure, Mum. And we have visitors."

Jemma stuck her head around the doorframe, while coiling a stray strand of hair back into her butterfly clip. "Oh! Hello, Rosie. Hello, girls. Are you staying for dinner?" The girls' shared glances, trying to portray a humble decline of not possibly dreaming of being such a burden, and yet almost simultaneously beaming at the prospect. Amid this, George Orwell seized his opportunity to enter the living room, padding determinedly on past the human feet in his way, all consumed by the simple aim to reach his watchtower on the windowsill.

Rosie screamed. "Oh that blasted cat!"

"Orwell won't harm you," Jemma said, already turning away to pre-heat the cooker.

"She's a cat-hater," Billie chided.

"I don't hate them," Rosie snapped. "I'm just not keen."

"Well, that's a shame," said Guy, scooping up his feline with one arm and then flipping him onto his back to tickle his chin. The cat lay there, limp and content like a baby with a bottle. "I couldn't possibly be friends with someone who dislikes Mr Orwell. Besides, what would we do at the joint birthday party? Orwell would have to be invited, and avoiding him would cause all manner of complications with the seating plan."

Rosie guessed he was joking and giggled – although just to be sure she spent the remainder of the afternoon dropping comments about how beautifully shiny the sun made his tortoiseshell coat.

After Margherita pizza and American-style French fries, Jemma Flower offered to take the girls home. To ease the risk of her acting as a taxi firm, the three friends insisted she drop them all at Sally's and they'd disperse themselves from there.

Neatly belted into her seat, Rosie inhaled the scent of pine needle air freshener, hanging from the rear view mirror in the shape of an evergreen tree. Her and Sally were in the back, and Billie was chatting away to Jemma in the front. The engine started and Jemma was just about to lift the clutch, when there was a tapping on the side window. Jemma flicked the button to let the glass slide down, revealing Guy's face.

"Sorry, Mum. Rosie's forgotten something. I need her to come back inside for a tick."

"What's she forgotten?" Billie screwed up her face in disbelief, knowing her friend had no personal effects of which to forget.

"Just a CD I said I'd lend her. We'll only be a second."

"Oh really!" Billie chastised, and wriggled in her seat at the annoyance of being left out. Sally and Jemma however, smiled silently to themselves as Rosie left the car.

Nervous, Rosie trotted down the garden path to keep up with Guy who had quickly disappeared back into the house. The door was ajar, and puzzled, she tentatively slipped between the small gap. The second her feet hit the hallway carpet, a waiting hand clasped the door shut behind her and Guy pressed his back to the frame, as if blocking her option of exit.

"Guy? I don't remember you mentioning a CD...?"

"Rosie, all afternoon I was just wishing we'd get a moment alone. So this is my last desperate attempt to have you to myself, however fleeting."

She felt her cheeks colour at his words. Her mind flicked back to the way his t-shirt hem had lifted and she felt an electric prickle on the back of her neck.

"I did want to give you something. But not a CD. Just...just... this..."

Slowly he leaned forward and carefully wrapped both of his brown arms around her tiny waist. He tilted his head to her height and as his lips pressed down on her own, she heard music so loud and clear that the gift may have been instrumental after all. For a moment she froze – terrified, breathless, fearing that now the moment had come she would be useless. Play it all wrong. Not know what to do. How was this supposed to happen? How was she supposed to be? How many girls had Guy kissed before? Maybe he was an expert and she would seem stupid and infantile in comparison to him?

Oblivious to her panic, Guy gently spread his lips and forced her own mouth apart, and she was able to breathe again. His oxygen into her lungs. At the base of her back she felt the balls of his thumbs rubbing in circular motions, and blissfully she relaxed. Enjoying this sensation too much now to worry about the unwritten rules, she reached out and entwined every one of her fingers into the loose yellow strands of Guy's hair.

This was how. This was it. This was everything. This was all.

They stumbled backwards and Guy pressed his palm firm against the wall to steady them from falling.

Neither was sure how long this wonderful experience had lasted, but the heaven was finally broken by a car horn sounding outside, which probably indicated that the moment had presided far longer than either presumed.

"That was amazing," Guy whispered, only just audible above the wild pounding of their matching heartbeats.

"Yes it was," Rosie smiled. Beamed. She knew she had never smiled like this before.

Never ever smiled.

Truly.

Really.

Until today.

An enormous cheer greeted Moss as he and his sister entered the dense clearing. The trimmed wildflowers which lined the circumference of this circular patch were all linked at the stem, hung with red and yellow bunting. The tapered flags fluttered excitedly, matching the mood of the crowd. At one end, crammed beneath the shelter of an empty, side-lying plant pot, various folk clutched wooden instruments in their hands and struck up a merry tune, to which many bystanders began to jig. People twirled one another around and then moved down the line, swapping partners. Some bellowed and yodelled, deep throaty calls of joy. Children not yet permitted to fly were hovering precariously off the ground in their euphoria, and overprotective parents ran crossly to their aid.

Moss scratched his head and glanced around, taking in the festivities. He knew he was well thought of by the Elders, but his mere entrance at Council had never caused quite so much celebration before.

Suddenly, flitting through the crowd, moving gracefully with an ever-present elegance all her own, Moss spotted his other sister. Carefully negotiating obstacles, she finally came to be at his side and threw her arms around him with such force that the pair almost fell backwards, feet over wings. She showered his cheeks with kisses and then bounced giddily on the spot, still clutching his hands in her own.

"Oh, Moss, we thought you weren't coming! We started without you! Even though I told them you wouldn't have forgotten and you'd be here soon and we should have waited…"

"Lace, Lacey, calm down, whatever's going on here?"

His sister continued to jump and as she did so her thick corkscrew ringlets of chocolate brown hair jiggled about on her shoulders. Moss had to laugh, even in his current quest for answers. Everyone close by had stopped to watch as his sister cantered past. He shook his head, and marvelled how the sweet little girl he had grown up with could be turning into such a beautiful young woman. The dress she wore showed off her shapely brown legs and long slim arms. Moss now regretted stealing the expensive white lace he'd used to make her this very garment, which perfectly matched her name, for her recent sixteenth birthday. It made her look far too old, and he didn't like the way older boys were looking at her. Their gaze rested on her figure far longer than was natural in greeting. Maybe they'd have to talk about this later.

"Lace, just try and get your breath back for a minute and tell us what we missed."

Fire placed her hands on her hips indignantly. "*I* didn't miss anything. *I* was here when it was announced. Some of us can keep time, Bro. The only reason I'm out of the throng now is because I had to come and fetch you." Fire didn't like the way Lace was looking anymore than her brother did.

"Hang on a minute! So you could have told me what had already been announced on our way here?"

"I could have but I didn't. I wasn't sure that you deserved it."

"Oh stop it, you two," Lace pulled her brother away from Fire and held him to one side. She had no patience today, of all days, for the bickering that had become a regular occurrence between her two siblings lately.

"What matters is it's happened. It was sooner than any of us expected. Oh, Moss, it's working. Everything is going to be alright!"

"You don't mean…? You can't mean…? The kiss! Already?"

"Yes, Moss. The kiss! It's happened! They were alone together for a moment and he did it. Just went and did it! There was no need for Council. Meetings were abandoned. Replaced with celebrations. Fluorite sent for the best bands, the best food! At dusk there will be fireworks!"

"Oh Lace!" Moss grasped his sister round the waist and swung her body high up into the air. On steady feet he twirled her round several times before letting go and allowing her own wings to spread and bring her lightly down to the ground with a grin.

Caught in the euphoria, Moss shamefully remembered his unnecessary ruckus with Fire and ran to her side to hug her too. Gratefully she pressed her cheek into his chest and smiled. Before long, an army of friends had drawn in to share the Agates' open display of pleasure. Everyone knew they had worked hard for this.

Another amiable cheer went up from the crowd and someone feeling flush blew a precious dandelion clock with such force that the seeds exploded above the clearing and showered the occupants in a wave of cotton snow.

All was well. All was as planned.

5

Helena Spotswood

Steeple High is a huge, imposing stone building which stretches its various blocks and faculties across the centre of Steeple Town like a tarantula spreading its many legs. Ancient in origin, it was rumoured to have been many things prior to its establishment as a school in the 1960s – a hospital, a library, a paper mill, a stately home, even an orphanage – though only some had accompanying paperwork to prove their legitimacy.

Despite the small population of Steeple Town and its neighbouring villages, the school was tremendously oversubscribed due to the high percentage of top exam results. Many young customers arrived from out of town to be taught here, and there was great competition to secure a place. Luckily, those who lived in the area immediately around Steeple Town were automatically deemed worthy, regardless of their academic bravado. As was usually typical of the blessed however, the local teenagers who crowded the halls on the first day back failed to see what all the fuss was about. Steeple High was just school. And the magnificent castle-like turrets and stained glass windows went unnoticed.

The sun was high in the sky. Golf-quality lawns were now invisible beneath the feet of hundreds of pupils waiting around for the first shrill bell of the new school year. The wide corridors within were equally packed and bodies jostled for space as they fought their way to new or familiar lockers and form rooms. Voices called out to one another, excited at seeing friendly faces they had missed over previous weeks. Vital gossip was exchanged and glossy holiday snaps swapped between eager hands with sighs of longing for the beaches they depicted. Squeaky new school shoes scuffed out a rhythm on the glistening chequerboard tiles. Doors swung to and fro on their sturdy hinges. Timetables were wafted like fans in the air. Footballs bounced disobediently out of owners' hands. Teachers called for discipline in the passages. And eventually the monotonous old clock in the hall heralded a five-minute warning.

Rosie prised open her steel locker door for the first time in six weeks. It had always been stiff and she bit her lip to stop herself swearing as the lock snagged on her knuckle. Peering in she was greeted by the patronisingly smiley faces of teenage Hollywood pin-ups – some she had circled with permanent marker love hearts and her initials. Tutting, she pulled them down and crumpled the flimsy magazine paper in her fist.

"Replacing them for posters of Guy, are we?"

Rosie grinned unashamedly as the locker door beneath her own swung open and Sally squatted at her feet to reach inside.

"Maybe." Rosie loved the thought. A photograph of the two of them together. Entwined. Now that would make it worth purposely leaving her locker open for passers-by to see. Maybe if they went on a date this week she could persuade Guy to go inside one of those booth things – where you get passport pictures taken. They would have to squeeze really close for that…

Rosie had, in fact, not spoken to Guy since the kiss. The thought of dropping by his house unannounced yet again seemed inevitably disastrous. Goodness knows what further ludicrous mishap fate might throw at her, and there was no way she was risking putting him off her a third time. Rosie had made her mind up that the next time she walked down his garden path would be on strict invitation only. Luckily the magic of that last, blissful moment had been more than enough to keep her floating in contentment. Otherwise the past two weeks of waiting would have sent her insane. Every passing minute she had prayed he felt the same, and each time she remembered his hands on her waist she knew for sure that he did. Happiness. It was great.

One thing which occurred to her was that in the flash of time before Jemma had driven her away, they had swapped neither phone numbers nor e-mail addresses. A crazy technological error in this day and age! At least that would have been a safe way of keeping in touch. She'd searched for his profile online but he must have had it set to private. She really must ask about that – as soon as she saw him today. *Today! It was finally going to be today!*

Sally was on her knees sorting through her new stationary. Various tools glittered in their cellophane wrappers on the floor. She had a pink ruler, a pink eraser, pink sharpener, pink stapler with pink staples, pink paperclips, pink post-its and several pink pens. All of these were lovingly dusted with a silk scarf before being delicately placed in a pink pencil tin and slotted neatly into a space in her locker.

Rosie smiled. "Pink overload, Sal?" She patted her own satchel with its diamante buckle. "Me too."

"Oh, you two pinkies make me barf!" Billie strode in, reaching for her own locker above Rosie's. Boldly she slapped a large poster onto the inside of her door and held it in place while she bit off tape to stick it. A severed head, dripping blood, with snakes oozing out of the eye sockets, stared grimly back at them.

"The logo of the new best band on the planet," she explained in answer to her friends' critical glare. "You know you really should check out the album. It's totally the direction we should be heading with our new stuff." The poster was actually too big for Billie's door and when she tried to close it, the sides caught in the hinges and tore. "Pain! That's what it's all about!"

Sally and Rosie shook their heads.

At morning break the three girls sat on the lawn in the heat. Between the library and the cafeteria the flat grass was lusciously mown like a soft green carpet, and students welcomed the opportunity to spread their limbs across its surface between lessons. In the space of two periods, an unlucky few had already been given homework, and discarded textbooks and worksheets were scattered between the bodies.

"Life is *soooo*...unfair!" Rosie held her head in her hands, while the other two sucked on the straws of squashy orange juice cartons. Guy had not been in their form room that morning, or any of their lessons for that matter. He'd been placed with 8E who were based in the science block, the complete opposite end of school to Rosie's class, 8C. Scanning the long lists pinned to the cork notice boards in reception, she'd also learned with a groan that he'd been put in a separate House to her. Out of Hazel, Ash, Blackthorn and Willow, she had been made a 'Willow' on arrival last year, and Mr Flower had now been labelled a 'Blackthorn'. Appropriate really, she supposed, since Blackthorns were generally stereotyped as the best looking and most popular Steeple students, but it did mean there was no chance of them sitting together in House assemblies, or celebrating wins together in House team games. *Grr.*

"Stop stressing, Rose petal," Billie patted her friend on the back and tossed her used carton into a nearby bin. "We'll get a message to him to come round to Sal's tonight. I invited Des and Deano to the garage to give their opinion on our new tunes. We could jazz up the event and make it a bit of a party. Nibbles and all! It'll do Guy good to get out and meet the boys. Make some new friends. No matter how big the crush he has on you, it's bound to mash his mind sooner or later, hanging with girls all the time."

"You did what?" Sally shifted her weight to her elbows and sat up straight. Anger flashed behind her eyes. "Our tunes are nowhere near ready to be heard by anyone else yet!"

"Oh, I know. I told them they may need a little reworking."

"A little! Billie, they're totally raw. I am not embarrassing myself. Besides, I haven't checked it with Mum. She might not like us having other people round. You two are one thing. She accepts you as part of the garage furniture – as much as Dad's beer fridge and the stepladders – but Des and Deano? I mean, come on!"

"What's with Des 'and' Deano anyway?" Rosie interjected. "I thought last time we spoke about them you said you had to choose between one or the other. I thought they were fighting over you?"

"They were. They are. But I really like them both. In a brotherly kind of way. And a little male competition is healthy for all concerned." She licked her fingertip and smoothed her eyebrows in mock pretension. "I can't help it if I'm irresistible."

"Irresistible? Ha! Please don't make me laugh! I wouldn't have thought Billie Featherstone and the word 'irresistible' could possibly go together in the same sentence."

A tall and extremely slim shadow had come to loom over them, flanked either side by a pair of equally trim matching shadow accessories.

"Doc Martins? Black fingernails? Dreary dark funeral attire? Irresistible? Wha'da'ya say, girls? More like *irritable!*"

A loud chorus of hyena laughter echoed at close range to accompany the snide remark. This could be no other than the Steeple High Super Bitch and her Queen Bee cronies.

"Drop dead, Helena."

"Oh wouldn't you just love that, Billie. Unfortunately I much prefer hanging out here and making your life misery. And frankly, in that overdose of eyeliner, you look like the dead one. Snuffed it long ago."

Another outbreak of high-pitched cacophony.

Helena Spotswood was dressed in tight leather trousers. They were a shade of dusty gold and sparkled like glitter under the sun's rays. Her high-heeled strappy sandals were of an identical texture, as was her hat-box shaped clutch bag which swung to and fro under her perfectly painted red talons. She wore a crop-sleeved white blouse, cut at the chest in a low V-line to emphasise the large jewel encrusted pendant in the shape of a letter 'H' which hung at her delicate throat. Both the belt which nipped in her tiny waist and the sunglasses on the top of her blonde head were leopard print.

Rosie wondered how long it must take to get ready in

a morning if you were Helena Spotswood. Did she line up her colour coordinated outfits and accessories by the light of the moon, long before the first bird had even thought about catching the worm? Despite her undeniable beauty and striking disposition, Rosie could not help but be reminded of Lego every time she saw Helena around school. Her expensive short bob-cut was stylish, yet harsh, and framed her face like a helmet. Rosie quickly pressed her fingertips to her mouth and fought to suppress a giggle as the image of a blonde Lego woman entered her mind.

The girls at either side of Helena were Tracy and Shelby Brook: twins with dark skin and masses of glossy, curly black hair. The matching pink velour tracksuits they wore with diamante flip-flops looked extremely pricey and designer. They were the style that belonged on a movie star's wife as she jogged with a personal trainer in Central Park, poodle in handbag tucked below arm. The sweatbands which held a large majority of their massive hair back from their pretty faces were naturally the same material as the tracksuits and Rosie felt dizzy from staring up at the three girls in wonder.

Helena had turned her malicious gaze on little Sally, who shrunk in the shadow cast on the lawn, a frightened deer in head-lights.

"Have you been away on holiday this summer, Sally? Oh, shame." She never gave Sally the chance to reply. "Couldn't your family afford it? I suppose not, with the kind of house you live in. One of the semis in the village, isn't it? Being from out of Steeple and living in the city, I tend to forget how the other half live. We went to Florida and Miami this summer. Absolutely loved it." Here, Helena tossed her head coquettishly over her shoulder, but her blonde bob didn't budge. "Mummy said I looked at home there. She's thinking of sending me to college in California when I'm sixteen."

Her companions gasped in awe at this remark, but Billie muttered under her breath. "Thank God for that. Then we won't have to put up with you anymore."

"Ah, jealous are you Featherstone? Just 'cos your idea of a big holiday would be Whitby to visit Dracula's lair!"

Tracy and Shelby squealed like this was the joke of the year, and grasped their idol's arm as though they could barely stand on their feet through the pain of the laughter. The whole debacle was extremely fake and forced. Students nearby turned to see what the disturbance was all about and when many of them, especially boys, saw that it was Helena Spotswood in their midst, they drew closer like dumb moths to a flame. Yes, the young, male population really were as pathetic and naïve as one would suspect when this threesome walked abroad. Boys went wild for Miss Spotswood, and now Rosie could see them tripping and bumping into each other as they forgot their direction whilst glancing at Helena's leather-clad legs. Really, the non-uniform code that Steeple had long ago adopted just wasn't all it was cracked up to be.

"Rosie!"

She jumped at the sound of her own name.

"I happen to have overheard you talking about a new boy-friend. I can't believe you'd even know what to do with one. I hope he hasn't tried to hold hands with you yet. I bet you'd run a mile!"

Helena's constant criticism had got too much for Billie. She jumped up from the grass and got right up close in the girl's face. They were both the same height. "For your information, Miss Fantastic, they are making out twenty-four seven!"

"Billie!" Rosie was mortified and sprang to her feet to dispel the outrageous remark from her friend.

"Oh, really?" Helena grinned at Rosie, delighted with this new tit-bit. "So she's gone from 'queasy' to 'easy', has she? You want to watch yourself there, Rosie. People will get the wrong impression. Especially boys, who are only after one thing. You're pretty. You've got style. Unlike your friends. In fact I never could understand why you hang out with them. You seem much more suited to my cool brigade."

And before Rosie could think of a suitable clever retort,

Helena Spotswood had turned on her high gold heels and gone, closely followed by her twin shadow puppets. Billie rang her hands together like she was squeezing the excess water from a dishcloth. "Oooo, I hate her!"

"Me too," said Sally. "She winds me up something chronic."

"Just ignore her." Rosie patted her friends on the shoulders. "She only does it because she's jealous."

"Jealous of what?" Sally spluttered. "What do we possibly have that could make *her* jealous?"

"I don't know. But my mum always says that bullies only taunt you because of some deficiency in themselves."

"I think she was dropped on her head at birth," said Billie, "and that's why she's such an arrogant, messed-up bitch!"

"Come on," Rosie smiled and shook her head, "we'll be late for Maths."

It was lunchtime in the cafeteria when Rosie finally got her first sight of Guy. She was sucking on a sugar cube and saw him walk in. He was wearing baggy jeans, pink and black chequered trainers without laces, and a pale salmon shirt open at the neck. Already he was surrounded by a dozen new friends, vying for his attention, but when he saw Rosie in a booth by the window, gently he extracted himself from their clutches and fought his way through the crowds to her side.

"Hey, I've been looking everywhere for you."

"Ditto. I can't believe we're not in the same form. Or even in the same lessons."

Guy pulled a crumpled piece of paper from his back pocket and spread it on the table before them. "Well, I've been looking into it. Where there are sets, it seems they've put me in middle ability groups to start with, so they can suss where I'm at. What I need to do is act like a real genius in English, and a real dork in Maths. Then I might get moved to be with you."

"Hey!" Rosie swatted him on the head with her purse. "Are you saying I'm thick because I'm bottom set Maths?"

"You can't be good at everything. I hear you pretty much rule

76

the school when it comes to literature. I was talking to the girl you sit next to."

"Well, you've certainly found your feet," Billie said from the bench opposite. "What is it? Three hours you've been here, and already you look like you've met half the Steeple High population!"

Guy laughed and his eyes twinkled. "Rosie Quartz, what on earth are you eating for your dinner?" Rosie froze, her arm suspended mid-air as she was just about to take another lick of her sugar lump.

"I know, it's disgusting, isn't it?" said Sally. "She's a weirdo. Does it all the time. We can't get her to stop."

Guy reached over and took the cube out of Rosie's fingers. The first contact of their skin in weeks shot electric currents through her veins. "Sugar rots your teeth, you know."

"We've told her, but she has an endless supply in her handbag. Nicks them from the cafe."

Rosie's cheeks reddened at this banter passing back and forth around her as if she wasn't there. She didn't want Guy thinking she was going to turn into a huge sugar monster, but at the same time she had never been able to fathom even to herself why she had such a huge fascination with anything immensely sweet. "Some people smoke, drink, take drugs, all manner of horrible things. I don't do any of that. I just happen to like sugar."

"We all eat sugar, Rose," said Billie, "But you – you suck it in cubes! Aren't ponies supposed to do that?"

"That's Polos."

"And sugar. Guy, just remember we warned you, you're dating a weirdo!"

Rosie flinched at the word "dating" and quickly looked at Guy to gauge his reaction. There was none. "Maybe you'd like some of my sandwich instead?" he suggested, reaching into the record bag slung around his broad shoulders. "Mum made them. Cheese and pickle." He tore off the tin foil and showed her the nutty brown bread. "Here, I'll break it in two." He halved the fat sandwich with his fingers as neatly as if he'd used a knife. Gratefully Rosie accepted and swallowed the sugar lump whole.

"Oh, how adorably sweet!" A voice came from above them and the accompanying figure stopped abruptly by their table. Rosie's happy moment was broken by the second appearance of Helena that day. "Are you going to introduce me to your friend, Rosie?"

"No. She's not," snapped Billie, who spread her hand over the gap on the bench so that Helena couldn't sit down.

But the girl had already wafted her blood red nails in Guy's direction, and held her smooth palm in a gesture to be shook. A diamond ring flashed on her index finger, and then went out like a snuffed candle as Guy smothered her waiting skin with his own. "Pleased to meet you. I'm Guy."

"Well hello, Guy, and the pleasure is all mine. Spotswood. As in Spotswood Plastic. My dad's the surgeon. I'm Helena. *Au revoir* handsome." Helena winked and picked an imaginary speck of dust from the hem of her blouse, before flicking it in Rosie's direction and leaving as suddenly as she had arrived.

Guy was captivated. "Wow! She seems nice."

"Nice?" Billie jumped in her seat. "She's a two-headed dragon!"

The bell rang to signal the end of dinner, and Guy shoved the rest of the sandwich into his mouth in one go. "I have PE next. Gotta shoot," he said between gulps.

"Wait! Come to Sally's tonight," said Rosie. "We're having a gathering in the garage. You can meet some more people." She was amazed at how brave she'd been, coming out with it just like that.

Sally huffed and rolled her eyes, defeated.

"Yeah, cool." Guy stepped out of the booth and squeezed Rosie's hand reassuringly. "Sounds good. Don't know where it is though, so I'll wait for you by the main entrance after school. You can give me directions."

"Fantastic." Rosie beamed.

"See y'all later."

As Guy crossed the floor of the cafeteria, Rosie caught sight of Helena hanging around by the exit door. Guy drew close, oblivious of the forthcoming encounter and Rosie saw Helena purposely allow her folder and books to slip from her arms and come crashing to the tiles, papers fluttering and fanning across the path Guy had just been about to take. Apologetically, he dropped to his knees and began to gather her belongings as though the accident had been his fault. As he passed the heap back to her, Helena flashed him a Hollywood, white-tooth smile, and touched his arm to say thank you. The pair walked off across the yard together, engaged in some enthused conversation which Rosie couldn't hear as they disappeared from sight.

Everyone sat round in Sally Nuttall's garage. Sally, Billie, Rosie, Guy, Des, Deano, and two more of the latter's friends whose names no one really seemed to know. The door was wound open and the sky outside was turning a deep, velvet blue at the sun's demise. A portable CD player sat on top of the fridge and the indie band sounded tinny and distorted in its dusty and aging speakers. Sally was at its side, constantly skipping to the tracks she liked best, and every now and then someone would complain because their personal favourite had been cut short. Deano sat munching directly from the giant bowl of crisps Mrs Nuttall had put out for them. He'd played his cards well, as after his grubby hands (covered with bike chain oil) had delved in, nobody else wanted to sample them. The two other boys who'd come were opening an old box of Subbuteo, which they'd found poking out beneath a stack of cobweb ridden shoeboxes. Happily, they pieced the faded stands together, marvelling at the headless players in their chipped blue and red shirts. Billie was showing Des her new guitar, but protectively pulling it away from him every time he got too close. Rosie sat next to Guy, breathing in the delicious scent of whichever deodorant he always wore. The pair of them sang along to the music, and occasionally twisted their heads shyly to smile at each other.

The Steeple Street framed before them was still and peaceful. A coal-black cat had passed once or twice on its way out for night mouse watch, but luckily Rosie hadn't noticed. She was too engrossed in her time with Guy. Her daydreams were deep, but not so concrete as to withstand a sudden noise, which stirred all the kids from whatever they had been doing. The pea-sized Subbuteo ball rolled to a halt on the felt and Billie forgot to stop Des putting his handprints on her beloved instrument. There was a roar and a screech, followed by a heady scent of fuel and tires. Loud pumping dance tunes drowned out the indie music, and a pristine metallic blue car snapped into view. Its exhaust puthered smoke as the engine over-revved in standstill.

"Wowee!" Guy jumped to his feet. "A Chrysler Sebring Cabriolet! Convertible! In blue as well. My favourite colour. Now that is sexy!"

Slowly the roof of the car slid back. Rosie saw two good-looking boys, both wearing sunglasses despite the time of evening – and both obviously a lot older than her and her friends. She wondered why they had chosen to make such a dramatic stop outside Sally's house. Her question was answered almost as quickly as it had formed, for as the roof's movement ceased, Helena Spotswood popped up her head from the back seat and raised herself to wave at the stunned faces.

"Yoo-hoo! How do you do fellow Steeple students?"

She had changed her earlier outfit for a purple skin-tight dress. Its silk material glistened against the stars, which had just started to come out.

"Jonathan, turn the music down. I can't hear my friends."

"Friends?" spluttered Billie in rage, staggering as she parted with her guitar. "Who's she kidding?"

The boy in the driver's seat lowered the volume on his dance track and the Ibiza beat faded to a distant pulsing sound. He was extremely handsome, although it pained Rosie to admit it, since she now knew from the name Jonathan that this must be Helena's older brother. He'd been mentioned in school. Many of her female classmates scrawled his name in biro over their pencil cases and "*Oooed*" and "*ahhed*" when he collected Helena from school – rainy afternoons when she couldn't possibly get herself wet. The eighteen-year-old, sports-car-driving Jonathan Spotswood was just one more reason for his pretty sister to be smug about their family's popularity. She revelled in it, and missed no opportunity to parade their connection right now, hanging out of the roof and homing in on Guy.

"This is Rob, Jono's friend."

The equally tall, dark and slick front passenger raised his hand in acceptance of the introduction, but couldn't have looked less interested in a garage full of kids, and began twiddling with the knobs on the stereo again.

Tracy Brook was also in the back seat, shiny and smiling. One of her hands played with the huge silver loops in her ears, but the other looked suspiciously close to Jonathan's denim-clad shoulder. Rosie wondered if Mrs Brook knew her twelve-year-old daughter was driving around with a college boy, even if it was her best friend's brother.

"Shelby couldn't come. She abandoned us for ballet lessons, so there's a spare seat in the car, and a spare cinema ticket going. We're thinking of going to watch the new Bond movie." Helena waved a rectangular piece of cardboard in Guy's direction. This select invitation was clearly meant for no one but him.

Guy turned to Rosie and then looked down at his shoes. "I... I can't. Thanks 'H', but I promised Rosie I'd hang here."

Helena pulled on the pleats of her dress. "Oh, shame. You look like cars are your thing. And this baby sure is smooth. You'd love the ride." As if to rub salt into Guy's growing wound, Jonathan revved up the engine and stroked the leather dashboard. "Sure I can't tempt you?" He was anxious to get going.

Rob in the passenger seat pulled a packet of cigarettes from the glove compartment, and Rosie turned away, feeling guilty even to witness the scene. Guy caught her arm and held her nose to his own. It was the closest they'd been since the kiss and her heart flipped. "Look, Guy," she said, not pulling away, "I can tell you really want to go. Who am I to stop you?"

"But I feel bad when I was supposed to be spending time with you." He glanced back at the vehicle out on the street. "I've never been in a Chrysler Cabriolet though."

"Exactly."

Releasing Rosie and holding her at arm's length, Guy grinned from ear to ear. "Hold up 'H', I'm coming!"

Billie had a face like thunder, and took several steps after him before stopping with her hands on her hips. "Oh, 'H' is it now?"

"Don't Billie," Rosie touched her back. "We don't control him. And besides, it's good that he's making new friends so soon and fitting into the school." She watched Guy as he effortlessly vaulted over the car door and landed in the back seat between Helena and Tracy. As the car made its final rebellious sound and shot away down Steeple Street, Guy Flower never once looked back.

Billie marched over to their own stereo and switched it off. All was quiet in the garage. Various members of the group began to pick up their jackets and slip them on. Buttons and zips were awkwardly fastened. Guy's sudden departure had seemingly destroyed the pleasant mood. Rosie grasped the handle of her own handbag and headed for the door. In the crescent moonlight she caught Sally's eye and tried to smile an amiable farewell, but the courtesy never truly met her face. Melancholy hung in the air. A strange atmosphere.

If the words she had just spoken were true – the ones about Guy's new friendships being a positive thing – then why did Rosie feel an incessant foreboding? As though something terrible was about to happen?

6

Making Contact

She first caught sight of them holding hands on a cold morning in November. The granules melted on her tongue but Rosie couldn't taste them. Sucking a routine sugar cube, she sat on her damp garden wall and thought yet again about the previous month.

Guy and Helena. Helena and Guy. No matter how people said the phrase, it had grown to sound right. Accepted. Familiar. Commonplace. And though the tears still frequently stung her eyes, even Rosie had to admit that in the grand scheme of things it made sense for the glamorous couple to be together. Blackthorns. Aesthetics. A logical communion. Appraised and approved by the mass body of Steeple High students who admired them and wanted to be like them. Having never known such a tumultuous high as Guy's adoration had brought her, Rosie hadn't been prepared for the waves of emotion that threatened to crush her at the sudden removal of his affection. She was a shipwrecked sailor drowning at sea.

It had been hard. It had been painful and hurtful beyond words. Especially the more she saw of the inseparable pair, talking and laughing, walking arm in arm, sharing an umbrella across the lawn when it showered. But always inside her was the voice which declared she shouldn't be surprised. Helena Spotswood was irresistible. Guy was bound to be bewitched by her. Who could blame him? It had, after all, been gradual. Guy had tried for weeks post-car ride to show enthusiasm for Rosie. Smile around her. Joke around her. But then, on cue, the coordinated couture of Miss Spotswood would loom in a nearby doorway and Guy would leap to follow like a giddy puppy freed from his leash.

The weekend before Rosie saw their first open display of comradeship by the library, Guy had walked Rosie home after school and paused at the foot of her path when she invited him in for drinks.

"I'm meeting Jono," he said. "I have to get washed and changed in time for my bus out of town."

Rosie lifted her heavy satchel from his shoulder, which he'd carried for her. "Jono, as in the great Jonathan Spotswood, I suppose?"

"Yes."

"And Helena will be there?"

"Yes."

"And that's the reason you're really going, isn't it?"

Guy shifted his weight from one chequered sneaker to the other and looked beyond Rosie to a threadbare autumn tree. It began to rain.

"It's okay, Guy. You can tell me. I know you've been spending an awful lot of time with her lately. You like her. I can see that. We should just be honest with each other."

"Jono knows some big football scouts. Professionals from the city. He says he can get me a trial." He reached for her hand. "Helena says she's going to talk to her father about getting his business to sponsor my mum's faery pottery!" A change in his tone. "She's not doing so well with sales at the minute."

"That's great, Guy. These people can obviously give you what you want. That's where you should be." The rain slid down her nose and she was thankful of the camouflage which meant she could cry undetected.

"Rosie." Tentatively Guy lifted a wet strand of her yellow hair plastered to her cheek. He smiled at her like the first time they had met – in the Flower's living room, in the sunshine, his teeth perfect, his eyes large. "Rosie Quartz, you are special. I hope we can always be friends."

"*Friends…*" Rosie whispered the word but it tasted like poison on her tongue. "Friends, yes. Of course we can, Guy." Wind hurtled through the gaps in the houses on Steeple Chase. A bleak November gale was taking hold.

He drew her towards him and held her really tight to his chest, the weather locking them together like Velcro. Although the embrace was a sad one, a final one, an inevitable goodbye, Rosie still appreciated every drop of the contact. For a long time neither one of them chose to move. Then over her back Guy looked at his watch.

"I have a feeling there's more to me and you. Something more…" he said before leaving.

And the next morning he'd kissed Helena by the library stairs.

Connecting the memories, raindrops began to fall in the present, and Rosie watched splashes make abstract patterns on the wall around her. Strawberry stirred by her side, turning her whiskered nose skyward to detect the intrusion.

"Come here, beautiful girl," Rosie murmured, lifting the lethargic rabbit. Her huge velvet feet stuck out at right angles and her lop ears tickled Rosie's face as she held her close. "If only people were as reliable as you. You've never let me down. Been here to cry on as long as I can remember. And you never answer back, never blame me like Billie. Or pity me like Sally. You just listen. And stare at me from under those big bunny lashes. That's what I need right now." Strawberry yawned and pushed her nose into the folds of Rosie's thick cardigan.

"It's not like I hate Guy or anything, you know Berry. I don't think I could ever hate him or blame him for what he did. Sally says she'd buy him a ticket for a coach ride over a cliff, and Billie says she'd gladly be the driver with the only parachute, but I just don't feel like that. In fact, if he realised his mistake and came grovelling back tomorrow, I'd happily forgive him. I wouldn't have the heart to be strong. But that's not going to happen, is it Berry? So I have to get over it. I have to let go and move on."

The rain momentarily stopped and Strawberry's long ears twitched. Her head shot round, alert. She'd seen something or heard something. Her nostrils flared and her eyes widened to vigilant saucers. As Rosie followed her stare, she noticed that a garden windmill-shaped ornament had fallen over onto its side. Maybe that had made Strawberry jump. Shifting Strawberry from her lap, Rosie reached out to push it upright, and then quickly retreated, gasping in shock. Something had moved inside it. The middle was hollow, and behind the tiny, fake windows and arched door, something had fluttered. A bird? A mouse? The motion made too much of an impact for it to be an insect.

"Come on, Rosie, pull yourself together," she chided herself. "A small animal can't hurt you...Or *you!*" She patted Strawberry, who had now curled up nonplussed on her haunches. "Bird or mouse, you're twice its size. You should be sniffing it out, not leaving me to be pecked or bitten." With one swift movement Rosie pushed the windmill back onto its base. Feeling braver, she peered into one of the top windows. There was nothing there.

Debra Quartz appeared on the porch step. "Rosie, honey, you're soaking! When did it start to rain?"

"I'm okay, Mum. I was supposed to be cleaning out Strawberry's cage, but then I kinda forgot why I was out here. I'll do it now."

"Well, Billie's on the phone. That's why I've come out to get you. Take it up in your bedroom. Your dad's watching a Roman documentary down here."

Rosie sighed. Talking to Billie was the last thing she felt like doing right now, but she told Strawberry to wait on the patio, and begrudgingly trudged indoors.

"Why don't you put up a fight? I don't get you, Rosie! You can't just give up."

"Yes, I can."

"But by standing aside and doing nothing, you're just letting that Super Bitch get away with stealing Guy and making your life misery. It's doing your reputation no good at all. People will think you're weak. I say you should punch her lights out!"

"That isn't going to solve anything Billie."

Rosie held the pink fluffy telephone receiver away from her ear whilst Billie continued her tirade, most of it gruesome explanations of what she would personally do to Helena if she had a chainsaw or knuckleduster. Bored, Rosie looked around her room and noticed that the framed photo of her and her parents which she kept on her bedside table had been turned around to face the wall. Her mother must have knocked it whilst she was cleaning. Stretching the cord till the coils pulled taut, Rosie leant across her bed and spun the image around. It showed her in the middle of Debra and Daniel, aged about six, the three of them golden brown on a holiday in Majorca. Despite her current despair, the warm familiarity of her parents' faces made her smile. She flopped down and braced herself for the next fifteen minutes of Billie's aggressive opinion.

Grey evening shadows had fallen when she hung up the phone and Rosie padded across the room to her standing lamp for a little illumination. Strawberry would need putting back in her hutch for the night. Scanning around for a jacket she could pull on against the cold, Rosie screamed. A chill went through her entire body which had nothing to do with the November weather. For a second or two she failed to breathe and her hand flew to her hammering heart. There on the bedside table the framed picture which she'd straightened moments ago was now upside down. Herself and her parents standing on their heads on the Majorca beach. She was so sure she had not placed the photo like that. But she must have, and now she shook her head at her foolish behaviour. How silly to hyperventilate at such a trivial mishap. Willing her heartbeat back to normal, Rosie placed the frame the right way up and went downstairs.

Strawberry hadn't moved an inch, her eyes tightly shut. Rosie walked straight to her cage and began to stuff it with hay for the cold night ahead. She tugged at the lawn and released a handful of supper – dandelion leaves for Strawberry to munch on. This familiar action would usually have had her beloved pet sniffing her own way homebound, so when Strawberry still failed to budge, Rosie tapped her nails against the chicken wire and whistled softly.

Strawberry's lop ears engulfed the rest of her face like a snug, comforting winter scarf. She looked peaceful, but somehow far away. Rosie watched her for a moment and then intuition took hold. A deep black hole opened up at her feet and her stomach lurched and sank down it. The horrible realisation set in.

"Mum, Mum, come quick! There's something wrong. It's Berry! She's not moving!"

Daniel Quartz took his spade from the shed and dug a low resting place in the rockery. His powerful torch propped on a boulder, shed a pathway of light onto the dark corner of the garden. Rosie stood close by as her dad worked, an old picnic blanket and her mother's arm draped across her trembling shoulders. She blew noisily into a wet handkerchief and her sobs shook her from within. When Daniel was finished, he placed the stone windmill on top of the fresh earth.

"We'll get a small plaque to put on the roof," he said. "In memory of Strawberry."

"Come on, sweetheart," her mum kissed her lightly on the forehead and steered her away from the grave. "Let's get you inside and make you a nice hot chocolate."

"Why is this happening?" Rosie tore the blanket to the ground and turned on her parents, red eyed. "What more could possibly go wrong for me? What have I ever done to deserve this?"

"Berry was an old rabbit, Rosie. You had her a long time. It was bound to happen sooner or later."

"But why now? Why is everything happening all at once? Why is nothing going right? I just can't stand it anymore!" Crying uncontrollably, Rosie ran into the house, up the stairs, slamming her bedroom door behind her.

It was a long night, through which she couldn't sleep. Her world felt shattered and disjointed. Thousands of pieces of an unsolvable jigsaw puzzle, scattered and carried on the wind. When she did drift into restless dreams, they were of Strawberry disappearing down a tunnel. Rosie called to her and chased her into a huge garden. It was vast and Rosie screamed as she lost sight of her pet, terrified that the rabbit would lose her way. Strawberry didn't know anybody here. Who would care for her and keep her company?

In the morning Rosie lay awake before her alarm clock sounded. Her entire body ached. Her chest felt hollow. Slowly, gradually, she eased herself to a sitting position, knees domed beneath the duvet. With a weak arm outstretched, she feebly swatted the bleating clock. Had yesterday really happened? Could it be rewritten? Had Strawberry really gone? Or was it merely one of the fragmented dreams between tossing and turning and lying awake?

"Rosie, I've poured you a drink. Come on down." Her mother. Fussing again. So, yes, it was real. Damn.

Standing in front of the antique mirror on her white Gustavian dressing table, Rosie rubbed her eyelids hard, hoping the action would pour some small sign of life into her shadow of a self. Her reflection oozed into view, like spilt ink spreading on a clean page. And sure enough, the sight jolted her harshly back into her bones.

"What the...?"

Rosie touched her head and leaned forward, the tip of her nose curiously drawn to the glass, as though she would tumble in like Alice.

"How can...? Who did...?"

She grasped her hair tighter, as though this would somehow reverse the damage. Every strand of her beautiful blonde mane had inexplicably been tangled into hundreds of intricate plaits. They snaked outwards, wiry and taut, like Medusa's slithering snakes in twisted, spiky, braided patterns. Now Rosie was used to the usual fluff and messiness from a night's turning on the pillow – she regularly straightened out the morning frizz – but this! This was something else.

"Muuuummmm!!!"

This could not possibly have been done by mere turns in bed. Gypsy ladies did this for you at the seaside and required decent payment in return. This had been done by another person. Some*body* had done this to her. *Someone* had crept up in the night and manically knotted her hair. But her mum or dad? The only other two people in the house? No way. Surely not.

"Muuuummm!!!"

Once Debra Quartz had explained for the umpteenth time that Rosie must have subconsciously fashioned this herself in the night whilst she slept, Rosie calmed down just slightly. Debra pulled a comb through the last of the plaits. Although the matted hair did vaguely resemble a bird's nest in texture, it gradually took on a more regular approach to gravity. Rosie sipped from a glass of milk and begrudgingly chewed through half a bowl of soggy cornflakes. A bobble was snapped around the offensive locks and Rosie trudged back upstairs to her room where the bed had been left unmade.

If a member of the family died, Rosie reasoned that her teachers wouldn't expect her in school the following day. The fact that Strawberry was a rabbit had never particularly excluded her from the Quartz household, but Rosie wondered if her form tutor would take that point of view on this occasion. Besides, her mother had not offered to write a sick note, which on top of the added hair incident undoubtedly foretold that she too expected Rosie to carry on as though everything were cheerfully back to normal. With a sigh she tipped her bag of exercise books out onto the duvet and began to sift which ones she needed today – Maths, English, History, Geography. Oh, and there was her English homework to be packed. She'd done it on a separate A4 sheet a few days back and placed it ready in the top dressing table drawer. They'd been told to write a poem on a subject which meant a lot to them, and Rosie couldn't remember whether it was out of laziness or genuine desire that she had used the lyrics of her most recent song. She'd typed them up neatly on her father's laptop and used font twelve in Times New Roman, just as Mr Anderson liked. Before she had a chance to forget about the poem, Rosie went to the drawer and reached inside. But it wasn't there.

She allowed her fingers to wander some more in the darkness, scrambling around to feel for the edge that must have been jammed. Then she knelt down to peer close, amid the rolled balls of paired socks and elastic headbands. Where had the damn thing got to? She knew for a fact she had put it here. She remembered the moment clearly. Although her head was full of many mysteries at the moment, this was one thing she was certain of. She had put the lyrics in this drawer. But they were gone.

Mr Anderson would give her detention. No second chances for him. He was just that kind of guy. And the infuriating thing was that she had done it and he would not believe her. Tears started to well in the corners of her eyes. She felt the flush of heat in her cheeks and knew she was going to cry. Angrily, she slammed the drawer shut and left a chip on the expensive white woodwork. If one more thing went wrong, just one, Rosie swore she was going to curl herself up into a human ball and not move until the world stopped turning and life came to an end. As it was, she just made sure the front door made an exceptionally loud bang on her way out to school.

There had been a severe downpour of rain in the night and the woodland stream had burst its bank. The excess water rushed hard and fast over upturned rocks, as if in a hurry to get back where it came from. As a result, the nearby houses were temporarily evacuated. Doors and windows were flung open to dry out the insides. Sodden leaves and petals were pegged to makeshift washing lines and a tuneful rhythm dripped in the soil below. Deep amid the foliage of the ground, an angry procession of tiny feet carved out mud-prints on their way to seek friendly neighbours whose homes had survived the flood.

Lace Agate watched them pass and sadly shook her head. From the height of the great hollow tree stump which formed the main body of The Agate Abode, she and her siblings were perfectly safe and protected from any type of freak weather storm.

"Maybe we should ask some of them to come in. I could

make some dandelion tea to warm them through, poor things."

"No chance, Lace," Fire snapped. "We're far too busy here for intruders, and knowing you, you'd probably have the entire Faery Kingdom cramped into our sitting room before you can say *sugar lumps*."

Lace turned from the window and its dried rose petal drapes with a sigh. She hated not to help a fellow faery in misfortune, but did realise that the task at hand called for her careful attention at present. Her brother and sister were sitting at the decoratively carved table in the centre of their communal dining hall. This was one of three large rooms which the Agate family shared in the ancient remains of the severed oak trunk; this along with a well-stocked kitchen and a comfortable cushion-scattered sitting room. The rest of the house had been crafted by their own hands. Three contorted branches projected from the stump in alternate directions and had been carved wide on the inside to form tunnels to the bedrooms, which sat slightly askew at the branch ends. These were fashioned from old, unused birdhouses that Moss and his friends had carried from nearby human gardens. The birds had never looked twice at them – senseless human inventions – but they did do very nicely as private accommodation for Moss, Lace and Fire. Humans did at times get things right but for all the wrong, unforeseen reasons. Each of these three offshoots had its own two matching windows and a low square door so that callers could go straight to their chosen Agate's acquaintance if so wished. Moss Agate's door was forest green. Lace Agate's door was pale blue. And Fire Agate's door was bright red. These were nothing, though, compared with the main entrance to the stump. Here the windows were bayed and lead-panelled, and the heavy arched door, once the original wood of the tree, now bore "The Agate Abode" on a shiny gold sign beneath a sheltering porch. It was everything they had worked for and it was home.

Lace pulled a chair between her brother and sister who sat at opposite ends of the table. She trained her eyes on the object of their contemplation. Consuming the entire surface of the wooden table top was spread a piece of white paper, tacked down in each corner with a pine needle pin so it didn't curl up at the edges. This carefully extracted paper was the missing homework belonging to Rosie Quartz – the lyrics of her most recently written song. All three faeries leaned forward to take a closer look. Moss pushed on a pair of thick-rimmed glasses and spread his wings. He rose from his seat to trace the path of neatly typed lines to the bottom of the page. He read each word aloud as he hovered above them, and then circled the table to settle back down where he'd begun.

Fire screwed up her face and folded her arms. "It's not very good is it?"

Lace rolled her eyes at her sister. "I like it."

"Ha! All that rubbish about '*you, you, you, do, do, do.*' What sort of a poem is that? It doesn't even rhyme. 'You', 'You' and 'You' don't rhyme because they're the same word."

"Does that really matter right now, Fire?" Moss cut her short, mid-tirade, displaying a rising annoyance of his own. "We're not here to be poetry critics. The song isn't important. What *was* important was that she realised that the homework being moved on top of everything else was an unquestionable abnormality and beyond the realms of sheer coincidence. Right now I don't see that happening, do you? And this is what we need to deal with."

"If you mean we need to deal with the fact that absolutely nothing is working, then yes, you are absolutely right!" said Fire.

"Look, we just need to sort this out. We need to slightly rethink things, that's all. Maybe draw up a new list of ideas and work our way down them." Moss was already reaching for a fresh shard of charcoal to jot his thoughts.

"So, on top of the homework and the windmill and the photo frame and the rabbit and the completely wacky hairstyle which took me goodness knows how long and a number of bruises every time she shifted her weight, you want to try out some more exceptionally bright plans, do you Bro? Oh, well, great. That's just great Bro. Except…COUNT ME OUT!" With that Fire lifted herself defiantly and stomped through to the kitchen where she slammed a pan down hard on the stove to boil some drinking water.

"Fine. Absolutely fine. I'll sort this. Me and Lace will go again tonight. Won't we, Sis?" Moss turned for his other sister's support, but found her totally oblivious to their conversation. She was far too immersed in the paper before her, staring intensely at the lyrics and singing the words softly to herself in a whispered breath.

Don't you know I've always thought of you?
And I have harboured all this love for you.
My life before you was just making do.
It seemed a hopeless task I'd choose to see through,
But I never changed my mind about you…

…It's beautiful!"

"Lace? Lacey? Are you listening to me?"

"Of course she's not." Fire walked back through to the dining hall nursing a steaming acorn-shell cup of hot dandelion tea. She had made only herself, and nobody else, one. "She thinks you're talking as much drizzle as I do, except she wouldn't dare say it to you!"

"What? Say what?" Lace snapped out of her reverie and sat upright, brown eyes bright and alert, guilty of having drifted to thoughts of her own.

"I was just saying that nothing's working, so we're going to have to try again." Moss spoke softly now but his deep irritations were clear, etched within the frown lines of his otherwise handsome face. "We do need to get her attention, Lace, and tell her to get this sorted out."

"Yes, yes, of course." Lace reached out for Moss's arm and stroked the fabric of his jacket. "I mean, we could have an absolute disaster on our hands here. After all, she signed "The Book". We've seen the signature with our own eyes. He has to say he loves her before their thirteenth birthday or we're doomed."

"Okay, we know the story," shot Fire. "Her thirteenth birthday is not until April and that is a whole five human months away."

Lace turned to face her younger sister with concern in her eyes. "But what if it's too late by then? What if the damage has already been done and it becomes irreversible, even by us? Guy could be lost to her forever."

"Let's not get carried away," Moss quickly interjected, sensing the gloom which had filled the hall and had nothing to do with the worsening weather outside. The diagonal rain had returned and was forming a pool on the sill of the open window. Dark clouds shifting overhead had wrapped the house and its inhabitants in a grey haze. "It's not the end of the world – yet. Like Fire says, we still have plenty of time. And besides, I just can't see it coming to that. We'll carry on doing exactly what we've been doing – the *three* of us, right Fire? And we'll give it till the end of winter. That can be our goal post. If we genuinely haven't made progress before then, I promise that we'll think about the next step." Moss tugged on his earrings and ran his hands across the stubbly surface of his head, the way he often did when he felt pensive. "If he hasn't done it…if he hasn't said 'I love you' before winter's end, then I'll have to go in and make direct contact. Just give it till the last snowflake falls…"

7

The Last Snowflake

I try to visit Steeple Village as often as I possibly can, because it is such a delightful place to browse around. But there is one time of year in particular when I always go out of my way to drop by, and that is the month of December. Christmas time in Steeple is the most uplifting sight you could ever wish to see. People walk the cobbled streets and their hearts fill with the sense of magic and wonder that these decorative festivities invariably instil.

The first fine scattering of snow powders the slanted roof of the ancient church. Surrounding beech trees are crowned with a white winter makeover and the iron gates which protect the cemetery are locked tight with frosted ice, glittering in the tall lamppost light. Individual gravestones are no longer identifiable in the churchyard, the family names and inscriptions hidden beneath clinging flakes. Large wreathes of holly have been laid by children from the local infant school who pass in nativity procession.

It was the Saturday prior to the last week of school when Rosie, Sally and Billie arrived, armed with pocket money for present shopping at the Great European Christmas Market in Steeple's Medieval Square. Many tourists flocked to the captivating canvas stalls packed into the small flagstoned area around the old stocks. Exotic smells drifted across their counters – mouth watering French baking, Italian handmade soaps and exquisite German incense. The girls were wrapped in their scarves, hats and gloves – Rosie and Sally in pink and Billie in black. They crunched their way through the snow and surveyed the changes the season had stamped across their residence.

The Steeple Village shop and post office, along with its neighbouring row of terraced houses, had been transformed by a web of twinkling fairy lights woven into the ivy-clad walls. A bell rang out above the chatter of busy shoppers, and the girls turned to see the landlord of The Crooked Steeple pub, ringing the handheld chimes outside his open doors to advertise warming hot pear cider.

But by far the greatest spectacle on show in Steeple at this time of year was the gigantic Christmas tree which towered twenty feet above the jovial carol singers huddled at its base. The branches were hung with enormous red and green baubles and bows, along with a collection of recent snowfall. As Rosie, Sally and Billie drew close, the performers were just setting out their song sheets on music stands with lanterns – flames flickering bright.

"We should have brought our own instruments," said Billie, "and really rocked this place off its feet. I do a mean version of 'Silent Night' on my electric guitar – and it's not too silent. "

A waft of cinnamon toffee apples led the girls to one of the market stalls, where they each bought the sticky treats before wandering into the cemetery through a gap in the privet. They found a rectangular monument with sculpted eagles, big enough for the three of them to perch side by side while they licked and chewed and listened to the carollers. The air was still here. The sky was almost tangible amid a dust of snow. Something moved, making them jump – a flash behind the gravestone opposite – but only Rosie had cause for concern when they saw it was Spooky, the white Persian post office cat. Round her neck was a tartan ribbon with a dangling star swinging to and fro, which Mrs Betty Strudel must have tied there. Despite shooing her away with several loud claps even Rosie felt slightly sorry for the feline in its unfortunate fancy dress. The brief scare had, however, reminded her of something she needed to say to her friends.

"What would you guys say if I told you that I keep *seeing* things…?"

"Seeing things?" Sally furrowed her brow. "What kinds of things?"

"Well, that's the trouble. I never really see them for long enough to figure out exactly *what* I'm seeing. But it's always like a flicker in the corner of my eye. Something out of focus beyond my vision. Put it this way; it's something you'd ignore and think nothing of it, if it wasn't for the fact that it's happening all the time."

"Glasses," said Billie. "It sounds like you might be needing glasses. The exact same thing happened to my dad just before he started wearing them. You should get your mum to take you down to the opticians in town."

"I can see perfectly fine, Billie. I don't need glasses. That's the whole point. It's because I'm seeing things *too* well that I'm noticing stuff more. Little movements. Like insects, for example. I think I could spot them a mile off. Tiny details – they seem huge to me. And it's not just that. It's the other things too. Especially the moving of my belongings. That's been driving me crazy – papers, photographs…And this morning, my pink sherbet lipstick. I put it down somewhere while I combed my hair, and I know for a fact exactly where I put it, and then I turn around and in just a split second it's moved to completely the opposite side of the room. I mean, that's just not possible, right?"

"Ghosts," said Billie. "It sounds like you might be seeing ghosts. The exact same thing happened to my mum just before she started reading tarot. You might have spirits attached to you who want to pass on messages to their loved ones."

"Talk about one extreme to the other!" grunted Sally. "If it's not glasses then it's ghosts. Get real, Billie. You're nuts!"

Billie shrugged and took the last bite of her toffee apple, controversially tossing the waste stick into the white graveyard grass. "I've been brought up on this kind of thing. You should come and talk to my mother, Rose. We have ghosts hanging round our house all the time. Although I'm sure on occasion she does just use it as an excuse if she hasn't washed and ironed the clothes I wanted. *Oh, I'm sorry honey, the ghost must have had it!*"

Sally expected Rosie to look as exasperated as herself, but instead she found her deep in contemplation. "Hmmm. Ghosts. Do you really think it might be something supernatural? I've never believed in all that before, but this is definitely out of the ordinary."

Billie was quick to offer more advice. "You need to ask them what it is they want. That's what my mum says to do. Next time you think they're hanging round you, or just when something strange happens, speak to them; say, *'Look, you're freaking me out and unless you say what you need from me I'd like you to bugger off and go!'* Just like that, okay?"

The girls walked back into the mix of market stalls and it was then that Rosie noticed a familiar face. Her heart stammered at the sight of Jemma Flower, leaning over to straighten a row of porcelain faery ornaments she was selling beneath a small yellow tent. Rosie stopped in her tracks, nervous to tread closer in case the attractive Ms Flower were to spot her. She pushed her flushed face further into the folds of her pink scarf, but Jemma had seen. She waved a hand in the girls' direction, half in greeting, half calling them over. Casting an uncomfortable frown at the others, Rosie sauntered in the direction of the faery stall, head still down.

"Rosie! How lovely to see you. It's been ages since our paths last crossed. How are you doing?"

"Just fine," Rosie smiled back, and for a lack of anything real to say, quickly picked up a winter faery to hold her attention.

Sally peered over her shoulder. "They're lovely, aren't they, Rose? Just look at the detail." All three girls began to peel off their gloves so they could better examine the ornaments in their hands. Rosie's wore a crown of holly berries and the full skirt of her dress looked like the hanging bell of a snowdrop flower.

"Yes, they're very pretty." The porcelain was initially cold to the touch but soon warmed intensely in her heated palm. A little shocked by the sudden impact, Rosie placed the faery back down on the counter. Jemma stared at her long and hard.

"I feel I must apologise, Rosie, for the foolish behaviour of that devilish son of mine. Of course I know it's entirely his fault that I haven't seen you around for a while, and I don't really know what to say...Maybe he'll come to his senses. Maybe not. And who knows, if he does someday soon, perhaps you'll have moved on and you can tell him where to stick it. You're a lovely girl, Rosie, and I wouldn't waste too much more time on a boy who's not yet mature enough to realise that. There's a wide world out there. Go and get it."

"Absolutely," chimed Billie, pulling her long gloves back onto her bony fingers, "and with that in mind, let's broaden our horizon and go catch the bus into Steeple Town. Further Christmas shopping awaits. Come on, it's due by the post office in five minutes. Nice to see you again, Mrs Flower. Let's go!"

"*Ms*," Rosie muttered, irritated.

Conversations aboard the Steeple bus rang hollow. The seats were uncomfortable and the framework clicked and trembled as the double decker rattled uncertainly round the country lanes. "Green Man Travels" they were called. As Rosie, Billie and Sally boarded the Green Man snowflakes began to drift diagonally and splatter patterns on the window glass. Rosie watched the formation of a Santa Claus face, whose beard filled out in fluffiness as the flakes picked up pace. Staring deep into the picture till her eyes lost focus, Rosie replayed continually the dialogue Jemma had spoken. Her heart was torn. Billie and Sally were chatting about their shopping requirements and the driver had commentary from an overseas cricket match playing on the radio, but Rosie blocked out the sounds and heard only regret from the mother of the boy she loved with all her being. "Maybe he'd come to his senses. Maybe not." Maybe she'd move on and maybe pigs would fly.

Sally must have sensed her reverie for suddenly she reached across the aisle and gently squeezed her shoulder. Billie noticed the gesture and cut short her rant about the cost of foil wrapping paper.

"Anyway, Rosie, forget Guy Flower. I happen to know that there are some really cute guys at school who just can't wait to get a look in where you're concerned. Take Jack Baxter for instance; just the other day during Geography, he leant over and tapped me on the back. 'Is your mate Rosie going to the Christmas disco at the Village Hall?' he says. 'Sure,' I say. 'Cool,' says he, ''cos I really like her.'"

Rosie groaned. Billie was making this up. And besides, she couldn't stand Jack Baxter.

It wasn't that she didn't know she should be moving on by now. She was quite sure her constant state of numbness must be wearing thin on her friends and family, boring them all to near death. But instead of blocking out the painful memories, Rosie knew that emotionally she was now in a place where she gladly enticed them. The fear was not in remembering what Guy's kisses had tasted like. The fear was in forgetting. Oh, to forget those days! To have them all slip away! What in heaven's name would she do if one morning she awoke and failed to recall the precise hazel brown of his eyes, the exact angle of his yellow fringe across his face, the elicit tone of his silky voice? What then? While she could remember the time she had spent with Guy, it would remain real. As soon as she forgot, it may as well have been imaginary. Like a trick of the light, a blink of the eye, in a moment – gone.

When the bus threw open its doors, a blizzard of icy white shot into the faces of the departing passengers. Stepping onto the sleek pavement, the girls clutched one another's arms for balance. In a tight three they waited for the Green Man to depart. It left them in the glow of another magnificent Christmas tree, stunning with a thousand yellow lights, guarding the main gateway to the high school. From here, the girls could see the path which led to a castle of learning: homework, text books, deadlines and demands.

"Only another week to go chicks," Billie called from deep within the hood of her parka, "and we'll be free of this place. It seems so long ago since summer."

The vast lawns of Steeple High were carpeted white and the stained glass picture windows of the library looked eerie against a backdrop of whirling grey. It was hard to imagine they had laid there in the sunshine, clad in crop tops and fanning themselves with maths papers.

In a chain they crossed the road to the mini roundabout with the World War soldier memorial. From here the town branched in three triangular directions: to the rear left were the endless school grounds and eventually housing estates; the rear right wound back through country lanes to Steeple Village; and straight ahead was Dark Lantern Lane, with its muddled row of quaint shops which some said had traded here since the beginning of time.

A couple of cars circled them carefully on the icy tracks and then they were safe to make haste to the corner of Dark Lantern Lane where the Steeple Print Newspaper Offices stood. Hanging in their high windows was a large banner saying, *"Steeple Print Wish All Our Readers a Very Merry Christmas and a Happy New Year."* Rosie still wasn't too sure whether she would be able to manage either.

If memory serves me right, the first building you come to here in Steeple Town is Cobweb Attic Antiques. It's worth seeing just for the window display. Enchanting archaic goods are stacked onto tiered shelves, jugs jostling for space, gilt frames hanging askew from the wooden ceiling beams. Not an inch of space; an emporium of secondhand and new but made to look secondhand household paraphernalia. As the girls peered in, their breaths cast steam on the glass. Their eyes ran over the brass hearth sets, cherub decked carriage clocks, paisley patterned tea services and tin retro washing powder signs. There were 1950s record players, replicas of the first Alexander Bell telephone and hatboxes bearing the ruby red lips of Marilyn Monroe. Billie wanted to go inside and buy her mum an elaborate, hinged tarot card box, so the girls crept below the swinging dried herb racks and squeezed between rows of dressmaker dummies and candelabras. A cacophony of ticking grandfather clocks accompanied their entrance and Mr Arthur Cobweb smiled warmly at them from across his cluttered counter, wire spectacles perched on the tip of his extra large nose.

"Now then, young ladies, what can I do for you today?"

Rosie's father knew him. They loved to discuss world history topics, but Arthur was eccentric to say the least. With a shiny gold pocket watch tucked into the breast of his chequered waistcoat and wispy hair defying gravity in a puff of white, he resembled a cross between Sherlock Holmes and Albert Einstein. Billie handed him the carved box and pulled out her purse.

"Indian or Egyptian in origin, who knows? The tarot's estimated arrival in Europe has links with the Knight's Templar after their crusades to the Holy Land. But it was the eighteenth century occultist, Antoine Court de Gébelin, who devised his own unique deck and claimed these seventy-eight picture cards held mystical significance." As he spoke, Arthur carefully wrapped Dahlia Featherstone's gift in thick brown paper and tied it with a piece of string.

"I know all that," said Billie. She took the parcel and tucked it beneath her arm.

"Rosie Quartz, send my regards to your dear old man and tell him I have those original Titanic newspapers he ordered."

"Will do, Arthur…Merry Christmas."

The girls were about to stroll on past Calm Down Café, when Billie caught sight of Des and Dean Airdale, sprawled across leather chairs, slurping from bucket sized mugs. They waved eagerly from their dry vantage point and beckoned Billie to come join them inside. Des wore the froth from his drink like a moustache and pulled a daft face as he mimed reeling them in by lasso. As Billie pulled open the door a tempting aroma of roasted coffee beans cut through the icy air, but still Rosie stepped aside and shook her head.

"I think I'll pass, girls. You go on ahead. I need to call at the bookshop next door and I may be a while. You can come and get me in a bit."

"Why, what's up?" asked Sally with a frown. "We could all do with a hot drink. Des and Deano are fun. It won't be long."

"No, no. It's okay. You go, I'll see you soon." Rosie couldn't speak her mind, her friends wouldn't understand. Socialising with the boys was like crushing one's self to death beneath a pile of house bricks. It wasn't their fault and they were rather sweet, but they held too much of a connection to time spent with Guy. Many nights the gang had curled lazily in Sally's garage, playing poker for matchsticks, listening to crackly music on the temperamental stereo – before Guy had finally fled and succumbed to the Spotswood charm. It was easier now for Rosie to avoid the triggers that could set off her tears.

Besides, Ye Olde Steeple Bookstore was one of Rosie's all time favourite places to be, so she wasn't entirely lying when she said she wanted to go there. The owners, Mr and Mrs Goodleaf must both be in their eighties, and had looked that way for a long, long time. Some say the bookstore has been there since Steeple High was first standing and that the kind, smiley couple have run it since then, but with estimations of the school building dating back to at least Elizabethan times, the only evidence to back up this fact would be witchcraft, wizardry or a philosopher's elixir which keeps the blood coursing through their veins.

As she pushed open the stiff door, the wood groaned like a sleepy child forced to wake on a Monday morning, and the doormat caught at the bottom, requiring an extra shove. The heat from a blazing fireplace rushed to her frozen cheeks. But it was the usual, familiar smell which she loved: the unmistakable and delightful scent of ancient books. It was a strange passion she had always possessed, and as she slipped off her gloves and unravelled her scarf, it was as good as coming home after a long, tiresome day. Dusty leather jackets with thick card pages and the fusty smell of first editions totally calmed her previous mood. The shop was full of narrow aisles, packed with mahogany bookcases which towered as high as the ceilings. Ladders were propped at various intervals, and the thousands of coloured covers dazzled the eye in every direction – copper lettering down spines, author's names and titles in elaborate italic.

Mrs Goodleaf sat in a rocking chair behind the counter, knitting what looked like a jumper for a dog. She greeted Rosie but her eyes never left the job, and Rosie wandered to the back of the shop where she knew she would find her favourite stories. Fiction. Fantasy. Fairytale. She gazed up at the shelf just above her eye line and stretched her hand across the bumpy spines. *Sleeping Beauty*. She loved this one. Something about the idea of a beautiful princess tricked into treachery and awaiting rescue from a handsome prince held reticence in her heart. It was sentimental, magical, and the final kiss that sealed the tale sent shivers down her spine. She tipped the cover till it slipped from its place on the shelf into her waiting palm. She smelt the old pages, like she always did, glimpsing the black and white illustrations then clutching it to her chest. She had to buy something to appease the girls, and this would do just fine. She stepped back into the aisle for one last glance at the higher shelves, but sensed too late another person behind her, and backed into them with a thud. *Sleeping Beauty* slid from her hands and landed open on the carpet.

"Oh I'm so sorry," she said, "I wasn't looking where I was going."

"No, I'm sorry, my fault."

The person bent down to retrieve the book and straightened to hand it back to her. Coughing nervously, he tucked his long sideways fringe behind an ear and smiled his lopsided grin. It was Guy. "Hey."

"Hey."

"What's up?"

"Not much."

"You okay?"

"Yeah. You?"

"Yeah, fine."

The pair looked down at their feet through the small talk.

"What you buying?"

"Nothing."

Rosie looked down guiltily at the storybook he still held. Quickly she snatched it away and tried to hide the cover with her arm.

"*Sleeping Beauty*. Cool."

"For my niece."

"You don't have a niece."

"Well…"

Damn him. And then she caught sight of his own purchase, tucked beneath the sleeve of his mustard-coloured shirt. *The Sword in the Stone*. Maybe they were both still children into fairytales.

Awkwardly they walked to the till together. Mr Goodleaf had joined his wife behind the counter and stood with his arm around her as she gathered up her knitting.

"You first."

"No, you go."

"No, you."

Rosie and Guy mumbled at each other before both plonking their books down and searching in their pockets for the correct change.

"Hope you're in the Christmas spirit young ones," smiled Mr Goodleaf. He winked conspiratorially at Mrs Goodleaf, who in turn made a show of tipping back her tight grey perm and looking up. There, tied above the till, hanging from a frayed red ribbon, was a large sprig of mistletoe – pretty to behold and unthreatening in any other situation than this one. Mr and Mrs Goodleaf laughed aloud. The traditional Christmas kissing plant for loved-up couples was hanging directly over their heads. If the faded carpet opened up and swallowed her whole it would have been a welcome relief to Rosie right now.

"Merry Christmas, Rosie, and I truly do hope you have a very happy new year."

Before she had time to react, Guy took her hands in his and kissed her ever so lightly on the mouth. It was over as quickly as it had begun but enough to send every nerve cell in her body into complete, unmitigated frenzy. For a moment she melted. For a moment she wanted him with every ounce of strength she had. For a moment nothing else mattered and the bookstore owners didn't exist and she prayed he would repeat the same unexpected action again. And again.

"Listen, Rosie, it's pretty cold out there. Do you want to get a drink next door?"

And just as quickly the moment was gone. Suddenly, she was furious at herself for being fooled by his false charm yet again. Guy was not genuine. He was not for real. And this was a chance to show him she was worth more. An opportunity to regain and reassert her value.

"No thanks, Guy. Nice of you to offer, but I have to get back to my *real* friends."

Taking a deep breath and calling upon a willpower she never knew she had, Rosie turned on her rubber-wellied heels and strode to the door. It opened a lot easier than it had when she'd come in and Guy was left with his mouth ajar, abandoned and deserted, like the copy of *Sleeping Beauty* which lay un-bought on the counter.

On a shelf high above the humans, a heavy book toppled over as three angry siblings slumped against it.

"The words *'bloody hell'* spring to mind!" snapped Fire Agate.

Rosie was positively glowing as she walked through the door of Calm Down Café. And it wasn't just to do with her dipping in and out of dramatic changing temperatures.

"I'll have a hot chocolate," she announced to no one in particular, "with two sugars, a squirt of whipped cream, a sprinkling of buttons and an extra large topping of marshmallows." She flopped down in a vacant leather chair while her instructions travelled to the ear of Miss Emma Mint, the pretty café manageress, who set about creating the indulgent concoction amid a whirring sound of steam.

Rosie's friends exchanged glances. "What's with you?"

The little white pot on the table was filled with sugar cubes and Rosie began greedily shovelling them into her mouth like an over-packed hamster.

"*Mmm-nnn-mmm-nnn-ma...*"

Billie raised her eyebrows.

Rosie was glad they couldn't tell a word she was saying, as she really didn't know what she was trying to say herself. Words. Sometimes they were just so overrated.

On Christmas morning Rosie could not fail to enjoy the familiar family routines which everyone in the Quartz household loved so much. The annual CD of modern Christmas classics merrily accompanied their slippered feet down the stairs, and the turkey already in the oven had begun to smell ravishing. After opening the pile of presents from her parents around the living room tree and gasping in delight at how spoiled she'd been yet again, Rosie stood to excuse herself and change out of her pink pyjamas. Before she left the room however, Debra presented her with one last package. A silver box with a curly green bow.

"This was dropped off for you yesterday. You might want to take it with you while you get dressed for dinner."

Puzzled, Rosie took the mystery gift and looked quizzically at her mother. Debra shrugged, giving no clues, and turned back towards turkey duties in the kitchen. Rosie pressed her thumbs firmly into the sides of the square shape as though that would somehow reveal the contents without her having to wait to open it. Like any young girl, she loved surprises, but something told her the surprise in this unexpected delivery was going to be bittersweet. Hesitantly she carried the box upstairs to her bedroom.

When she reached the folds of her butterfly print duvet, she placed it dead centre and sat at its side to pull the bow. This gave way and enabled her to lift the lid. There were layers of white tissue paper inside which crackled beneath her fingertips. A small note, handwritten on a piece of card, caught her eye. The words read:

To Rosie,
Jemma Flower Porcelain Faery Collection
The "Nothing is Ever as it Seems" Faery
With Love & Best Wishes For A Merry Christmas
J. x

The ornament was wrapped in another layer of tissue, but already Rosie was smiling brightly at the thought she at last owned one of Jemma's fabulous inventions. She held the delicate, detailed creation in her palm. It was beautiful. A tiny faery girl with long black hair swept across her bare shoulder, and a serious expression set across her face as she pondered life from her perch on a hollow log.

"Thank you, Jemma," Rosie said aloud. "I shall place this on my windowsill to remind me what a lovely person you are. You shall always be dear to me, even when our paths don't cross."

She set it down in the glow emanating from the mounds of snow outside and then noticed there was something else protruding from the bottom of the silver box. She lifted a corner and instantly the realisation of what she was looking at shot jarring bolts of emotion through her veins. Tentatively, she lifted and stroked the aging cover of *Sleeping Beauty*. Hands trembling, she tilted the pages to her nose and inhaled. It smelt of the fusty shelves and passageways of the Bookshop. This was it. This was the one. The very book that could only have been purchased by one person. She turned back the first page and in small, neat print, next to the dusty eraser mark where the secondhand price had been rubbed out by the Goodleafs, Guy had written in the top right hand corner:

I thought you wanted this???
So let it be a gift from me.
Sleeping Beauty for a Steeple Beauty
Lots of love from Guy XXX

Tears welled up in the corners of her eyes, but whether from sadness or joy, she was not entirely sure. Either way, she hugged the book as tightly to her chest as if someone were about to storm in and whisk it away from her. She gripped it with all her might and the force rocked her to and fro on the bed. A sound rose in her throat. It started as a giggle but grew into so much more.

"Ha, ha, ha, ha! Ha, ha, ha, ha!" Rosie was laughing out loud and she couldn't stop herself. Guy had bought the book. He'd gone to the trouble of purchasing it for her even though she'd left him in the lurch. That surely meant something. Didn't it? And he'd called her beautiful. The inscription there in his own handwriting clearly labelled her so. That was his opinion of her. A beauty.

"Ha, ha, ha, ha! Ha, ha, ha, ha!"

How wonderful.

He must love her after all. He must. He must. He must.

All of a sudden, there came a very strong smell of lavender, intensely overpowering. Indeed it must have been potent to dispel the roasting turkey, and even more so to distract Rosie from her romantic thoughts. Turning in the direction of the new scent, Rosie realised it came from the windowsill where she had placed her new faery. And then every hair on her body stood on end. She was quite literally terrified.

The faery ornament which just seconds ago had possessed black hair and a serious scowl, now had blonde hair and a dashing smile. Furthermore, she no longer sat on a log, but stood with legs ajar and hands on hips, oozing self-confidence. Rosie coughed and spluttered, a sign from her body to get some oxygen back in her lungs. Was she going mad? Had she gone insane? The faery now looked just like her.

8

Spring in the Step

Take a map. Any map will do. Hold it in your hands or smooth it down flat on a table surface. Whether it's a modern street map or an ancient ordnance survey, faded russet brown with age, the results are much the same. For imagine now placing a transparent sheet of one map over another. You can still see the sites of the first through the territory of the second. They coexist, both a part of the same thing. The names of buildings and regions surviving independently, yet somehow intertwined. And so it is with Faery Land.

The world these beings inhabit is not a separate location to our own. Other story books would have you believe that the existence of such a place belongs somewhere long ago and far away, across the seas, over the hills and under the dales. No, no, no, my dear friend. Do not be mistaken. The Faery Land is as near to you now as your mind can comprehend. Right there at your fingertips. Right down at your feet. Faery Land is everywhere. Wherever we may be in our boring chores of day-to-day terrestrial life, we are never more than a few feet away from a faery. Overlaying our kitchens and bathrooms and living rooms, intersecting our gardens and patios and pathways, there pulses an ulterior energy of faery magic and glamour. The children of Mother Nature flow about us every second. So why then, I hear you say, are we unable to see them for ourselves? You might be able, if you are of a particular frame of mind. The right kind.

The term "Faery Land" means all the places inhabited by faerie, whereas "Faery Kingdom" applies only to an area occupied by royalty and overseen by a royal court. A Kingdom must have its own King and Queen, Princes and Princesses, and undoubtedly a Palace. "Faery Dwelling" is any individual house, be it tree, plant, bush or flower, where a faery makes its home. But turn your attention now to the phrase "Faery Realm", for it is this which enables us to understand why some people can see faeries and others cannot. "Realm" explains the dimension in which faeries exist. A dimension which is of a much higher frequency than our material world of physical needs and possessions. Like a dog whistle seems soundless because it is beyond the pitch-range of the human ear, so we must turn up our inner volume if we truly wish to hear the noise. We are each made up of a trillion atoms and molecules, all spinning and vibrating at designated speeds. The atomic make-up of a faery moves at a far faster pace than we do and so to bridge the divide between their world and ours, either side of the two parties must make a conscious decision to alter their energy levels. Faeries must slow their vibration down, whereas we must raise ours higher. This is far more tricky than it may sound and very few can manage to achieve it. However, though I mention the exchange being a "conscious" decision, there are those lucky few who seem able to do this naturally, without giving it a second thought. Some call them "mediumistic", others "clairvoyant", at times in history they've even been labelled "witches", but whatever, their exciting ability makes you jealous, doesn't it?

It was the month of March, a time of transformation. The season kisses the winter wonderland goodbye and makes way for the shy, peeping buds of the Spring equinox. The things we take for granted at this time are never overlooked by the faeries. They know that every single flower is a masterpiece of Mother Nature's art and no two blooms are the same. Shape, scent, colour, medicinal purpose: all are unique and sacred. Patches of the last snow can still be seen, and occasionally the odd snowflake will dare drift from the heavens and settle upon a cowslip petal, but faeries know the worst of the frost is over once the familiar creatures of the earth return to play. For generation upon generation, millennia upon millennia, the Animal Kingdom has willingly served the faery community as both friend and loyal servant. It's a mutual and harmonious agreement that works both ways. Much of the food eaten by faeries – plants, flowers, berries and nuts – is shared with their furry neighbours and in return for help with the manual labour of collecting supplies and cultivating the land, faeries will use their magic to protect the animals and their habitats from potential human disturbance. Insects and birds, too, are firm friends and despite faeries having their own wings, remain popular modes of transport.

Some animals, however, do *not* serve the faery community and should be avoided at all costs, but we shall speak of these at a later date.

To continue our story, we must go back to the clearing where you witnessed the celebrations last summer. The overturned terracotta pot today formed the schoolhouse and lessons were taking place within and without on the thinning grass. Several small groups of students were scattered about, each class engaged in a separate project with their subject teacher – one of the five designated Elders.

Madame Celestite had her pupils seated on shells with their handcrafted instruments perched on shoulders or knees, ready to be played when she finished talking. The old music teacher was a stickler for perfection and rightly so, since these youngsters would one day play for the elite Faery Band. Faeries quite naturally from birth can produce the most heavenly music and one may ask why indeed they need orchestration lessons at all. Well, if ever you were to be blessed for just a second with hearing the beautiful sounds which eternally accompany the air in the Faery Realm, you would realise that only the best have been carefully selected to conduct the continuous stream of music which plays night and day, never ceasing, across the Land.

"If you are one day chosen to play among your esteemed brothers and sisters, then you will by and by be asked to take your rightful place at a regular Musical Shift. The Council will decide which Shift you are most suited to, depending on your particular talent, but when The Changing of the Shift occurs, whether a singer, a harpist, or a hornblower, you must work hard to ensure that the music continues at all times and that there is never the slightest hint of a pause. Although the mood and tempo may morph and change, the music must never ever cease."

Madame Celestite tucked a stray wisp of hair back into the coil of her grey bun.

"The Night Shift requires a different sound to the Morning or Midday Shift, and of course there are ulterior melodies for the summer season compared to the more rustic notes of autumn. Today we shall focus on depicting the sweet sounds of spring, and perchance one of you may be asked to perform at the opening of our new Sabbat Ball."

Tapping the grand conductor's baton dramatically across the flat palm of her other hand, she swept across the ground in her long Victorian-style black dress which hid her feet from view. Being an extremely tall woman, frightening in both stature and disposition, the young faeries often wondered if she kept a pair of stilts attached to her legs beneath the dark folds of fabric, just to make her more intimidating to the children she taught.

Amy Thyst, an exceptionally beautiful child blessed with a heavenly soprano voice, began to sing the first verse of their homage to Spring. The tender flow of words would sound foreign to our untrained tongue, but the incantations spoke of hope, faith, trust, peace and love – of the ultimate respect for a power far greater than we ourselves can imagine – Lady Gaia, the worshipped Mother of Nature.

Beyond the plant pot walls, Sir Hematite held a captive audience in his stare as he told his seated circle of students how they each possessed a great persuasive power to inspire receptive humans. Musicians, actors, artists and authors were particularly susceptible to receiving this divine intervention from the Faery Realm. Although they would take credit for it, seemingly having come up with a grand idea or blazing talent all by themselves, the faery influencers would gain great satisfaction from knowing it was indeed them who had planted the seed of success in the humble human brain.

"The key, however," Sir Hematite was saying, "is how you make that first connection. As humans become increasingly engulfed in their one-way vision of how life should be, they find it harder and harder to venture past their boundaries of possibility and welcome the unknown and unheard of into their heart. Whilst it is true that the ones who possess creative gifts in the arts – a dancer or a painter for example – are naturally more able to hear us whispering advice as that 'inner voice', it is still a hard task for the faery to administer."

The students nodded in agreement, hanging onto his every word and dramatic hand gestures. Sir Hematite was well admired. Not only was he young for an Elder and extremely handsome, with square shoulders, dark hair and chiselled jaw, but he also had many famed victories to boast of in his area of expertise. Some of the world's greatest sports stars had taken stimulation from his attachment, pushing themselves that extra mile to win a race, shoot a hoop or save a dreaded penalty in extra time. Celebrity songbirds had hit notes they'd previously struggled with. Poets had finished those lines which seemed like they'd never come together. And on every such occasion, humans would state, should they be asked, that these inspirations were accompanied by a tiny tinkling of bells. Seemingly far off and in the distance, but none the less still there, chiming gently *somewhere*.

"Bells," Sir Hematite told his class as he re-crossed his legs beneath the long, scratchy woollen jersey he wore which made him look all the more like a dashing, Arthurian Knight, "should always be carried at times of human contact. We may think it incidental, but the mystical ghost-like sound shall stay in the memory of the receiver, and haunt their subconscious, however they may push it to the back of their minds as fancy. Girls, you can wear them in you hair or at your throat as a necklace. Boys, you can slip them on the buckle of your belts or wear them at your heels upon your sandal strap."

A Wand and Spells lesson for Beginners was also being led today by Madame Sodalite, who was instructing her students how to use their first magical extension tools to grant wistful wishes and heartfelt desires to *deserving* humans. The excited young students sat turning their shiny new wands eagerly about in their hands. Students of school age had to carry these items as proof that they were still in the practice stages – an adolescent of magic. Once they'd graduated at the age of sixteen, the tools became worthless. The learned adult held all the knowledge they would ever need in their mind and at their fingertips.

"Of course, some older faeries do still like to carry the wand and the spell book about them in person," Madame Sodalite told her class, "but this is purely for ornamental and decorative purposes. An extremely developed faery will do it on occasion, especially when seen by a human, merely to establish their identity. For some strange reason humans are far more likely to recognise us in a tutu and tiara with a star shaped wand flashing fireworks from its tip." She sighed. "Complete nonsense and degradation in my opinion, but it's not always for me to say." She paused.

"A Fortune Teller, such as Apatite who once lived among us, may well keep ancient books which hold all the wisdoms of the ages, mysteries which journey far beyond the capacity and capability of one faery mind. In cases such as these the books are like a museum, an archive we can access in times of great need. But I doubt any of us here will ever want such cryptic prophecies. So again, it's not for me to say."

Madame Sodalite was an Elder of extreme beauty. Like Sir Hematite, she was fairly young to hold this sacred and coveted position, but becoming an Elder was a predestined birth right, and indeed the attractive Madame had continually demonstrated way and beyond that she deserved her place here as well as any deity in the Faery Realm. She was strong and determined, a focused businesswoman with her pupils, and she accepted no nonsense. Absolute application in getting the job done.

"Granting wishes has become such a cliché in recent years, as if the good faery folk have nothing better to do than go hopping around waving their wands to bring happiness to one and all, no matter what the cost." Madame Sodalite spoke in her clipped Queen's English with a hint of irritation in her tone. "I'm not, of course, saying that you shouldn't use your gift for the good of others. By all means, if it takes your fancy, then give gladly and ye shall receive threefold in return, but what I do imply is that you consider carefully the object of your affection and ask yourselves whether they truly will benefit from the gift you are about to bestow. It is so common for a faery to become infatuated with a human and want to help them all they can. But humans have this awful tendency to think they want something so badly and then, once they have it in their grasp, to see all too clearly that it was never a good idea in the blooming first place and that, in actual fact, it well and truly sucks."

One or two of the young faeries giggled at this point and then guiltily hid their rosy faces behind the pages of their still-wrapped spell books when Madame Sodalite shot them a look of condemnation. Shaking her head, she went back to her lecture.

"We faeries, however, are blessed with the bigger picture. Our eyes see what theirs cannot. We see the ever-giving universe constantly at work for those who ask for themselves. Lady Gaia – our beautiful Mother Nature, and The Law of Attraction – never fails those who can self-attract. Hence why we faeries so rarely use wand magic for ourselves. We know that the power of thought manifests anything we desire. So there. Lesson learned. Just think carefully about what may benefit your friendly giants in the long run."

A handful of students looked quizzically up at their teacher, before a braver one among them asked, "But Madame Sodalite, what of the humans who believe in our existence, and upon that wave of faith ask outright for our help, sometimes even leaving us gifts in encouragement? Sugar cubes, plastic buttons, copper pennies and milk bottle tops...Are we to refuse these treasures if the wish is better not granted?" The question had come from Jasper, a cheeky Puck-faced sprite with ears as pointy as upturned ice cream cones. His friends nodded in unison, and tentatively Madame lifted her dog violet skirts to sit down in the grass beside her prodigies.

"Accept gifts if you will dear children. The most deserving may well leave you a treat. But ultimately the decision will fall on you as to how to use your magic. That is the great power of being a faery. I am here to teach you the ways of the light and the dark, but you will do with it what you will."

Jasper's large ears twitched and stirred and his eyes grew round as saucers. "The light and the dark? So Madame, is that the reason why some faeries go bad? Like what happened in the Faery Kingdom? To the King and the Queen? With Sulphur and his Sect?"

"Jasper!" In a flash Madame Sodalite flexed her fingers in an action which transformed Jasper's hazel wand to a strip of sticky pond weed, leaping from his hands and plastering itself across his lips, taping his half-open mouth tightly shut. "You do not speak of such things and you know it! He will not be mentioned in the safety of this Land. Just the sound of his name is enough to bring us to his attention. Do you not think that his crows sit all about, waiting for opportunity to strike? One such foolish outburst from the likes of you could cost us all our refuge here. I will hear no more about him. Or his Sect. From any of you. Is that understood?"

Silence.

"Do I make myself clear?"

The weed withered and died, sliding from around Jasper's mouth like a sad let-down balloon at the end of the party. "Yes Madame Sodalite. I apologise Madame Sodalite." Jasper hung his head in shame, and although he had been the one to mention it, his classmates having thought similar things, also began to apologise quietly in timid breaths. What happened in the Faery

Kingdom was a tragedy they had long since learned not to speak of, and doing so was an error they should know better than to make.

But Madame Sodalite was a kindly teacher, loving of her students, and seeing how upset they all were in the dim shadow of such poisoned words, she sought to soften the blow and shook imaginary specks from her skirt as she stood to face them, each and every one. With a warm smile and a glint in her eye, she spoke in a hushed yet bemused tone. "Do not forget my children, we faeries are also renowned in many a fireside tale for causing harmless havoc and mischief. Perhaps then it would be sheer negligence if once in a while we did not dare to live up to our names. I say, why not reap the seeds they sow? We can all benefit from a little fun at times. And remember we spoke of humans *deserving* the implications of our magic. Well, what human doesn't deserve a little pixie trickery? A little poking fun of, hey?"

A loud cheer went up among the class of Madame Sodalite, causing other lessons to pause and look their way, as they danced giddily, waving their wands on the spot.

"'Truth Tongue' is a particular favourite of mine. I delight in placing this spell upon an annoying human, who from then on, no matter how hard they try, just cannot help but tell the truth. Oh, it's hilarious to see a mean spirited vagabond pay for his sins by openly admitting them to the world against his will!"

Two or three feet in the air, the fourth and final lesson was taking place. The Art of Flight by merry Sir Rhodonite. The cheeky young faeries labelled him merry for this he always was, despite their rebellious and irresistible teasing of him. With a bright pink complexion to match long red robes which he often tripped over in a fluster, Sir Rhodonite was jolly in the face of adversity. He had a stutter which impaired his deliverance of instructions at times and the students often mimicked him behind his back when he wasn't listening – as well as when he was listening too. The lovely Sir Rhodonite was too gentle to reprimand even the most insolent of faery youth. His scolding went along the lines of; "Now, now, there, there, enough's enough now, thank you."

Although a faery child began to sprout and develop their wings from around the age of nine or ten, permission to use them for actual flight was not granted until complete graduation at sixteen. Lessons were given to teenagers on how to use their wings to the greatest advantage, but experimentation of this sort was only allowed within school time and any public display of fluttering or levitating of any kind was strictly prohibited. The lure of potential flight was of course just too tempting to some teenagers and punishment for breaking this rule was among the highest given by any Council of Elders in any Faery Land. The stronger and fancier the flyer, the more attractive the faery. Or so at least the youngsters saw it. Flying was a form of flirtation which many a headstrong puck just couldn't resist to attract a mate.

The other exciting thing about wings was that you just didn't know which kind you were going to get. Until they had fully grown, every single faery could do nothing but wish and wait for the right type to emerge: large ones, small ones, thin ones, thick ones…Wings made of petals or of pure light. Wings shaped like tree leaves or some insect-like. Each individual had their own opinion on which were the best ones and which they most desired, but at the end of the day, you had to settle for what Mother Nature gave you. Much like the human philosophy on looks and appearance, I suppose.

These young faeries were today trying out the makings of their recent acquisitions and Sir Rhodonite had not yet quite got the hang of controlling his class in an orderly manner. A series of wails and whooshes accompanied the giddy students as they soared at the speed of lightning overhead, zigzagging to and fro, leaving white streaks of speed in the air as they turned. Swerving and evading one another like a break-neck game of dodge cars, the students hollered and high-fived their peers as they tumbled past in somersault.

"C – c – c – calm down, k – k – k – kids!" Sir Rhodonite

called as he kicked his own heels together to join them in a plea to settle. "L – l – l – let's take it easy to start. Just a few s – s – s – small circles around the green to begin with."

At that moment, one young faery called Peridot took an extra daring dive, and not noticing the new figure emerging in the clearing below, knocked a tall, pointed hat clear from its owner's head.

"What in Mother Earth's name is going on here?" roared the superior voice of the ancient Elder as he clutched his back and bent to collect his royal blue head gear depicting golden suns, moons and stars, from the dirt into which it had fallen. "Sir Rhodonite, for the sake of Lady Gaia, get a grip on that unruly class of yours!"

"Y – y – yes, Sir Fluorite," called down the merry tutor, a little flushed and embarrassed at this stage.

Fluorite, having just arrived on the scene, gazed around him at the array of lessons taking place in the clearing, and shook the long tresses of his snow white hair in disbelief. "By my beard, I leave this place for half an hour and the whole thing's gone to pot!" He ran his wrinkled fingers through that waist-length beard and growled deep within his round belly to relieve frustration. Fluorite was the leader of the Elders, the oldest faery in the Land, and the Head of Table at Council. He was the designated Protector and therefore a little unnecessarily grumpy at all times.

He winced at the ear-splitting cheer drifting from the patch occupied by Madame Sodalite and her wand-waving lunatics. He grimaced as he turned to the terracotta pot and heard a wrong note hit by an out of tune violin. Begrudgingly he surveyed the circle around Sir Hematite and the moony-eyed girls digesting not one educational word he said. And finally, the last straw, he ducked again as another of Rhodonite's tearaways missed decapitating him by the breadth of a single white hair.

"Damn and blast, you young scallywag! Right, that does it! All of you. Come on down here at once!"

It was not yet break time, but in his rage, unable to bear the frivolities any longer, Fluorite reached deep down into the blue depths of his long over cloak and pulled out the silver hand bell which indicated that morning respite was upon them. The familiar and welcome sound brought everyone to a standstill. Even the sky trippers, regaining their breaths, dropped lightly to the grass. Equipment was hastily packed away and at the centre of the clearing Madame Sodalite and Sir Hematite met with the usual basket of chopped sugar cubes which were dished out as rewards for a morning's hard work. The students invariably fought over the largest ones and who seemed to be getting more than another, but generally the treats were well distributed by the two teachers and the children's squabbling was superfluous.

Fluorite allowed the fuss to unfold as it must, knowing full well that once the students had scattered he would be having a firm talk with his teachers. Irritably, he tapped the base of his oak staff upon the ground and scratched at his bristling moustache. As he did so, he noticed the perimeter fence of pansy petals lift and Moss Agate stride purposefully through the clearing. Tanned, tattooed shoulders pinned back, and shaven head held high, he made the striking statement of a keen warrior on a mission.

The children turned to see him enter and rejoicing at the sight of their much loved hero, dropped their cubes and came running to surround him. When sugary treats were forgotten you knew you were at the height of popularity. Moss smiled brightly as they skipped his way.

"Moss, Moss, have you come to play for us?" A few of the music class shoved their guitars in his direction; but gently, Moss pressed the wooden instruments back into their hands.

"No kids, I'm afraid not. Not today. I've come to talk with Sir Fluorite."

Patting the smaller boys on the head Moss turned aside to speak to the Elder. Serious and grim, Fluorite scowled at Moss beneath his one long wiry brow. Moss also now grew solemn as he levelled with the old man.

"It is time?" questioned Fluorite in his gruff tone, meeting the eyes of the younger faery with no apparent emotion to define.

"It is time," replied Moss. "I am going to speak with her today. Myself and my sisters shall leave shortly. I thought it best I come and alert you first. Please call Council and let the other Elders know."

Fluorite shook his head in agreement and consent, but again his wise expression revealed nothing of his disposition.

"I shall not fail," said Moss firmly. "I am certain we can do this. By nightfall, Rosie Quartz shall be home."

9

The Faery Ring

The paper made a satisfying crunch as Rosie reduced it to a fist-sized ball in her hand. The words she had scribbled down a moment ago were tossed to the floor to join several similar eliminations piled on the soft, cream carpet. The clock at her side showed it was well before dawn, but she was unable to sleep. Taking a deep breath, she reached inside the drawer of her dressing table and drew out a fresh sheet to begin again. Laid across the cleared table, the paper was temporarily invisible upon the whitewashed wood. Only as Rosie began to fill it with her dreamy scrawl, did its existence become apparent. A few lines down and she stopped. She reread the words and shook her head, tapping the pencil up and down to create tiny flecks of lead, like insects across the page. This was just not coming together, but she needed something to occupy her while the rest of the house still slept. There were times when words would pour out, song lyrics for the band buzzing in her fingertips to be set free, clamouring at her throat to be recited aloud. But at other times, such as now, Rosie found herself in that awkward and frustrating land of writer's lockdown. Everything she thought of seemed to sound wrong and unpoetical. She crossed out a full line of prose, digging the pencil tip deep into the paper. Magic was not at work.

A lavender smell distracted her momentarily – a pleasant aroma which cast a wave of warmth through her nostrils and into her lungs. Though her curtains were closed, the window was slightly ajar, so she presumed her mum had planted something new out in the garden to brighten the borders, since the winter frosts seemed to be behind them for good.

Rosie turned her mind back to the page.

Don't you know I've always needed you?
Last night I sat and wrote a note for you.
I let the breeze decree its way to you.
I spoke the words I hoped so hard that you knew,
And I prayed the wind would take them to you.

But the smell grew in intensity and as it enveloped Rosie entirely, she began to feel slightly nauseous. She patted her cheeks to check if her skin was as hot as she suddenly felt, and finding her face clammy to the touch, she placed her pencil down and crossed the room to peer outside. She pulled back the curtains. The flower beds looked exactly as they always had. There was nothing to identify the cause of this heady pungent scent. Frowning, Rosie pulled the window shut and secured the catch. As she turned back round, she was again forced to stop in her tracks. A fine tinkling of bells came close to her ears. They were instantly strange as they were dim enough to sound far away but simultaneously clear enough to seem near. Her ear lobes itched like the bells were right by her, inside of her, part of her, and frantically she scratched like a fly had just rested in the recess of her head. As her mind spun, turning over the possibilities of where this strange yet beautiful sound could be coming from, the gentle chimes turned from musical tones to melodic words.

"*Ro-sie.*"

"*Ro-sie.*"

"*Rosie Quartz.*"

It was so subtle that it could definitely have been a dream, so temperate that the words may have been nothing but pure fancy of the imagination. And yet Rosie had had too many of these unusual experiences of late to turn the episode away as irrational.

"*Ro-sie.*"

"*Ro-sie.*"

"*Rosie Quartz.*"

She turned her head. Spun a three hundred and sixty degree circle on her tiptoes. Every possible direction to identify the voice.

"*Rosie Quartz, we know you can hear us, so speak in reply.*"

The second voice was both louder and harsher than the first. Unlike the previous whisper, this was clear enough and piercing enough to be another person right in the bedroom beside her. Rosie shot round. In a flash her eyes had examined the bed, the table, the wardrobe and the door.

"Show yourselves. Where are you?" Rosie screamed, frightened now. There was no mistaking that she wasn't alone.

"*To show ourselves is exactly what we want to do, but we may need to go out into the garden to do that.*"

She flung the duvet up in the air, scattered the cushions onto the carpet, dropped to her knees and clutched at the chair leg for support.

"Who are you? What *is* going on here?"

"*Come out to the garden. Sit by the rockery where Strawberry is buried. Don't be scared. We know you're afraid, but all is well, and we'll meet you there.*"

Rosie jumped to her feet and grabbed her grey cardigan from where it hung on the bottom post of her bed. Her bare legs were trembling below the turned hem of her cotton shorts and as she made her way downstairs she clung onto the glossy banister like her life depended on it. A million disorientated thoughts were speeding round her brain. What was going on here? Was this the work of Sally and Billie? Some elaborate game they had set up to freak her out? Well if so, it was working. It was pretty damn cheap to scare her like this, however funny they may have thought it. But it was far too early for them to be up and about. And it wasn't just that. Deep down Rosie knew that this was nothing to do with her friends. Or her parents. Or any other human being for that matter. This was something altogether stranger, something far more sinister. Supernatural occurrences had been flocking to Rosie for months now. The porcelain faery on the window ledge had transformed several more times since the first alteration that Christmas day, and no matter how much Rosie may have admired the tremendous sculpting talent of Jemma Flower, she knew in her heart of hearts that even *she* couldn't achieve that.

Tentatively Rosie stepped out into the garden and sat down on the grass. She drew the cardigan around her and tucked her crossed legs beneath her. For a moment all was still and calm. There were no sounds and Rosie began to think maybe she had gone insane after all. And then by the side of the windmill, as had happened before, Rosie saw a flicker. She stared hard at the spot where the movement had been, determined this time not to lose focus and let it pass. Three tiny shapes emerged in her vision. They started blurry, like the distorted view through a dirty windscreen, but then grew clearer as she followed their path to the windmill roof and out onto the spokes which never stirred, so gentle were the footsteps. Roughly two inches tall, but apart from that, entirely human looking: a boy and two girls. Rosie blinked once. Rosie blinked twice. Rosie balled up her hands and rubbed them deep into the sockets of her eyes to clear any debris. But the people did not change. Looking right up at her and sensing her sudden recognition of their existence, they began to wave and applaud. Rosie felt the blood rush to her head and in utter disbelief her bones gave way and she fainted.

Gradually, Rosie opened her eyes and regained consciousness of her surroundings. She was lying on her back, flat out on her raised garden lawn. It was lucky she had fallen this way and not in the opposite direction, onto the hard patio flags. Her eyelashes fluttered. She could feel last night's mascara sticky and smeared at the corners of her eyelids. Another moment was needed to raise her upper body onto her elbows, and as she did this she realised her back was a little sore from where she'd hit the ground. There was a tickle across her bare midriff where her t-shirt had lifted, and as she peered down at her own flat belly, there again were the three miniature faces, cause of the whole calamity. Though exquisitely tiny, Rosie began to pick out the slightest details. The boy was dressed in shades of green and brown. Knee-length shorts and a waistcoat hanging open, both of which seemed to be sewn from forest leaves. He had a shaven head, a horde of golden earrings glinting at his ear lobes and an unusual swirling pattern of tattoos carved across the evident muscles of his tanned arms. The girls were as opposite in appearance as was possible. One had short orange hair which flicked itself stylishly about her freckled face in stubborn spikes. Her flower petal skirt matched this approach by fluttering round her thighs in jagged edges, which looked like dancing flames. The other girl had thick brown hair which hung in long corkscrew curls. She wore a simple vest-dress of white lace and looked so delicate that Rosie thought she may break her just by breathing too harshly in her direction. With this in mind, she held her oxygen intake for just a moment and then let it out far gentler. This particular creature, Rosie mused in absolute awe, was the most perfectly beautiful being she had ever seen in her entire life.

"Uh! Yuk! I told you, she's just a big ugly and bony girl! She can't possibly be the one." The redhead placed her hands on her hips.

"Of course she's the one," the brunette was smiling brightly, happiness and excitement evident in her tone.

"But she's so big!"

"Right now she is. But not for long."

"Wait a minute!" Rosie pulled herself up a little further, though still carful not to disturb her miniscule visitors. "This can't be happening to me. It really can't. I mean, *what* are you? *Who* are you? *Why* and *how* am I seeing this?"

The creatures astonishingly rose from her midriff, hovering without the aid of any apparent apparatus, and it was then that Rosie noticed they had shafts of fast vibrating light protruding from out of their shoulder blades. They had *wings*.

"Whoa...whoa...whoa! You're...You *can't* be! You're...You *are*! You're *faeries*!"

"Oh, she does have a brain after all!" snapped Fire. "Well done, kid. Ten points to the genius!"

Rosie arched her knees and the three of them now settled there like watchmen on a castle tower.

"Hi, Rosie." The male faery spoke for the first time, setting himself apart from the others by drifting to her left knee alone. "I'm so glad to see you. Or rather, I'm so glad that you can finally see us! We've been trying to make contact with you for months. You've been a pretty tough cookie to crack, I can tell you. Anyway, that doesn't matter now. I'm Moss. Moss Agate. And these here are my two sisters, Lace Agate and Fire Agate. Fire's the grumpy one. But you'll get used to her soon enough. She's lovely really."

"Shut it, Bro!" barked Fire, folding her arms in total disagreement.

Moss held out his hand, as though for Rosie to shake. She looked down upon him, her face a picture of incredulity and mistrust, and he must have realised the absurdity of her being able to grip his palm, as with a trace of embarrassment, he tucked it back into the pocket of his leafy shorts.

"So I'm right then? You guys are faeries? But I always thought you didn't really exist. I mean, we're always taught you're just a thing of myth and legend. Some made up story. This is amazing. In fact, this could change the world. When people find out about this, everyone's just gunna totally flip!"

"Slow down, missy!" Fire slid down her leg and burst back onto the edge of her t-shirt hem with a vengeance. For such a tiny creature, she definitely knew how to do intimidating. "You humans think we're make believe for a reason and it's going to stay that way! We're only talking to you 'cos we have to. It's not by personal choice, okay? As far as I'm concerned, you made your own grave and you should lie in it. Besides, even if you were to blab and tell, who in their right mind would believe you?"

"You're right," said Rosie, running her fingers through her dishevelled hair. "Nobody would believe this. Not even Sally and Billie."

"Rosie, we *are* faeries," said Moss, "pixies, deities, nature spirits, sprites, whatever you want to call us. The problem is this. We have something that we very much need to show you and you're going to have to come with us in order for us to do that."

"But...how can this be? How am I seeing you right now? If you really are faeries and humans really aren't supposed to know you exist, then how come I can see you? Why me?"

"Basically, Rosie, what you're doing right now, is you're using your sixth sense. That fabulous ability all you human beings have, but far too few of you ever actually use." Lace was speaking now, and there was something about her sing-song voice that made Rosie feel instantly calm and normal. As if maybe this wasn't so strange or big a deal after all. "You're clairvoyant. You're mediumistic. You're able to tune into the higher vibration and sense us there. This is going to make you feel pretty exhausted very quickly, so in a moment we're going to make things much easier for you by moving you into our dimension. Once you're there, things will come naturally and it won't feel like such hard work anymore."

As Lace explained Rosie felt less like questioning and more able to let go. If this was a dream, then she'd wake up soon enough and simply be back where she started. Life as normal. And if it wasn't her imagination and this all was for real, then sooner or later she was going to have to give up gawping and get used to it. Plain and simple. There was nothing to lose.

"Faeries," Rosie said, and then repeated the word again. "*Faeries*. Apart from picture books and cartoon films, which could be totally wrong interpretations, *what* are you?"

"What are we?" Lace sighed whimsically, turning the thought around lightly, like it deserved careful contemplation before answering any old way, but Fire cut in before her.

"We are the ones who take the things that go missing – the human objects that get moved. We are the ones who tangle your hair in the night and knot it at the roots so that no amount of brushing will get it out. We are the ones who tie your shoelaces together under the tablecloths, so hilariously you fall when you

130

stand. The ones that set the shop alarms off as you walk out of the censored doors, even though you haven't done anything wrong. When you can't turn the door key in your lock, we are the ones pushing it out at the other side. We are mischief and mayhem and we love wreaking havoc on the bumbling fools who think they're the superior race on this planet!"

"Fire, really!" Lace scolded her sister abruptly. "How could you? Rosie, don't listen to a word she said. She's impossible! Why, that makes us sound just about the most monstrous species that ever lived!"

"No, but it's true," chided Fire, sticking her tongue out behind her sister's back.

Rosie giggled. She raised her hand to her mouth for fear of the sound blowing her companions away, but found that she couldn't control the amusement. Quivering like jelly, Rosie let the laughter unfold, hiccupping ruthlessly at the delightful characters.

Lace wasn't sharing her glee. She had reached her own perfect answer. "Faeries are the ones who lovingly tend pink blossom on the trees. We paint the poppy vibrant red and shape the daffodil's elegant petticoat. We polish your apples to make them shine and sweeten the juice of the tangled bilberry bushes. We are the sound of the wind through the leaves and the clean cool rain on the skin. We shake off old clothing from ancient trees in the autumn and open up pinecones for insects to creep inside. We sprinkle the first fine scattering of snow and comb the robin's bright breast. We are the changing of the seasons, the earth's balance upon its axis, and we scrub the stars twinkling in the sky at night. Faeries are the children of Lady Gaia, the great Mother Nature. We are her humble servants and we do her bidding to keep this earth as fresh as the day it was born."

Like a small child by her mother's feet, hanging onto every word of a bedtime story, Rosie listened intently as Lace recounted these beautiful things. She was utterly captivated, spellbound.

"Okay, there's that. But the other things I said count as well," said Fire. "Anyway, are we gunna get on with this or what?"

Rosie stirred. "You said you had something important to show me. That's why you're here, right?"

"Yes, that's right," said Moss, "there's something you have to see."

"Well come on then, I'm ready. After this, there's absolutely nothing that could shock me today. You couldn't possibly show me anything else more extraordinary and unbelievable."

"We'll see," Moss grinned. "I have a feeling you're going to regret saying that." He followed the girls as they dropped from Rosie's lap and settled on the grass by her side. "This way."

"Where are we going?"

"To Faery Land."

Have you ever seen a Faery Ring? I doubt it, and even if you had you would probably not have recognised what it was or realised the power it possessed. Such magical circles of poisonous red and white spotted toadstools are a rare portal which bridge the gap between this world and the next. Some call them *pixie hoods*, others prefer the term *elf caps*. Me, I like the phrase, *faery saddles*. But regardless of what we label them, their presence in any garden or woodland should never be taken lightly. Find a Faery Ring and you have guaranteed access to the Faery Realm. The faeries may not want you there and they may be awfully annoyed at your sudden intrusion, but they are completely powerless to halt your discovery. You have unique and unprecedented entry. Until, of course, the enchantment wears off. And how long or short a period of time that may be is anyone's guess. Every experience is entirely different. Mine was a matter of seconds but it seemed like hours on the other side. My very first innocent and unintentional visit was via a band of speckled saddles nestled deep, almost invisible, among the buttercups in the field at the top of Steeple Lane. The wonders I witnessed have haunted me my whole life long, and I often wandered back in search of that same Ring. But inevitably it was gone. No doubt they had moved it. And I have never seen one since, no matter how hard I look. The faeries, however, know exactly where they are hidden. Keeping track of their locations comes in handy on occasions such as this in our story, where the concentrated magic serves their purpose just right.

Rosie shook lawn trimmings from her clothes as she stood and followed the siblings across plants and boulders in the rockery. Reaching the green wooden shed, they took a narrow gap between its flaky painted wall and the spiky hedgerow. Rosie realised she was going to have to really squeeze herself flat to slide through this thin crevice, and for a split second she glanced around, feeling silly and self-conscious. Was she seriously doing this? What would people think if they woke and saw her? But she needn't have worried, as the instant she placed her foot within the circle of toadstools on the other side, she was gone. Totally invisible to the human eye.

It was a part of the Quartz garden where Debra never went. She had never bothered to clear or weed this area since it was tucked away out of sight behind the shed. Wild foliage grew so high that the toadstools were well hidden, but true to their eternal promise, once in their middle, Rosie was transformed. Her head spun and the dizziness reminded her of the time at her cousin's wedding when she and Billie stole a bottle of sparkling champagne and took turns swigging it in the toilets. They'd regretted it later and been totally reprimanded by her parents but it was that same disorientation she felt now. Her heart raced giddily, her thoughts a mixture of excitement and fear. In fact there was one other time she had felt this way – her first kiss with Guy. Pressed against the doorframe of his house. Bolts of lightening. Twinges of electricity. *Ah, Guy.* Maybe not. It was good, but not that good.

Rosie was getting used to losing and regaining her consciousness. But this time when she came to she had the biggest surprise yet. Moss, Lace and Fire Agate were the same size as her.

"You've grown!" she said, amazed.

"No honey," Fire sarcastically retorted. "You've shrunk."

"Oh, Rosie, dear. You are so much prettier now. Not that you weren't pretty before, but now you're just as exquisite as I thought you'd be!" Lace took Rosie's hands and danced around before hugging her close. Bells tinkled as they turned and Rosie now saw that she wore them in her hair. The heady lavender smell perfumed Lace's skin, but now it was homely and familiar, and Rosie drank it in like a welcome cocktail.

"Well, just for the record, I still think she's a big ugly girl," said Fire, rolling her eyes at the soppy exchange.

"Take a look around you, Rosie," said Moss, "take in your surroundings."

She was standing in what appeared to be a huge rainforest, jungle-like creepers towering grand above her. Voluptuous plant heads vanished upwards, making their enclosure dim and tranquil. Every sound was accentuated, a musical breeze suddenly apparent, and a hundred scurries and scuttles of invisible creatures in jagged mountains scattered as far as the eye could see. No one stood a chance of crossing these perilous summits on foot. Where could she possibly be that had such hazardous terrain? What made the penny drop was unclear, maybe the amused smirks on the faces of the other three, but all at once Rosie realised she hadn't travelled anywhere at all. The forest and peaks around her were not some far off Faery Land but the very same grass and soil which she had stood upon just moments ago. A patch of untended foliage in her parent's garden now spread out infinitely like a vast tropical paradise.

Rosie stroked her clothing and massaged her skin. The white t-shirt and grey cardigan, the pink trainers and cotton shorts, all still fitted her just fine. But there was no mistaking the truth in Fire's words.

Rosie was now two inches tall.

10

Homecoming

The first emotion was fear. It occurred to her that if her parents were to wake, they would find her bedroom empty and presume her missing.

"Where you're taking me – is it far? Will I be gone long?" asked Rosie, panic in her voice as she pictured her mum ringing round her friends, growing frantic. Rosie knew never to leave the house without explanation or a note.

"You'll be there and back in no time at all," Moss offered reassuringly. "The time differences, they alter the path of the clock. A whole hour in our world is only a fraction of a second in yours. In fact it's already midday in the Faery Realm now."

"Weird," said Rosie, as the second dreadful picture formed in her head. She imagined her father's giant foot crashing down and squashing her into the soil.

"And is it completely safe?" Rosie asked, scanning the faces of the three faeries surrounding her.

"I wouldn't say it's *completely* safe, no." smiled Fire wickedly. "There's always the chance you could be squished, stolen or eaten. But doesn't that make it all the more exciting? Now can we please just get on with this?"

Moss held out his hand to Rosie for the second time that morning, only now she was able to take it. As his fingers slipped though hers, she realised how strong and powerful his grip actually was, now that she was in equal proportion to his size.

"You're going to have to hold on to me tight," he said. "My

wings are enough to carry us both, but you can't let go. And if you don't mind – forgive the personal intrusion – but I need to grasp you a little more like this..."

Rosie felt her cheeks turn red as Moss manoeuvred his arm around her waist and pulled her left hip close to his right, their sides locked together like magnets.

"Are you ready?"

Rosie swallowed, releasing the nerves stuck in her throat. "I'm ready."

The faery boy struck the heels of his leather sandals together and catapulted the pair of them up into the air. Suddenly the leaves and stones, which just moments ago seemed gigantic, were once more insignificantly small as they rose high and left the patch of tangled weeds behind. But now there were new objects to contend with. The garden shed which had once stood not much taller than herself – in fact Daniel Quartz had to stoop considerably to reach inside and take his tools out – now appeared the largest construction she had ever seen. Moss's wings propelled them above its rusting roof. But wait – no! There was her house. How big? Could it possibly be? Oh my goodness, she felt sick. Every single brick was enough to house her now, let alone the monster dwelling which never seemed to end. En route, she noticed her bedroom window and the faery ornament displayed there. How ironic the sight of that was now!

The two girls had set off after Moss and Rosie, but now over-took them in the rolling sky. They looked so graceful, treading air and looping back round, beautifully at ease with the motion of flight. Their wings of pure white light batted so quickly that all Rosie glimpsed was a flashing pulse of energy. It was the way they made it look effortless that kept Rosie feeling safe.

"Perhaps now you'll begin to appreciate the greed of the human race which we see so clearly from up here," Fire called as she disappeared out of sight.

"Never mind her," said Moss, hugging Rosie tighter. "Get ready. This is where it gets really good."

Having made their climb to the height Moss required,

clearing the house and the network of other rooftops which capped Steeple Chase, Moss now focused on sheer speed. He shot like a lightening bolt at a horizontal angle, slicing through the air, his free arm fixed before him like a guiding spear. *And*, Rosie thought with a breathless smile, *a little like Superman*. But the next moment she feared for her life…

In open space, Moss flipped them headfirst to dive bomb through the now bright blue sky that opened below. Like a pair of fish in water, changing direction with a swish of their tails, Moss shifted his wings to fling them back up again. Once more they accelerated, and once more they dropped. Unable to stop herself she let out a scream and then followed it with a prayer. Eyes watering and heart pounding, Rosie realised they had done a full circle loop upside down. She begged Moss to slow down, but in the next breath begged him to repeat. She was laughing and crying all at the same time.

Fire and Lace drew close and chuckled at the acrobatic display.

"Okay, Moss, that's enough. We're here. Let's take her down." Lace reasoned with her brother.

Gradually, like someone taking their foot off an accelerator, Moss relinquished and the pair slowed to a steady pace. They were breathless, both grabbing at air in short, sharp bursts.

"Do you usually fly like that?"

"No. That was just for your benefit."

Rosie was going to jab him but then remembered he was the sole reason she was suspended in mid-air.

"You can relax a little now," he said. "Your fingernails are gouging my skin."

Everything had changed. They were floating gently. All was still and calm. The afternoon breeze was warm and brushed gentle ripples of wellbeing through the very un-faery-like clothing she wore. They were roughly five feet above the ground, and although this was usually the height she walked around at, it now seemed pretty high in the grand scheme of things. Glancing all around, Rosie realised they were in the woodland by the Steeple Willows housing estate – the uncharted terrain behind

Guy's house – and the connection sent a stab of unexpected pain across her heart. But only for a moment. In a blink the memory was gone, for now she saw in this woodland things she had never seen before. Things of which she could never have dreamed.

Plants and flowers and tree stumps below were all fashioned into faery houses. She realised she had a panoramic view of an entire little person's neighbourhood. A cluster of orange primroses with red flecks at the heart served as a bungalow. She could see steam rising between petals where the chimney had been implanted. A glossy, green hillock whose rounded belly had been perfectly mown despite the wild grasses elsewhere, hid a wide-mouthed tunnel. Various designs greeted her eyes, no two dwellings were the same. A fat mushroom with windows carved into its broad hood and a door with a number and a knocker dead centre of the thick base.

A little plump old woman with an upturned bluebell hat was pegging out washing on a string by the mushroom by threading pine needle pins through the fabrics. The woman looked hot and flustered. She mopped at her brow as she worked and muttered something about *chores never ceasing round here*. Fire laughed and swooped down, purposely clipping the wash basket with her feet and tipping out the remaining contents. The woman turned quickly skyward to identify the perpetrator, squinting into the sunlight and shaking her fists in anger.

"Just a little faery fun!" Fire quipped, re-joining the others, but Rosie couldn't help think the cheeky incident had been purely for her benefit. Fire sure seemed to like showing off.

Further on a group of children were playing butterfly tag in a field. Beautiful, vibrant coloured butterflies flocked airily among them. The young faeries danced figures of eight from one leaf to another, but the butterflies skipped on, always an antennae out of reach.

"They like to think they're faster than us," said Moss, "but it's only because those kids can't fly yet. In a few years time they'll give as good as they get. They're nice fellows though, the butterflies. Especially Cabbage Whites."

"You're friends with butterflies?" Rosie asked, aghast.

"Of course, best of."

"But how do you communicate with them?"

"By *talking*." Moss sounded sarcastic.

"So butterflies can speak?"

"Yes, but through telepathy." Moss smiled at Rosie's clueless expression. "It's all in the mind, all in the mind. You can talk to any living thing on this whole planet if you just take the time to listen. Animals, insects, trees, rocks and water."

The school was below them now and afternoon lessons had resumed.

"That music," said Rosie, "I've heard it all the time since my shrinking, but it's louder now. Where's it coming from?"

Moss pointed and Rosie saw the students in the plant pot with their instruments.

"It's divine. The most magical sound I've ever heard."

"It never stops," said Moss. "Not if they can help it. You get used to it after a while and your ears take it for granted. There are some who say that if ever the Faery Band stopped playing, all in Faery Land would die and the Faery Realm would cease to exist. It's probably true but no one need worry as it would never happen."

As they flew on Rosie saw a mountain of leaves, nuts and berries beside a number of brown field mice. One mouse had a wooden, two-wheeled cart attached to its back. Cleaning her face with her front paws while she waited, the mouse appeared unperturbed by this unusual mode of transport strapped to her behind.

"What's happening?" Rosie begged of Moss, each new sight more fascinating than the last.

"Food collection" he stated simply. "The mice help transport for us. She'll pull it to one of the nearby storage cupboards. We protect them in return. From cats mainly."

Rosie shuddered. "I hate cats. I have a phobia of them."

Moss grinned. "Now you know why."

"What?"

"Never mind. You'll see in time." They moved on, but he added as an afterthought, "At best, cats are one of our daily dilemmas, at worst, they're our sworn enemies."

Losing height all the time now, the foursome passed an assembly of sparrows darting alongside them with faeries on their backs. Nestled into the russet feathers with arms looped about the birds' necks and heels tucked safely into the pocket of their wings, the faeries smiled warmly in greeting.

Rosie frowned, confused. "Why would you fly on a bird when you have wings of your own?"

"A few reasons really," Moss answered. "You humans can walk but you still catch buses, don't you? Also, as I said before, young faeries are not permitted to use their wings until they're sixteen."

"Oh," said Rosie, a little put out, realising that in Faery Land she fell into this *young* bracket. It also meant that Moss and his sisters must be considerably older than her if they were allowed to fly.

"And finally," said Moss, "if you could get from A to B on the back of a bird, wouldn't you, just for the fun of it? It's the most wonderful feeling." Rosie watched their neighbours laughing and waving and had to agree.

"Hello, Rosie Quartz," they called, "Welcome, welcome, welcome indeed."

"H – how?" Rosie stuttered in shock. "How do they know me?"

"Everyone knows you here," Moss said with a laugh.

"They do? How?"

"Don't worry about it right now, Rosie."

"You keep saying that, Moss, but I want to know. I want to know everything."

"I might have guessed. You have Quartz blood in your veins."

"What do you mean Quartz blood? You mean you know my parents?"

Moss never answered this question, for the next moment they touched the ground. They landed softly in the woodland without the slightest bump. Rosie never even noticed her feet connect with the path and was suddenly surprised to find they had. Moss released his grip and her hands fell to her sides. She felt a little dizzy, windswept perhaps, but other than that, perfectly fine. Before them stood the enchanting Agate Abode – the great hollow tree stump and its three remaining branches capped with birdhouse turrets. Its arms twisted skyward, casting an unusual, disfigured shadow on the threshold where the inhabitants and their guest now stood.

"This is our home, Rosie." Moss gestured toward the central arch with its porch roof and shiny sign. "Let's go inside and we can talk in private."

There were no steps leading to the entrance and Rosie realised that to reach the front door she would once again have to take Moss's hand so his wings could lift them both. She had no idea why this made her blush as she held out her arm. There was no need, however, as Fire abruptly stepped forwards and scooped Rosie up for herself. With a tough grasp, considerably rougher than her brother's, Fire cleared the short height in a single motion and pushed Rosie through into the dining hall. Staggering forward, Rosie took in her surroundings. To the right a neat kitchen, to the left a sitting room stacked with plump cushions, and between the two an impressive table lined with ten carved chairs. Lace Agate came to stand beside Rosie on the thick crescent-shaped rug which lent an instant impression of comfort. She smiled at Rosie's wide eyes and planted a friendly kiss on her cheek.

"I'll pop the kettle on. Dandelion tea all round, I think."

The three faeries busied themselves and Rosie was left alone in a home she had dreamed of as a little girl. It was something straight out of the books her mum had read her. Enchanted, she crossed the space, running her hand across the thick oak table. To the rear of the room was a round, lead-panelled window set deep into a pretty curtained alcove. The view beyond showed the beautiful woodland, hanging bowers and the twisting stream. Incredible that in her normal form this stunning panorama would be no more than debris she'd flatten with her shoe. She inhaled the lavender scent and drifted to a small bookcase packed with yellowing hardbacks. The books were shoved, stacked and piled in any old fashion. Intrigued by what a faery may read, Rosie coaxed out the top two and was surprised by the titles: *Great Expectations* by Charles Dickens and *Wuthering Heights* by Emily Brontë. So classics really did stand the test of time – and space – and world! Finding a name she didn't recognise, Rosie clasped the heavy cover and lowered herself into an armchair strategically placed by the shelves. Opening it, she found that the pages inside were blank. She flicked a fair way through but still there was nothing. Her puzzlement was interrupted by Lace arriving with an acorn shell of hot, steaming liquid.

"Try it," she said, setting the drink down on a low pedestal table with a feathered reading lamp.

It's all like doll's house furniture, Rosie thought, *except I'm the doll.*

Swapping the empty book for her dandelion tea, Rosie drank and found she thoroughly enjoyed the sweet nectar which trickled down her throat.

"It's beautiful, Lace, thank you – the nicest thing I've ever tasted. And your home is amazing too. I love it here. It's so cosy."

"Well you make yourself comfortable, my dear. We have a lot to tell you."

Relaxed, Rosie tucked her feet up on the paisley cushions of the armchair, cradled her tea and watched Moss as he tentatively approached. He pulled up a footstool and sat down before her. He ran his hands across the stubble of his head and played with the loops in his ears. Rosie thought he looked nervous, a little unsure of how to begin. Lace and Fire, standing close behind him, urged him on with expressions of intent.

"So, Rosie…" He knitted his fingers together and rested them on his knees. "We said we brought you here because we had things to discuss with you. Important things."

"Yes."

"She knows that already! Just get on with it!" snapped Fire.

Moss continued. "Rosie, haven't you thought before now that you're different? That maybe you don't fit in with the other kids at school? Have you ever realised that you're special?"

"Special?" Rosie raised her eyebrows. "No. Not really. And as for fitting in, I seem to do okay. I have Billie and Sally and... well...I did have Guy."

"But surely," Lace said hopping impatiently from foot to foot, "you must have felt it when you arrived here."

"Rosie," Moss said slowly, looking her squarely in the eyes, "Rosie Quartz...you are one of us. You are a faery."

Rosie laughed. "Well, yes, I guess after the mental time I've just had, I certainly feel like one of you now."

"No, no. What I mean is that you always were. Rosie, you were born that way."

"What? I don't understand."

"You are one of us – or *were* one of us once, and then you chose to change."

"Okay, just say that for one minute, what you're saying has any chance of being true – which of course is completely impossible – but just say that for a second I was hearing you right, then why on earth would I ever have decided to become a human being when it's altogether nicer here? You live in this dazzling, perfect world, so much more exciting and beautiful than anywhere else imaginable. Why in heaven's name would I have chosen to leave *this*?" Rosie had leapt from her chair and was gesticulating wildly around.

"For the same reason anyone makes crazy decisions in life, Rosie." Moss placed his hand lightly on her arm and coaxed her back to her seat. "You did it for love."

11

At the Agate Abode

"So just tell me again, Moss, how this whole *time* thing works. My head is starting to spin with information and it's getting dark outside. My parents will flip if they find me missing. My mum likes to know where I am at all times."

The world beyond the Agate Abode had turned a dusty grey and the woodland view was no longer visible through the picture window, save for a few spindly shadows which depicted the outline of trees. Candles flickered orange in a jumbled assortment of holders, which Lace had just dotted about. They sent jumping spidery images across the walls. Lace had also set a small fire burning in the hearth of the adjacent sitting room. Evening wanderers passing by the house would have seen circles of smoke oozing through the chimney up towards human height.

Moss was being patient, although he had already tolerantly explained things to Rosie several times.

"The length of time you have spent with us today may seem like hours to you, but in actual fact it has taken up no time at all in your world."

"And this is because...?" She still didn't follow.

"This is because of the contrasting frequencies which exist in the two alternate dimensions. Old Father Time is a mysterious figure you know, Rosie. He moves entirely differently between one space and the next. The human world is far courser and heavier than ours, so in it time drags. The Faery Realm is light and free so time merely trips upon it like a leaf on the breeze.

One whole faery hour is a human second. You can spend an entire day here and only have been gone from the place you call home for twenty-four seconds."

As unbelievable as this seemed to Rosie, the penny was beginning to drop.

"So, if I were to spend a full week with you, I'd have only been missing for…erm…one hundred and sixty-eight seconds… that's two minutes and forty-eight seconds. And for my parents actually to notice I'd been gone for the equivalent of an hour, I'd have to have been here for…" Rosie paused and scrunched up her face in mathematical concentration. Defeated, she sighed. "…A long time."

"Just over three months," said Moss, grinning.

"Wow, that long? That's seriously spooky."

"There are times, however, when that rule goes completely out the window," Fire chuckled. "Faeries will be faeries and all that."

Lace tutted and batted the comment away with her palm, as though it were a living entity which force could remove from the house. "She's talking about when a mischievous faery will use his or her magic power to trance the clock. We can hypnotise the passage of time and train it to do whatever we want. Backwards, forwards, flip it and reverse it or stop it dead still. But that's another story and quite irrelevant right now."

"This is all truly fascinating," said Rosie, mainly looking at Moss, since he seemed to have been her lead source of information so far, "but what happens now? Let's get back to the original point of *why* I'm here. You've been so kind to me and I thank you for that, but I'm just really confused. You said you wanted to show me something and you got me here like you wanted. You could have just left me in ignorance, none the wiser. Why now? I come here to your home and you tell me I'm a *faery*, which quite seriously stretches even my imagination, and you talk of love but mainly you talk in riddles, and in all honesty my head really hurts and I just want to go home."

She knew she sounded like a small, whining child and that

in all probability this was still a dream from which she'd soon wake, but it was late and she was tired and she needed answers. Or was it late? If she was to believe Moss, back home it was early morning and her parents were still tucked up in their beds. So why did she feel like she now needed a good night's sleep?

Lace came to sit by her side and gently took hold of her hand.

"As for what we do now, Rose, I'm not entirely sure. Our role was merely to bring you here. The Council gave us the job of getting your attention and coaxing you into the Faery Realm. Now that we've done that, for us Agates, it's mission accomplished and what happens next, Gaia knows? Perhaps we've said too much already."

"I seriously doubt you've said too much," said Rosie. "As it stands, I feel severely under informed."

Moss rose and began to pace the room, back and forth. "Strictly speaking Lace, what you've said about our role isn't true. It was also our responsibility to guide Rosie on the right path. She needs to know about the *Book* and the *Spell* and then we need to get her to take the right action."

"*Book? Spell?*" Rosie was shouting now. This was just too much.

"The spell the Elders are so concerned about you mucking up and wrecking!" Fire folded her arms defiantly and fixed Rosie with an icy stare.

Determined to keep the peace, Moss placed himself between her and Rosie. "Look, Rosie, there's a Council of Elders who were elected to take charge and guard the Kingdom now that there's no longer a King and Queen."

"No King and Queen?" questioned Rosie with sheer sarcasm in her tone. "Why do you have no King and Queen? I thought all faery worlds had to have a set. No self-respecting kingdom would be without one, right?" She laughed. "Every book I've read says it's so. What about Oberon and Titania? Surely they're around here somewhere." She knew she was being rude but Fire had begun to annoy her.

"Actually, they're in Glastonbury," said Moss. "All areas

of your country's map coincide with ours. Just like you have Members of Parliament and Lord Mayors to reside over each separate town and village, so we have our own Kings and Queens. Steeple is no exception. Or at least it wasn't. Sadly, the Steeple royalty died." He hung his head and Rosie sensed genuine distress.

"Murdered," said Lace, a cheerless whisper under her breath. "They were cruelly murdered."

"Murder?" Rosie echoed in disbelief. "Surely violence doesn't happen in your world? It doesn't even happen in Steeple."

Once more Fire shot her down. "Girl, you just haven't got a clue."

"So these Elders you speak of," Rosie continued, unphased by Fire, but a little guilty at having previously made light of the Faery King and Queen's downfall, "what are they doing about it?"

"They're waiting for their precious little pathetic Princess to return," snapped Fire with venom.

"Hold it there, Sis," Moss cut her off before she had a chance to say more. "That's enough. I think Council business is one thing it's really not our place to discuss. In the morning I'll take Rosie to see Apatite and she can tell the rest."

"What?" Lace was up like a shot, hanging by her brother's side. "No way, Moss. You've got to be kidding."

"I've already made up my mind. We'll visit Apatite tomorrow. She'll know what to do."

"Oh yeah, she'll know what to do alright! Probably turn the lot of us into slimy croaking toads!"

"Apatite? Who's that?" said Rosie.

"She's one of the Elders."

"No," said Lace, surveying her brother like he'd lost his mind. "Strictly speaking, she's *not* one of the Elders. She's an outcast."

"Well, she *was* one of the Elders once," said Moss, "but now she lives in the Woods."

"Why is she an outcast?" Rosie ventured timidly, looking first from Lace and then to Moss. Lace pulled a face as if to say *don't ask*, but Moss muttered, "Just differing beliefs, that's all."

"And this Apatite, how can she help me?"

"She's also known as the Fortune Teller," said Moss, ignoring the awkward glares of his sisters. "She knows *all*. From times past to times ahead. If anyone knows what to do, it will be Apatite. We'll visit her in the morning."

Lace began to collect the empty cups. She hoped that her tidying would effectively bring the day's events to a close. She hated to disagree with her older brother, whom she normally idolised, but a fear crept over her at the thought of where such meddling may lead. "It's getting late and I think we're all ready for bed. Everyone's tired and saying things they don't really mean. We'll function better with clearer heads after a good night's sleep. Maybe then we can reassess this in the morning."

"So you're taking me back home?" Rosie asked her.

Moss was quick to interject. "No way. It was hard enough getting you here in the first place. I'm not risking having to go through all that again. Now you're here, you are staying here. Besides, Rosie, we've been through this. The time difference means that a full night's sleep will be but a dot on the horizon of your absence at home."

Fire snatched the acorn shells from Lace's hands and marched with them through to the kitchen, calling over her shoulder as she went. "Regardless of time this and time that, blah, blah, blah, I think Rosie needs to go home and sleep in her own bed tonight."

"No, it's out of the question," said Moss. "Rosie is welcome to stop in my bed and I'm happy to sleep on the sofa."

Cups dropped to the floor and rolled around like spinning tops on the wood. One by one they hit the edges of cupboards and cabinets and stopped. Fire stood frozen in the spot where they'd slipped through her fingers. "She'll what?"

"Sleep in my bed. I'll go and clear the room for her now."

"But...but...Lace?...How about your room?...Erm...I'm sure if Rosie *has* to stay here, she'd find it far more comfortable sleeping in your bed. In a girl's room. Yes? What do you say, Sis?"

Lace chuckled while pulling some spare sheets out of a chest and beginning to make up a fourth bed in the sitting room. "I don't know. What do *you* say, Sis? If you're suddenly so concerned about Rosie's comfort, how about you give her *your* room for the night?"

Fire's cheeks burned the colour of her name. She looked positively furious.

Lace pounded two pillows to plump them up before setting them on the sofa arm. Rosie thought they looked like white cottonwool balls, the kind she usually used in the evening to remove her mascara. "Not that you're not entirely welcome to my room of course, Rosie. I just thought Fire sounded extra anxious for your wellbeing."

"Girls, girls," Moss called, irritated. "There's nothing to discuss. Rosie will have my room like I said."

"Well, just for the record, I still think she should go home tonight," Fire spat in disgust before turning on her heels and disappearing down the corridor which led to her own section of the house.

"Well, I must admit, I am tired," said Rosie, trying hard to stifle a yawn as she spoke. She stretched her arms above her head and suddenly wanted very much to lie down and close her eyes.

"Come on," said Moss, "this way."

He led her to the mouth of a tight passage, similar to the tunnel down which Fire had just made her dramatic exit, except this one ran from the left side of the house, and Fire's had sloped from the right. The space inside was limited and Rosie had to follow behind Moss in single file. He moved quickly, with one of the candles fluttering in his hand, lighting the way before them. The branch had been carved to a hollow corridor, the twisted walls of which glittered with gold-framed portraits of faery ancestors, and Rosie wondered, not for the first time, how the faeries had set about building and creating this place. Their workmanship was sheer genius. Ancient eyes watched her from askew angles as she climbed the remaining steps into Moss's chamber.

The room was sparsely furnished but overwhelmingly warm. The floorboards were bare and the extent of decoration was a bed and side table, a wardrobe, a chair and a chest of drawers beneath the window, all cut from the same oak wood as the walls. A small pile of books and papers sat upon the chair and a pair of black, thick-rimmed glasses balanced on top. Exhausted, Rosie only cared that the bed looked like the most comfortable thing she had ever seen.

Moss set the candleholder on the side table and pulled the rose petal drapes together at the window. While his back was turned, Rosie hopped beneath the covers, still wearing the shorts and t-shirt from home. She buried herself in the folds of thick duvet and felt her head sink and mould into the cottonwool cloud of the pillow. Almost instantaneously her thoughts drifted away.

Moss stood for a long while at the foot of the bed, watching her gently breathe. Once he was sure that she was fast asleep, he gave a wry smile, blew out the candle and tiptoed out of the room.

In the morning, Rosie felt the bright light of the sun prising open her eyes. Her lids flickered but the heavy sheets were still so cosy around her body that she didn't want her sleep to end. Eventually it was noise that got the better of her, curiosity for the buzz of voices at very close range. They were made up of many different tones so she knew that there had to be more than just the three Agates with her in the room.

"Hush," said one, "keep your racket down, she's starting to wake."

The sound dropped to a whisper while Rosie trained her focus on the blurred silhouettes. The outlines hardened and she found she was looking upon at least a dozen faeries of all ages, shapes and sizes, crowded round the foot of her bed. Jostling for space and nudging each other's elbows to get nearer than their neighbour, the inquisitive pixies stared shamelessly.

"She's far prettier than I remember."

"She's beautiful."

"She seems to be blonder than before."

"Her cheeks are pinker than when she left."

Lace Agate was in the background, flapping around and trying to push her way through the crowd. "Guys, guys, she's really not ready for visitors just yet. I know you're excited to see her but we are running a tight schedule today and Rosie can't get up and dressed until you lot clear out of the way."

Gradually but reluctantly the uninvited guests began to disperse. They looked over their shoulders, grumbling and chuntering as they went.

Rosie sat up and bunched her messy hair into a handheld ponytail. "What was all that about?"

"Oh, them?" Lace looked at Moss's green door, by which they had just left. "They heard we had you here and on and off people have been arriving since dawn. I tried to keep them out but some came down the chimney. After that it seemed pointless even trying to maintain order."

"Why did they want to come and see me?"

"You're creating quite a bit of a stir, girl. You're famous, after all. Everyone wanted to be the first to catch a glimpse of you. They can't believe it's true that you've returned."

Rosie rolled her eyes. So it wasn't a dream. She was still here and the new world around her was still proclaiming her a faery.

Lace stood with a crocheted, powder-pink dress hanging over her arm. It was perfectly pressed and smelled of clean soap. "I picked this out for you to wear today. Hope you don't mind. I thought it would be slightly less conspicuous than those trendy teenage street clothes you've been trotting around in."

"Thanks," said Rosie. She played it down but secretly thought it was a beautiful dress and couldn't wait to put it on. As she flipped her legs over the edge of the bed, Lace met her feet with a basin of warm water to wash in, then filled and emptied a porcelain jug over her skin. The dress slipped over her head and fit perfectly. Rosie viewed herself in a silver hand mirror while she brushed through her hair.

"I look so...so..."

"Gorgeous," Lace offered with a smile.

Rosie hated to admit it, but she'd expected to feel mortified this morning at having no make-up to put on. The mascara and eyeliner she relied on were stashed in her vanity case back home. Instead, the reflection she saw in the glass was undoubtedly the most attractive she'd ever been. Not only had she magically morphed to two inches tall but she'd also become an exquisitely more beautiful version of herself than she'd ever thought possible.

"Lace, how long have I been missing from home?"

"About twenty seconds."

Twenty hours here. Twenty seconds there. This satisfied her worry. Her parents would still be asleep right now.

Moss and Fire were at the dining table when Rosie and Lace came down the passage. Pots and pans were scattered around them. Moss was wearing his black glasses and reading something which looked like a newspaper. The headlines screamed out at Rosie in thick, bold lettering: QUARTZ PRINCESS RETURNS! And a subtitle underneath stating, AGATES TRIUMPHANT! She recognised her passport photograph in black and white and then a less professional shot which she knew Billie had taken in the Buttercup Fields last Summer. Appalled, she groaned, which Moss mistook for hunger.

"Breakfast?" he asked, pushing a plate towards her. "Have some tea and toast and then we'll make a start."

Despite the dramatic change of size, Rosie recognised much of the woodland which she and Moss now made their way through. Glancing up, she saw the barbed-wire fence and heard the babbling of the stream. It was just the two of them. Lace and Fire had stayed behind and Rosie knew by their fixed expressions that they were still not happy about the outing. Moss clearly had final say on the matter.

"My ex's house is by this woodland," Rosie told him. "I know it's silly but it still freaks me out. I feel a little funny walking by. Not that he'd be able to see me right now."

"Yes," said Moss, "but we're going quite a bit further than Guy's house today. It's a long way to Apatite's tree."

Rosie stopped. "You used Guy's name. You know about him then?"

"Yes, Rosie, I know all about Guy. More than you do at present in fact. But there'll be time to discuss that later."

Rosie had learned it was useless pushing Moss if he was not ready to talk, so instead she chased the questions from her mind and concentrated on her footing across the dangerous terrain. The surface got worse the further they travelled: jutting rocks, poking sticks and slippery leaves. A number of times she tripped on the changing ground and would have fallen headfirst were it not for Moss clasping her firmly round the waist. Gratefully, she'd nod thanks and then dust herself down. They walked in silence until a branch snapped underfoot and the volume to her now tiny ears seemed to deafen. Rosie shrieked and jumped up in the air. Absentmindedly, she reached for Moss's hand as support. Embarrassed as she was, Moss didn't seem to mind and the pair of them walked on that way, hand in hand, for the rest of their journey.

"Why are we not flying there, Moss?"

"We want to remain as inconspicuous as possible today. I'd rather we get there unseen." The trunks got thicker and grew closer together and though it was still morning, they began to lose light.

"So tell me again about Apatite. Who is she and why do you think she can help me?"

"She is what we call a 'Faery Witch' as she has tremendous psychic powers. She can tune into the past as well as the future. She has a crystal ball, which can show her events as clearly as if they were on a movie screen. The ball itself is quite worthless. It's her own unique ability that provokes the response from it. I know because a group of cheeky faery youths dared to steal it once, back when she was living in the Palace, and despite saying all the magic words they knew, nothing happened. Apatite is the only true Fortune Teller in this Kingdom. It's her third eye that does the work. The ball is just a tool she uses to focus. Even without her tools, she's extremely wise. Probably the wisest woman in all of Faery Land."

"You say *when* she lived in the Palace. Why did she have to leave? Especially since her gift must have been so valued."

"There has always been a Council, a circle of Elders, who support and protect Faery Royalty. But when the King and Queen were murdered, six specific Elders were elected to be Guardians of the Kingdom. It became their job to make sure things ran as close to normality as possible. Three males – Fluorite, Hematite and Rhodonite; and three females – Celestite, Sodalite and Apatite. Nobody quite knows why, but there seems to have been some discrepancy, a heated argument over something, and as a result Apatite fled. The remaining Elders declared her outcast and a powerful fixing spell was placed on the Kingdom walls. It's woven so tight that it will never allow her back in. And so she crept into the darkest recesses of the Woods and made her home here. There's an old tree known as the Bearded Bark. It's the largest and most ancient tree in Steeple, and it's deep within the roots of this that she makes her home."

"Moss, how do you know all this? How do you know that this is where she'll be?"

"Because from time to time I come and visit her."

Rosie decided that there was altogether more to the relationship between Moss and the Fortune Teller than he was letting on, but she also sensed that this was not the time to probe further.

A brown owl sounded high up in the branches above and Rosie almost jumped out of her skin again. She squeezed Moss's hand harder and saw his jaw tighten to suppress the pain. The owl watched them intently, turning its swivel head to follow the pair, never shifting his beady eyes from their path. Cautious and timid now, Rosie shivered and it was then she spotted the first of the signs. They were all around, painted on wood in messy, childlike writing and pinned to every available hard surface: rocks, branches and overturned debris.

GO BACK NOW!
TURN AROUND FOOL!
DO NOT ENTER IF YOU WANT TO LIVE!

"Moss! Moss! Have you read those signs? Do you see what they say?" Rosie's voice had risen several octaves as she spoke. "Lace was right, wasn't she? This really doesn't seem like such a good idea. It's not safe!"

"Oh, those old things? Just ignore the signs. Apatite put them there herself to keep people away." He laughed. "Judging by the look on your face, it works pretty well too. Come on, Rosie, don't be scared. We're almost there."

Rosie eyed the vicious warnings warily as they walked between them. Each step sent creepy chills down her spine. The sky grew blacker and eventually Moss came to a standstill. Rosie looked at him and then followed his gaze upward to reveal the source of the huge shadow that enveloped them. It was cast by the most enormous, gnarled and chiselled oak Rosie had ever seen. Even in her human form it would have been a giant among trees. The thick, twisted knots set within the trunk seemed to show the wrinkled face of a grumpy old man – two veiny eyes beneath a furrowed brow, a pointed, hooked nose and a moustache capping a crooked frown. The tree man towered before them and Rosie knew without a doubt that they had reached the Bearded Bark.

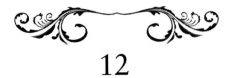

12

The Fortune Teller

At the foot of the tree where the trunk was widest, the thick roots of the Bearded Bark could be seen to tunnel their way deep into the earth. Moss and Rosie made their way through the curved hollow entrance at its base; or rather, Moss took the strides and Rosie was pulled in tow. The tree face seemed to look bemused as it watched them go inside. Rosie was sure she glimpsed a raised eyebrow and heard a low laughing sound.

It was pitch black inside until the hallway opened out to a circular room lit by airborne shimmering lanterns. Rosie looked to see what was supporting the lamps above her and then remembered that to seek practical explanations in a place such as this was totally impractical. The lights were, of course, suspended in mid-air by sheer faery magic. There was no ceiling, as far as Rosie could see. The spherical space seemed to stretch on and on, upwards forever. She hadn't been able to see the crown of the tree from outside and it was no different within. Around the circumference was a never-ending circuit of shelves. They lined every gap, occasionally housing books, but mainly displaying an immense assortment of glass bottles and vials. These appeared to have a life of their own and the bright, clotted liquids inside jumped and gurgled like they were screaming to be set free.

Spells and potions, Rosie guessed. Moss had mentioned a spell had played a part in bringing her here and maybe that was why this was the perfect place to find answers.

At the centre of the room, a fire was burning. An iron cauldron rocked over it on rickety tripod stilts. A broomstick was also resting there and Rosie remembered how Moss had referred to Apatite as a witch. This lair was about as stereotypical a witch's house as you could get. The only thing missing was a black cat purring by the flames. Maybe Apatite would appear wearing a pointy hat and a billowing cloak. But as Rosie was soon to find out, the Fortune Teller was anything but the stereotypical witch.

Moss called into the void above where his voice echoed loudly, "Apatite! Madame Apatite, are you home? It's Moss Agate. I've brought someone special to see you. I know you knew we were coming. Please let us speak with you."

A shuffling noise came from the shadows – the sound of a scratchy material dragging on the dirty floor. Although Rosie tried hard to mind her manners, she instinctively gasped as the Fortune Teller hauled her appalling carcass into view. Apatite was a hunchback, which meant that her back was twisted over and locked that way. She was forced to walk as though she were bending to retrieve something from the ground and her hands hung limp before her like a mole's muddy claws. She had cavernous, wrinkled skin, dull grey in colour, and for this she appeared to be unfathomable hundreds of years old.

Rosie dared not breathe as she drank in the sight, but she feared her heart was hammering audibly in her chest.

The Fortune Teller was half bald, and then at random intervals hair sprang white and wispy upon her head – an odd, alopecia patchwork. But most shocking of all was the fact that Apatite had just one large, round eye in the centre of her forehead. Just above the bridge of her crooked nose, the eye flickered incessantly, turning every direction in the socket. It shot first to Rosie, then to Moss, and then to the archway by which they had entered, checking there were no further intruders.

Rosie felt her stomach turn. This must be what Moss had meant by saying Apatite could see things through her *third eye*. Where her two normal eyes would have been there were charred grooves and badly sewn eyelids. Red, swollen and covered in scabs, the angry scars shamelessly desecrated her face.

Living in a tree had somehow turned Apatite into a tree-like creature herself. Her dress hung in torn rags, scraps of rough sack sewn together, and from the holes of this pathetic garment, branches and weeds protruded. Grass, fern and dandelion leaves poked through the hems at her neck, wrists and ankles, and where her back hunched over and forced the dress apart, an entire stinging nettle plant had sprouted there. Rosie turned from horror to wonder to empathy. Did this cause her discomfort or pain, or had she grown so used to the personal garden that she simply accepted its existence? The Fortune Teller wore no shoes on her filthy feet. Instead, her toes were buried beneath a clump of rotting leaves.

Moss Agate cleared his throat and bowed low before her. Rosie watched and then feeling she should do the same, mirrored the gesture. She trembled all the while.

Apatite's serious expression never faltered, but slowly in a gravelly voice she began to speak. "I have indeed been waiting for this meeting a long, long time. Step forward Rosie Quartz, let me take a good look at you."

Rosie looked to Moss for reassurance. He nodded his consent, so cautiously Rosie inched closer to the woman she found extremely frightening.

"A-ha, yes." The Fortune Teller began to move around Rosie in circles, her rags and weeds shuffling, her single eye scanning her visitor up and down. "Just as I thought. There's no doubt you are 'The One', The Royal Quartz Princess. The only daughter of Smoky and Snow."

Rosie opened her mouth, about to protest that she was the daughter of Daniel and Debra, and maybe Apatite was not such a great psychic after all, but Moss placed a finger to his lips signalling for Rosie to hold her tongue and listen carefully to what the woman had to say.

"How I loved your parents, Rosie Quartz. They were fine faery folk: beautiful, pure and true. No greater rulers of this Kingdom have there ever been. And how they loved each other. Their love enabled them to achieve great things. The Kingdom was alight and alive when they sat on the throne, and all revered them. I can still hear the music and laughter from their renowned parties, to which all were welcome. Yes, I loved them and I served them well. Especially your mother, whom I nursed since she was a little girl, much younger than yourself. Her mother before her had kindly taken me in as palace maid. So proud I was of my important job, helping to raise a little princess into a strong ruler of the Land."

Rosie tried to picture Apatite as the Palace maid and wondered if she'd always looked so old and overgrown. How had the Queen endured such a creature? Strangely, a vision of an elegant and attractive young woman appeared in her mind, and Rosie guessed it had not always been so.

"From a young age your mother was always particularly interested in the Spiritual Laws and mysteries of magic. These were my own passion and expertise and so I revelled in teaching her all I knew about the wonders of the universe and the secrets it held. Your mother could have been a great Fortune Teller herself, you know. She had the gift of the third eye. But as is usually the case, those who are worshipped and adored also attract loathing and jealousy. For where there is light, there is also dark. Never forget that, Rosie Quartz. And dark exists even in the Faery Realm. There were those who resented what your parents represented, the power they could never achieve themselves. The evil that brought about your parents' tragic demise still exists and until it is defeated once and for all none of us can ever truly live in peace. *He* is one of those who crave only the dark. And now only one other has the ability to defeat him – the only living descendant of the deceased Faery King and Queen. Legend has it that the Quartz Princess bears white light within, and the pure, true beauty she possesses can reflect back into his rotten soul and dissolve the evil in his heart, destroying him once and for all."

Rosie thought she had read this clichéd fairy tale a thousand times, and now couldn't believe that the conversation they were having was about *her*. The fire in the centre of the room crackled and the broomstick slipped to rest on the floor.

"Madame Apatite?" Rosie had learned to address her as such from Moss. "I've heard about a book and a spell. What of these? They seem to be important to my being here and you haven't mentioned them yet."

The Fortune Teller looked genuinely crestfallen at this. Her hunched body seemed to bend and fold even more like a shrivelled flower. Rosie had stepped on delicate ground and the witch's one eye watered and glazed over.

"The signing of the Book was how we two first fell, Rosie Quartz. The spell you asked me to create was the reason I was banished."

"Pardon? The reason you were banished was *my* fault? That can't be possible. How? I don't understand."

"Of course you don't child. It was a 'Forgetting Spell'. The spell we chose required you to forget all that had gone before."

"Madame Apatite?" Now it was Moss who spoke. "I believe the Forgetting Spell is our current problem now. Although we have begun to tell Rosie about her past, the very nature of the charm renders her memory useless. While the spell is at full strength, Rosie cannot recall any of her life as a faery. In order that we keep her safe and stick to the plan, the Council have had to intervene. They sent my sisters and I to keep her on the right path. As things have become more desperate we feel we must quickly inform her of her purpose. Great Apatite, I trust your judgement. What do *you* suggest we do now?"

The Fortune Teller stared into the flames. For a time she was still, and then she shuffled to a low shelf where a black cloth covered something at arm's reach. Brushing the velvet aside she revealed her glistening crystal ball. The quartz glass sent diamond orbs dancing around the dark walls. Clasping the globe in her grimy hands she carried it to where Moss and Rosie stood in awe. All watched smoke rise and change within, but only Apatite read the meaning.

"Moss Agate, you must take Rosie Quartz back home to the Quartz Palace. The spell will be weaker there and the power of her bloodline will infiltrate her thoughts. There she will find her old bedroom and her old diary. These words will awaken her soul. And that is our only hope."

Apatite lowered the ball and walked back to the shelf. She blessed it with a sign before returning it. "I pray for you both," she whispered.

Moss said he would be in touch, as he placed a protective arm around Rosie's shoulder and ushered her outside. Rosie's mind was so spinning with the overdose of information that she forgot to say bye or even thank you.

In the Woods Rosie and Moss sat side by side on a low, overturned log.

"Rosie, I know it's a lot to take in. I can see you're worried. But I totally believe we did the right thing. It was wise of us to go."

"I just...I just can't get my head round it all, Moss. *Royal parents, murder most horrid, an evil lurking and a final battle.* I've heard this one before. Only I'm not supposed to be in it!"

"I know. Look, before we go to the Palace, let's do something fun. I have a surprise for you." Turning his head over his shoulder, Moss let out a shrill whistle. The loud call was impressive to Rosie who could not whistle at all and the sound was obviously heard a long way off, as now it was answered by a pounding, like a heartbeat racing through the woods. Rosie saw the cause of the ground's pulse and squealed in delight. Grinding to a halt by the log where she sat was her old beloved rabbit. Though she was now the scale of an elephant, her doting owner would have recognised her anywhere.

"Oh my goodness! I can't believe it! Strawberry?"

Rosie leapt from her seat and threw her arms about the rabbit's front legs, losing herself in the soft, familiar scent of her fur. Strawberry bent to lick her with slobbery kisses across the face and Rosie relished the warmth, giggling with joy.

"This is so wonderful. But, Moss, how is it possible? Strawberry...died."

"Rosie, nothing ever *dies*. Our bodies are made up of energy. Energy cannot be destroyed. Not ever. It can only be changed into something different. When the body Strawberry used in your human world grew old and tired, Lady Gaia stopped it working and it was time to return it to the earth. Strawberry, however, can only continue. She rises to the higher dimensions. Like here, with us. I've met with her on numerous occasions. In fact, she's a fabulous mode of transport."

"Transport?"

"Sure. Climb on board." Moss jumped down and offered his cupped hands to hoist Rosie up onto her pet rabbit's broad back.

Amazed and a little scared, Rosie perched precariously in a kneeling position, tightly bunching tufts of Strawberry's coat in her fists. Moss used his wings to lift himself behind her and settled gently. Again his presence made her brave and she noted the unusual array of pictures that patterned his arms as he slipped them tightly around her waist.

"Moss, although obviously she's much bigger, Strawberry looks entirely as I remember her."

"Of course she does. She's your Strawberry. Why wouldn't she?"

"But you said that when our bodies grow old, we have to change into something else."

"Yes. Pure soul. But how would our loved ones recognise us if we didn't show up in our old clothes? Strawberry can choose to look however she pleases now. Like a silver chinchilla if she wants. But she'd hardly do that to you on your first reunion. You'd never know it was her."

Rosie was not entirely sure she understood, but any further conversation was cut dead as Strawberry set off, careering straight ahead as the world flashed by them. Grass, plants, rocks and shrubs, all of which they had walked through earlier, now whizzed past in a green-brown blur. It was exhilarating, like flying with Moss last night, a rush like you're invincible and somehow born again. As her rabbit slowed, however, Rosie couldn't help wonder whether it was the swift motion of travel which had taken her breath away or whether it was more to do with having Moss Agate so close beside her.

"Strawberry will have to leave us here," said Moss. "She has brought us to the Palace Gardens, but now we must dismount and journey on alone."

"Gorgeous, gorgeous girl," sang Rosie as she slid down with Moss's help. She ran a hand across the rabbit's sleek side. "I love you so much and thank you for our ride and I know now I'll see you again." The rabbit nudged her gently in the ribs and then as fast as she'd first appeared, with the same giant rumbling, she was gone.

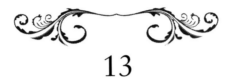

13

In the Quartz Palace

"Where are we now? I don't recognise this in relation to the human world. With the Bearded Bark, I knew we were somewhere in the woods behind Guy's house, but now I seem to have lost all sense of direction." Rosie turned around before tall iron gates, painted white and twisted ornately into two kissing doves at the top. She could hear the sound of water but it wasn't from the stream.

"Any Faery Palace is always purposely well hidden, for obvious reasons," said Moss, "but the perimeter of our Steeple Faery Kingdom is where you would know the Buttercup Fields to be."

"The Buttercup Fields? At the top of the lane? We've seriously come that far? But it didn't seem…" Rosie allowed her thoughts to trail. Stop thinking logically yet again, she scolded herself.

Moss unlatched the gate and the two doves momentarily parted as they stepped through into the Palace Gardens. The royal grounds rendered Rosie speechless. They were enormous and gave life to every single species of flower she had ever seen, not just yellow buttercups as she'd imagined, but plants she had never even glimpsed before. All the colours of the rainbow, but brighter. Vibrant, pulsating shades which seemed to pierce her eyes with their brilliance. Exotic and peculiar shapes with heads which turned to follow the visitors as they passed. Sometimes the strange hoods snapped shut, making them jump, but the tiny bugs who fluttered between the stems were nonplussed as they drew invisible vitamins and goodness from the petals.

The potent lavender smell she had come to associate with Faery Land was stronger than ever and she breathed the intoxicating aroma from deep within her lungs. The Gardens oozed a special magic which made all in them feel peaceful, and there were comfortable benches set in the alcoves and recesses of the many blossoms where a faery could sit and read or simply contemplate.

Now Rosie saw the source of the water sound – gushing waterfalls were dotted between the beds of flowers, each one with a stone statue at its middle in the spray. The elaborate sculptures seemed to be of important faeries, previous generations of royalty maybe, as most were depicted with crowns, tiaras, armour or swords. Some of the effigies had bare torsos and long fish tails in place of their legs. *Mermaids.*

Rosie turned to Moss. "Don't tell me that mermaids actually exist too?"

"Are you kidding? Of course they do. Mermaids are just another *type* of faery – the water version."

Rosie rolled her eyes. What had she expected?

Privet hedges shaped like animals also trimmed the massive gardens – swans, flamingos and dolphins – and tucked into the bottom of these carved masterpieces were acorn-shaped speakers emitting the heavenly faery music always played by the band. For a brief yet strange moment Rosie had a vivid flash of herself as a younger child, running around these hedges, playing hide and seek with faery friends she'd long since forgotten.

Then she saw the Palace. It was surrounded by a moat of calm, blue water with an arched footbridge to the main entrance. Everything was white, translucent, crystal or diamond. The whole building glowed with a sparkling radiant light, as though a constant moon hovered above it. There were twelve pointed turrets high in the sky but the ground level was Roman in structure, like an ancient temple with smooth, stone columns.

Rosie and Moss passed through two tall entrance pillars and found themselves dwarfed in a vast hall with no furniture. Their footsteps echoed on the polished marble floor. The ceilings were high enough to have accommodated even humans.

"It's so quiet and so still. Where is everyone?" Rosie's sentence echoed back at her.

Moss pushed his hands into his waistcoat pockets and stared at his feet. "Nowhere, Rosie. Smoky and Snow are gone, remember. No one lives in the Palace now. The Elders closed it all off as a mark of respect. Occasionally, they use the main meeting auditorium to hold a conference, but only for important things." He laughed to lift the mood. "Things like *you* for example. The conversations about your future were all held in here."

"But who keeps the gardens so beautiful?"

"Faeries, silly. That's what we do."

At the back of the hall was a raised platform with carpeted steps leading to two flamboyant, jewelled thrones. The precious gems still gleamed brand new. Above the spectacular seats hung two large portraits in frames fashioned from coral and seashells. They showed the King and Queen – Smoky and Snow Quartz – her mother and father. Supposedly. Although that was not possible. Her parents were Daniel and Debra, the waitress and high school history author. Always had been, always would be.

"Your mum and dad were quite the celebrity couple in their day, Rosie. The masses adored them – *the nation's sweethearts*, they were called. Paparazzi flocked wherever they went. Every magazine in Faery Land fought for their picture. Whatever your mother was wearing, faery girls wanted to copy. Your parents had their own fragrance, designed their own sunglasses range, all that kind of thing. When you were born, the special edition newspaper spread sold out in seconds."

Rosie arched her eyebrows in disbelief. The Faery Realm had celebrities? She shrugged. Well, why not?

Stepping up onto the platform, Rosie walked around the back of the thrones to get a closer look at the portraits. They were so beautiful. Smoky so handsome and Snow so pretty. But despite the white-blonde hair which framed both of their faces and the cream gowns with high, fur collars, there was something familiar about the eyes and the smiles and even the cheekbones. Rosie made a binocular with her thumbs and fingers and zoomed in on the innermost section of their perfect complexions. The revelation sent her tripping backwards and caused her to gasp out loud. The King and Queen *were* Daniel and Debra after all.

"How is that possible? That can't be!"

"What?" Moss stood beside her and was gazing up at the pictures too.

"My parents! Those portraits are of my parents!"

"That's it, Rosie, exactly. You're getting your memory back. The spell is weakening now you're here."

"No, no, that's not it. I mean these are my *real* parents. The ones at home. My human parents, Daniel and Debra Quartz."

"Ah, no, not quite." Moss looked disappointed that she hadn't remembered. He saw there was yet more explaining of the Spiritual Laws to do. Rosie never quite seemed able to understand.

"When a human decides to incarnate, before they are born, they carefully select who their parents will be. It's a long and drawn-out process. The choice has to be just right. Who will bring them up on the path they are planning to take? Who can teach them the lessons they are coming to learn? Because you knew you were going to need a lot of moral support and comfort along the way, you chose parents who'd remind you of home. Daniel and Debra were the closest human resemblance you could find to Smoky and Snow."

"That's ridiculous." Rosie shook her head.

Moss merely smiled.

At the top of an impressive spiral tower of steps with a banister of pearl, which seemed to swirl upwards like Jack's giant beanstalk, a landing opened out – a cream carpeted corridor as huge as the hall below them. There were long passageways hiding hundreds of rooms, shooting off in every direction. Moss peered behind every door. "Apatite said your room would help us. We have to find it."

"But there are so many rooms. How will we know which is the right one?"

"I'm hoping you'll just know."

Each room was whiter and barer than the last, with little in the way of decoration. Many of the items which did remain were covered in large white dustsheets which shed an eerily abandoned atmosphere upon the Palace. Rosie shuddered.

They reached a fork in the corridor where Moss turned to go off one way and, to save time, she went alone down the other. Right at the bottom she spied a door slightly ajar, and through the gap could see the frame of a four-poster bed. The white posts were carved with pictures of suns, moons and stars – a bed fit for a princess! Rosie ran the rest of the way and flung the door open. Never had she seen such a perfect room. It was the most delightful bedroom an aspiring princess could imagine, and unlike the other rooms this one still felt lived in, as though it had been left completely untouched with all of the owner's belongings still scattered mid-play. Both the bed and the large windows were hung with transparent silken drapes and there was curvaceous, white Gustavian furniture, the very same as she'd begged her parents for at home. There was a rocking horse with porcelain dolls stacked on its back and a doll's house replicating the very Palace she stood in. Exquisite pink gowns embedded with sequins and stones hung on dressmaker dummies. Rosie caught her reflection in the oval dressing table mirror and saw that the pink, crocheted dress which Lace had leant her was now muddy and torn from the day's events. But, she told herself, patting her cheeks and smoothing her hair, she still looked healthier and happier than she had in a very long while. A music box stood on the table with a fine pirouetting ballerina on top. Rosie gently wound the key in its back to hear the tune play. It took time to get going, having not been turned for an age, but gradually the notes began to form...*Da da da da da da da da da*...She recognised this song. What was it? Wait a minute – it couldn't be. It was.

Don't you know I've always thought of you?
It started long before I met you.

168

I've spent my childhood scouring clouds for you.
I guess it's something that I just had to do,
'Cos I never could stop thinking of you.

Her song. The one she had written for their girl band. She'd thought it unique and her own. How had it come to be playing on an old ballerina music box in this abandoned room? Unless… unless she *had* heard the tune before, long ago, and stored it in her memory…

There was a broad windowsill, the kind you can sit on, with luscious cushions padding the ledge. The wide windows were open, making the drapes flutter back and forth like a ship's sail, and through them Rosie saw a stunning view, overlooking the Palace Gardens. As she sat she noticed a hardback journal on one of the cushions. The cover was silver with a picture of a white unicorn on it whose horn was made of real, light-catching diamonds. This must be it, the diary Apatite had spoke off. Rosie felt her heart quicken as she traced the shape of the unicorn with nervous fingers. Slowly, she opened the cover, terrified of what she may find. But the first page was blank. She turned again. So was the next. The breeze took hold of the pages and flipped through them from back to front. There was not a word on any of them. The journal was empty and she felt her heart sink. Whatever miracle she'd expected to find was an illusion.

Moss appeared in the doorway. "Rosie, your room, you found it!" Excitement rose in his voice, just as it had in her when she'd sensed it was unmistakably hers. Now she scowled.

"Save your breath. There's nothing here. The only book is empty. There's no diary to read." Bitterly disappointed she cast the journal down on the window ledge.

"Here, let me take a look at that." Moss picked it up and opened it as Rosie had. "Doesn't look like nothing to me."

"What?"

"You wrote this diary in faery ink, Rosie. It's invisible writing."

Irritated, she stomped back over to his side. "If it's invisible, then how do you know it's there?"

"Because I'm a faery, so I can read it. You're still in your pig-headed human frame of mind."

Something dawned on her. The books in Moss's house. The one she'd opened on arrival and found the pages bare. Had that been faery ink too? "So how can I see it?" Rosie asked. "How do I make the words appear on the page?"

"You need to start to *believe*. Begin thinking like a faery again. Swap your negativity for pure unconditional trust. Do you think you can manage that?"

Rosie was determined to prove that she could. Especially to Moss. She pulled the diary from his hands and wrinkled her face in concentration. Nothing. But rather than throw a strop, she took a deep breath, counted down from five in her head, and then tried again. This time something happened. A dust seemed to shift on the page, a small scattering of specks scampering to and fro. The particles moved and grew and soon they began to form silver writing in neat rows across the page. But not just any old writing. Her *own* handwriting. Astounded, she flicked through and more dust began to swirl, revealing a full journal undoubtedly written by her. Some of the pages were song lyrics. The words she had already written at home, but also ones she'd not even thought of yet. Or at least not in her human form.

> *And there are times I fear we'll never make it...*
> *This dream's so real, I'm almost scared to break it.*
> *You'd be so good for me,*
> *And I'll be all you'll ever need,*
> *Let this magic bind us tight,*
> *If we only have tonight...*

A gust of wind turned the page again and settled on a new chapter. Hungry for more of her own forgotten work, she began to read the diary entry mid-sentence...*and I feel so bad for feeling that way. Honest I do. But it's not like I haven't thought this through. I've sat and pondered my options for hours. This is not something I take lightly. But every time I argue with myself,*

I am always brought back to the same conclusion. So I have to go through with this. I know I do. There is no other way. Yes, I love my parents with all my heart and soul, and yes I shall miss them tremendously. It will break my heart to say goodbye. As it will to all of my family and friends who I so love here. But in time that will ease. Apatite says she must place a 'Forgetting Spell' within the 'Transformation Spell' so that once it is done I'll have no previous memories of the life and the people I've left behind. That should make it easier. That I can live with. Especially when compared with the other loss, which I just couldn't comprehend. To lose him would be like having my soul ripped out. There is no point in life if we can't be together. My love for him now is so great that I can hardly contain it inside me, it consumes every part of who I am. My heart flutters like a caged butterfly in my chest in anticipation of all the excitement that lies ahead. Me and him together forever. My happily ever after.

Apatite, I honour you always for giving me this opportunity and will never be able to thank you enough. You have been a true and wise friend. I appreciate your words of warning and concern, but know that I shall not need them. This will all go to plan, so I needn't worry of the things that could happen should it not. I can't wait for the morning light so we can begin to put our great adventure in motion. I will hardly sleep for thinking about it. If only he were here now, holding me in his arms…

"Rosie," Moss broke her dreamy reading trance with his voice. She looked up, startled, forgetting for a moment where they were. His expression was serious and his eyes seemed to be searching warily about, like he'd heard a noise not to his liking.

"Moss, are you okay?"

"Rosie, we need to take the diary and bring it back with us. We must reach the safety of the Agate Abode as soon as possible. We've a long journey ahead and we have to complete it prior to nightfall."

Rosie didn't want to leave the beautiful princess bedroom, but reluctantly she stole one last glance at the toys and the clothes and the bed, tucked the book under her arm and followed Moss out.

They made it back as a waning moon appeared over the three Agate birdhouses. Moss flew Rosie straight to his own bedroom door. "You'll have privacy here. Feel free to spend as long as you want. I'll be in the main house if you need me."

Rosie was tired but she had no intention of sleeping. She moved some of Moss's belongings to the floor and settled into his chair. This time, she turned to the beginning of the book. Once more she began to read.

14

Dear Diary

Dear Diary,

I just have to tell you about what happened today. I should have known something amazing was coming. I had a feeling when I woke up this morning that strange and fantastic things were in store, although I almost had it stamped out of me when I came down for breakfast. Mother and Father were nowhere to be seen and I'd wanted to run my new song by them. I'd had the tune in my brain all night and had risen at the first sign of sunlight, singing the words out loud. Instead, I had to make my own dandelion tea and sit at the table alone while they and the rest of the Palace were busy making arrangements for the latest fancy dress ball. I love their grand parties, but they don't half take a long time to prepare, which means they spend less time with me. I was bored and unsettled. I'd read every book in the library and wondered how I was going to spend my day. You know, being a princess isn't all it's cracked up to be. While other teenage faeries my age get to socialize and mingle and go about helping nature, I'm forced to stay safe and sensible, missing out on all the joys of aiding Mother Earth. But not today. I had made up my mind. While Mother threaded quartz pieces onto the napkin rings and Father draped peacock feathers from the ceiling, I slipped past the servants, who were also too busy with food sampling to notice me, and walked out into the Gardens.

Despite having lived here for nearly eighteen years, the Gardens never fail to enchant me. I know I'm so lucky to have them at my feet. I wandered through the alcoves, touching each leaf and flower. But today I ventured further, further than I knew I was supposed to go. If you walk far enough there are patches of grass which are not such luscious green, more of a russet brown. The ground gets hard and stony, purposely difficult for delicate glass princess shoes to step on. So I kicked them off, hoisted my skirt and skipped over a rock, using my wings to lift me. This change of terrain marked the edge of the Faery Kingdom. From here I was no longer on royal territory, but free to fly with the rest of the jolly community of Faery Land. Of course this meant I risked running into danger: dogs, cats, farm animals, and most importantly humans. But none of these could deter me. I felt able to handle them all! Anyway, humans can't see us unless we particularly want them to, and even then it can be exceptionally hard work – a bit like banging your head against a wall.

I picked my way through a misty yellow sea of swaying buttercups. Cows were mooing and chomping in the distance, but they didn't bother me. On I tripped until something broke the golden blaze. It seemed to be a kind of gigantic burrow. A concrete tube which I'd heard humans call a 'flood tunnel'. The water inside was pretty deep to me, though for them it would just be a shallow puddle. I believe it's used to catch rainfall in stormy weather. I clung to the sides of the concrete and skirted round the stream. It was dark inside and smelt unpleasantly dank and damp. Careless humans had, as usual, crammed the space with common litter: drinks cans, crisp packets, chocolate wrappers, chewing gum foil…I think I've heard faeries talk about this place before. They come here on regular operations to clear up the mess. It's the cause of puzzlement as to how it collects here. Yes – I've heard faeries say to each other, "Meet me at the Rainy Bridge." Well, it's actually not a bridge at all, but that's what they've christened it.

Grateful of the rare opportunity to behave like a normal faery, I began tidying up the litter, enormously satisfied to touch the objects and watch them disappear, when all of a sudden a large shadow was cast outside the tunnel on the grass. A human. I could tell instantly. The shape and the loud heavy breathing gave it away. And from the broad shoulders of the silhouette it was clear that it was male. I held my own breath. He was throwing pebbles into the water and one just missed me. I drew my long dress tight around me and was suddenly terrified. They always seemed so much bigger in real life, and I'd never been at such close range before. I edged inside a bottle and crouched low, peeping over the rim. The human stared intently into the flood tunnel, watching the ripples his pebbles were making and concentrating on the sound. I hid for a while – needlessly, I know – trembling, till my mind began to function and I remembered that the chances of him being able to see me were practically zero. Unless he was psychic or clairvoyant, and again that was exceptionally rare. He couldn't see me unless I willed it to be so. This made me relax and gradually I mustered the courage to leave the bottle and creep nearer. Slowly, slowly, I crept to his white trainer. The laces were messy and not properly tied. The bottoms of his jeans were caked in mud, probably from the walk here. Beyond that it was difficult to see up past his long legs so, bracing myself, I hopped to his knee and from there managed to get a good look at his face.

Recalling this now, I realise it's a miracle that I didn't faint. For this was one of those precious moments that you replay in your mind forever. Seeing him for the first time was so extraordinarily special because he himself was clearly so extraordinarily special. This boy was gorgeous. GORGEOUS! I have never, ever seen anyone or anything quite like him before. I will try to describe him here, but words may fail me.

He had rather a lot of straight floppy hair, which hung in streaks of brown and yellow across his tanned, slightly freckled face. He had perfect teeth, whiter than snow, and he was chewing gum, which I caught flashes of as he turned it round constantly in his mouth. His eyes were large, animated and hazel brown. He looked serious, even a little perplexed. I wondered what was going on in his mind and I think during this same time I had forgotten how to breathe. In. Out. Inhale. Exhale. That was it. That was the way. Had this strange boy got me under some kind of spell? Was he a wizard hiding a wand in his pocket? I wondered whether I should turn and fly as fast as I could straight back to the Palace. But instead I just stared, noting again and again how intoxicatingly fine he smelled. He had an aftershave on, so I moved further up to his shoulder where I could sit and drink in the scent from his neck. There was a trace of stubble across his cheekbones and from this I guessed he was probably about twenty years of age. I don't know what happened next, but I think in excitement my wings came unfolded and they fluttered lightly across his skin. The boy jumped quickly to his feet, scratching frantically at his neck, as though bitten by an insect. Totally unprepared for the sudden movement, I lost my balance and fell backwards off his shoulder, tumbling to the ground. I was stunned. Usually humans can't even sense a passing butterfly, let alone a faery in a different realm. But he had felt me. He had registered my touch. And it had unsettled him enough to make him leave. He began to walk off. I watched him all the way. Till his outline was a speck no bigger than me.

And now I'm home, my head is spinning, my thoughts are whirring around. How long will it be before he goes there again? Or will he ever go at all? I have to find him. I have to see him once more. If not at the Rainy Bridge, then anywhere. I'll track him down. I'll seek him out, whatever the cost. For I never knew anyone could be so perfect.

Dear Diary,

I've seen him again! He was there again today! He was even more beautiful than I remembered. He had on a sort of checked shirt which hung open over a tight white vest and made my heart do forward rolls and back flips. It was such a surprise to find him waiting at the Rainy Bridge, in the first place I looked. Things are usually so complicated and dysfunctional with humans, I'd felt sure I was going to have to move mountains in order to locate him. Overjoyed as I was, I was careful not to get too close. I didn't want to scare him off like before. So I watched from the opposite end of the tunnel and counted the number of pebbles he successfully skimmed across the shallow water. Occasionally he moved his hair from his eyes and how I wished I could flutter across and do it for him. Now I can't sleep for visualising his face, I can't eat for remembering his eyes, I can't hold a conversation with my parents for hearing his breathing and I can't concentrate on my lessons for fantasizing about what it would be like to touch him again.

Dear Diary,

I am so sorry that I have not written for nigh on a week, but I do have the greatest excuse in the world for my lack of attention. It is because I have spent every single day sneaking off to the Rainy Bridge and watching him. He goes there every day, and now so do I. The same time, the same spot. I'm immensely glad that one of the magical lessons I really mastered in class was Trancing the Clock, so I can adjust the passage of my time to fit with his without worrying about taking too long. On his human clock, he probably sits there for little more than a half hour, but this can take up my entire day, and I'm perfectly happy for it to do so. Besides, my parents are so busy with preparations for my eighteenth birthday ball that my absence is easily missed. Mother did ask me the other day how my Princess Studies were going (I have to have passed all my final etiquette qualifications before my eighteenth), but I just smiled and said, "Great", and that lately I preferred to take my books and writings out to the benches in the Gardens since the weather was so nice.

I've started to think that maybe the smouldering look in his hazel eyes is actually a trace of sadness. I sense he is downhearted. If not, why would he keep going to an old flood tunnel in the middle of a faraway countryside field? I have a reason for going – him! He doesn't even know I exist. How I wish he did, though. I so long to speak to him, to ask him his name, to find out things about him. Real things. Things about his life and not just the latest colour of his shirt or style of his shoes.

One day this week I arrived and he was not there. Lady Gaia, how I panicked! I waited for hours and shivered in the cold. Trudging back to the Palace with my head hung low, I honestly thought I was going insane. I threw myself on my bed and cried and cried, until I ached deep within my core. But then the following day he was back. I felt my body grow lighter with tangible relief. The way I feel for this boy – this man – who I know so little about is a new and frightening sensation, which I struggle to control as it seizes full hold of me. Maybe it's the fact that it's secret which keeps it burning, the knowledge that I have no one to talk to or share it with. There's definitely no one in the Palace who would understand. Maybe it's the fact that he's human and not one of us and so far removed from all with which I'm familiar. The fact that he's forbidden. Either way, I know that I have to do something about it. Something drastic. Something quick.

Dear Diary,
Today I went to talk to my mother. She was at her dressing table, brushing her hair. I sat on the bed behind her and watched her reflection shine in the pearl mirror. She was so very beautiful.

"Hello, sweetheart, this is a nice surprise. To what do I owe this pleasure?"

"Mother, you know I'll be eighteen in a few weeks time and allowed to use magic whenever I wish with no restrictions, well, I wanted to ask you about one magical spell in particular that I've heard of…"

"Okay, go ahead."

"It's the one where faeries can change their size. Like shape shifting – to more of a human form. I've heard of it happening, but I just wondered – is it possible?"

"Rosie, why in the good name of Lady Gaia would you want to know that?"

"I don't know. Just for fun, I guess."

Mother broke off from brushing her hair to lift a small china cup of dandelion tea to her cherry coloured lips, and then slowly replaced it.

"You need to be careful, sweetheart. Being eighteen doesn't automatically mean you can go around using magic however you wish. With age also comes responsibility. Especially since you're a princess. You must show you're wise and mature and can use it with discretion. Only ever for the good of others, remember."

I thought about what she said. Were my intentions truly for the good of others or were they built entirely on selfish reasons? No. Having the opportunity to speak with him would ultimately help him out too. I was sure of it because he always looked so sad.

"Come and kneel beside me then," Mother said. "Since you ask, I'll tell you what I know."

I joined her eagerly, gazing up into her blue eyes.

"It can be done, yes, but it can't be held for a very long time. It takes far too much effort and drains your energy. I think the most it's ever been done for is one human hour. And that's pretty impressive. It's in the Faery Record Book."

"Have you ever tried it, Mum?"

I was sure she hesitated, just for a second.

"No. Here have a sugar cube." She reached into a silver pot on her dressing table.

"Ooo thanks," I said, but the way she then patted my back and ushered me out of the room made me feel she had just offered it to change the subject and get me out of her way. She was avoiding further questions.

Of course I went straight off to practise. I knew I had to do it outside the Palace for the risk of suddenly shooting upwards, so I flew all the way to the barren farming village of Lock Marshland. In those bleak and desolate fields I actually managed to get up to about two feet high. This startled and thrilled me at first, until I realised that was about as far as I could go. It's nowhere near enough. I'll end up looking like some freaky garden gnome beside him…I'll frighten him to death this way, or at least repulse him. I have to be just the perfect height by his side. Well, I reckon he's about five foot eight, so in that case I need to be around five foot three or four. No more, I don't want to overpower him. Practise makes perfect and I am not giving up until I get this right. Not with such a dream prize in sight!

Dear Diary,

That's it. I'm giving up. I am never ever going to be able to get this right. I have tried and tried this stupid growing thing for days now and I can't do it. I've tried saying the words differently, I've tried standing differently, I've tried it at different times of the day, and I've tried wearing different clothes, but nothing helps. The most I've managed is three foot five. Three foot five! And while, yes, that may seem huge in comparison to my regular two inches, it is simply no good for meeting the man of my dreams. I'd still be way too small. And besides, I can't hold it for long enough anyway. Ten seconds and I'm done, crashing back down to what I was before. Damn this magic thing. Call myself a faery? This is ridiculous! Aaaaaaaaaaaggggggggggghhhhhhhhhh!!!

Dear Diary,

I've cracked it. I still can't hold it for long. It's still ten seconds tops. But I've got to five foot three and that will do just fine.

So yesterday I went down to the Rainy Bridge and there he sat. I flew to the opposite end of the tunnel and waited till I was sure he was focused on the water. Relishing that new sweeping sensation of the world falling away beneath me and the sky dropping down to my head, I watched my reflection appear on the glassy water. It took him several seconds to register it, two seconds to drink it in, and then another one to realise I'd gone. Ten short seconds – over so fast! And yet each one was enough to frighten the life out of him. He screamed – a manly type of scream, I hasten to add. Then he jumped to his feet, like he had when my wings brushed his cheek. He looked genuinely terrified. And this is not, of course, a good thing. Not quite my desired effect. But he didn't run. He didn't turn to leave. Instead, he shouted into the tunnel, "Hello? Who's there? Who is it? Hello?"

He cupped his hands round his mouth, like this would somehow help me answer. But I'd done enough. I'd set the wheels in motion. And now the fun could start.

Today I know he came to the Rainy Bridge for different reasons. He was desperate to prove what he'd seen. To certify, if only to himself, that he wasn't going mad. I appeared again – a flash of white across the wall of the tunnel – to satisfy his

180

curiosity. This time he laughed to himself, "I'm seeing ghosts. I'm insane or I'm seeing ghosts."

As soon as I'd lost my size, quickly I started over again, materializing directly before him. The tips of our noses nearly touched in the brief moment I managed.

"Oh my…What the…? Bloody hell!!!"

His heart hammered. I could hear it from my place back down by his feet on the ground.

"Who are you? Are you real? What do you want? Are you a ghost?" He paused. "…Because I really hope you're not a ghost, since if you are, you're the hottest ghost I've ever seen!" he laughed aloud at himself again. "A fit ghost, bloody hell, I really am losing it."

He called me fit. I can't believe he called me fit. And a few seconds was all it took to make that impression. Oh yeah! And most importantly he saw me. He actually saw me. Which means, he has the capability to sense the other realm. Or I am particularly skilled in my ability to vibrate at his realm. But what does it matter. The fact is it's happened and I suddenly feel like our lives will never be the same again.

Dear Diary,
I can hold the shape for longer now. I've practised and practised and I can do one full hour. This means we can meet.

Dear Diary,
Guy.
   Guy Flower.
   His name is Guy.
   Guy Flower. Guy. Guy. Guy.
   The word is like music on my lips.

*

Rosie dropped the book and the hairs on the back of her neck stood on end. Of course she had realised whilst reading that it

181

had to be Guy, but the sight of his actual name on the paper, snapped her out of the story's trance and back to her present-day thoughts. When she bent to retrieve the unicorn diary, she realised her hands were shaking. Beads of sweat had formed on her brow, but she had to read on...

*

I crept from behind the tunnel like I'd been there all the time, a shocked and hesitant expression on my face, as though it was him who was disturbing me. I'd given careful thought to my clothes and wore denim cut off shorts with a checked shirt, like the one I'd seen him in previously. I'd tied it in a knot so you could see my bare waist, swung a basket in my hand and was well rehearsed in my speech about bilberries, hoping I looked suitably kitted for a fresh spring walk. There are many bilberry bushes sprawling near the Buttercup Fields, and though I know that the berries are incapable of growing at this time of year, surely he wouldn't know that. He didn't strike me as the gardening type. And this was the only cover plan I had. I was out in the countryside collecting them for my sweet little grandmother who liked to bake bilberry pie. Did that sound too twee? I wasn't sure, but it was the best I could come up with.

"Whoa, you scared me! I thought I was alone here. You totally took me by surprise." He jumped up and ran his fingers through his hair, which I'd come to recognise as his personal sign of apprehension.

I took a step back, clutching my basket tightly, my pulse racing.

"Wait, hang on, you're the girl I saw the other day." He laughed at himself, cooler and calmer now. "Yes, of course you are, I recognise you. Thank God for that. I knew I wasn't going crazy. I saw your reflection in the water. I thought you were a ghost. Ha, ha, ha. What are you doing here?"

"What are you doing here?"

"Me? I come here all the time."

"So do I."

"Well, I've never seen you before. Well, okay, I have, but just briefly. Hey, are you stalking me?"

I felt my cheeks flush with embarrassment, but quickly righted myself. "Ha, you should be so lucky. Are you stalking me? I'm just here to pick bilberries."

It was a good start...ish. I told him I lived in Steeple Village and just about managed to keep this up, even through his insistence that I couldn't possibly live here as he was sure he'd have noticed me around before. I maintained my story of a modest semi-detached house with my parents, and, well, I was only partly lying since Steeple is my home after all – just not at the level he's familiar with. But then he started to mention things I properly struggled to keep up with; human things like cars and department stores. I think I nodded in all the right places and made all the right noises, but I was only hypnotised by his smile, lost in his warm, friendly gaze. Finally he began to comment on the blue and white stripes he wore, which depicted his favourite football team, and I had to admit defeat.

"So then, mysterious girl, which local club do you support?"

"Club? Er, well, to be honest, I've never even been to a football game before."

"What, never been to a match? Gosh, you are such a girl."

"Yep, that's it I guess. I'm such a typical human girl."

He looked at me quizzically, his thick brown eyebrows raised, and he shook his head from side to side.

All this time I had been ultra conscious of making sure my wings were concealed from view. For some reason, the shape-shifting spell did not include eradication of my transport, and transparent as they were, wings were still pretty obvious to a close standing outsider. I'd managed to fix the shirt over most of them, but the upper blades were stuffed down at the neck, which meant I had a kind of hunchback feature going on. Not a pretty sight. So whilst we spoke, I kept my back to the arch of the tunnel. A couple of times he moved closer, and as much as I welcomed this, every time, I had to step back.

"You're weird," he said, "aren't you?" He looked me up and

down. "Slightly mad, but I like you. My name's Guy, by the way. Guy Flower."

"I'm Rosie."

"Rosie. Like the flower too?"

"No. Like the stone. Quartz."

"What?"

"Never mind."

For a moment we stood there awkwardly, just facing each other in the field. Again, he inched forward. This time he took hold of my hand and I couldn't get away. His lips hovered precariously close to my own. I could feel his breath against my throat, smell the peppermint of his gum. I trembled. The world stopped. And then he broke away.

He shifted his weight from either foot and looked around. Embarrassed at the very near kiss. "Yeah, well...right, yeah...I best get going...see you around, Rosie...I mean, maybe when you're bilberry picking again. By the way, you didn't get too many."

And that was that.

Dear Diary,

Today he told me about Helena.

Aaaaaaaaaaggggggggggghhhhhhhhhh!!!

Helena! I could spit at the word. I have never ever met Helena Flower. For all I know she could be the nicest, kindest woman on the planet, but she makes me feel sick. I can feel myself boiling with hot fiery jealousy right now, just having to write down her name. Helena Flower – née Spotswood.

His wife.

He's married.

My whole world crumbled around me. I thought I had automatically shrunk back to my faery size when he told me, as my conscious seemed to slip and slide. How had I not noticed the wedding ring on his finger? I'd studied every other detail of him a thousand times over. I was sure there was nothing I'd missed. How could I have been so foolish?

"We've been married three years," he said. "I was nineteen."

184

I wanted to choke but didn't show it, and he seemed genuinely oblivious of my turmoil.

"How old are you, Rosie?"

"Eighteen." It was a little lie. I have a while to go but if he's twenty-two, I don't want him thinking I'm a child.

"That's the age. The time I'm talking about. You'll know exactly what I mean. Everything seems possible at that age. Nothing is unachievable. You have the world at your feet and you can grab your plans and dreams in your hands. They're almost visible, they're that clear. But if you let them pass you by, and you get to where I am, you find they're gone. Lost. Missed. Dead."

There was that sadness. The one I'd seen in him on every occasion before we met.

"Don't say that, Guy. Dreams are never dead. Age has nothing to do with it. The Law of Attraction is at work whether you're aware of it or believe in it or not."

He hadn't heard me. He threw a pebble past me into the water and it made a clunk before sinking.

"Sorry for boring you. It's just, that's why I come here. To get away for a bit. Things between me and my wife, Helena, aren't so good. We married far too young and I think maybe we've grown apart. We've been together since high school, since we were kids. I sometimes wonder if I've missed seeing the world through my own eyes and somehow just ended up seeing it through hers."

"There's nothing wrong with your eyes, Guy," I said, thinking what a miracle it was that he was so easily able to see me.

He suddenly looked at me then, as though for the first time, a renewed fascination stamped on his face. "This must sound so annoyingly corny, but I've never known anyone like you, Rosie. You're so unnaturally beautiful. Like a creature from another world. Ha! Just listen to me. I have never sounded so cheesy! I think it's sitting for too long in these fields that's doing it. Rosie Quartz, can I take you out for a drink one night?"

Panic. This was the part where of course I wanted to say yes, but reality sank through my brain like an iron anchor in sea.

"Can't we just continue to meet here?"

"Here's weird. You've got to admit we're both a pair of oddballs for coming here so often. It's dark, damp, and it stinks. Hardly the kind of place a man should be taking a beautiful woman."

"But, Guy, you're married."

There was a long silence, which seemed to stretch on like a void.

"Yes, yes I am. For some reason when I'm with you, I start to forget."

I was brave and touched his hand. Our fingers entwined and I felt the gold metal of his wedding ring. It made me jump like I'd been burned by a hot coal.

"I have an idea," he said. "I could take you to the football match instead. There's no harm in that. It can just be because you've never been before. I can tell Helena I'm helping out a friend, educating you about the wonders of offside and four-four-two."

"No. Seriously, no. I would love to, honest I would. But I can't. I'm sorry, I have to go."

"Rosie, Rosie, wait."

But I'd gone.

Dear Diary,

Today he brought me flowers.

Admittedly, they weren't the greatest kind. Slightly droopy from his long walk and a little crispy at the edges from being in a shop. Absolutely no comparison to the blooms at the Palace. But because they were from him, they were the most beautiful flowers I'd ever seen, and I made a mental note to make some new curtains out of the petals for my bedroom, so I'd sense him near when I missed him at night.

I'm up to three hours now. I can hold my human height for just over that long. I guess I've grown stronger with all the practise. I think that'll be it though now. I seriously doubt I'll ever beat this. I can't tell you how much I'm dying to tell my mother. She would be so impressed that I've beaten the record she talked of. But I daren't mention it in case she starts to get suspicious and wonders why I'm doing it in the first place. She's bound to pry and that could blow things forever.

Oh yes, perhaps I should have mentioned this first.

Today was also our first kiss.

He handed me the bouquet and said he was relieved I'd come as he'd feared I wouldn't. My back was pressed to the Rainy Bridge and slowly he leaned forward, wrapping both of his tanned bare arms low around my waist. As his lips finally pressed down on my own, I realised that five foot three was absolutely perfect. We were made for each other. Two jigsaw pieces slotting together. Gently, he forced my mouth apart and, blissfully, I relaxed. Enjoying this too much now to worry about broken rules, I reached out and entwined every one of my fingers into the loose yellow strands of his hair. I can't be sure how long it lasted. Time is such a flimsy and irregular measure of things. I just know that afterwards, I beamed. Truly smiled like I had never smiled before.

"Guy," I whispered.

"Rosie," he whispered back.

Never ever smiled.

Truly.

Really.

Until today.

Dear Diary,

Today we kissed for hours and then I sat with my legs outstretched on the grass, his head resting in my lap. With one hand I coiled his fringe around my finger and with the other I stroked his cheek. Both of us stared out across the Buttercup Fields. He was pulling at loose weeds, rolling them between his thumbs and then emptying them onto my ankles.

"Rosie, I have to say this. I have to get it off my chest… I think I'm falling in love with you."

"Guy, I don't think that, I know it. I fell in love with you a long, long time ago."

And then he drew me down towards him, grasping me tight. I let myself fall forwards, and in one swift motion he'd rolled me round, pulled me on top of him and locked me onto his chest as we lay on the ground. It happened too fast. I had no time to think. In horror, I realised my carefully concealed wings had unfolded. They'd spread like a great ship's sail and burst out of my dress buttons in all their glory.

Guy sprang to his feet and stumbled several times, trying to right himself.

"What the hell…? What the bloody hell are these?"

15

Truth Tongue

Rosie realized that the small room had grown dimmer. The candle on the bedside table had nearly burned out. The wax was just a splodge of goo, feebly supporting a weak flame. She shifted her position on the wooden chair and snapped the diary shut. Her back ached and she yawned. She'd been reading for more than an hour. Footsteps came up the passage from the main rooms of the Agate Abode and Lace stuck her head through the archway. "Hello, can I come in?"

"Of course you can."

"Are you okay?"

"I'm not sure." Rosie placed her flat palm on her own forehead to check her temperature. She felt like she was burning up. "I mean, really not sure, Lace. This diary. It's turned me upside down. I can't believe what I've just read. Except I can. I can totally believe it. And that's what's tearing me apart. It's like everything makes sense now. I'm only halfway through the pages, but I can already see what's coming next. It all fits."

"Well, that's brilliant, isn't it?"

"No – yes – there are so many questions. Still so much I don't understand. One thing's for sure, I have to get home to Guy. I have to show him this."

Lace sat herself down on the edge of Moss's bed. "Rosie, I don't think your work here is done yet. Moss says you have to read the diary fully before we decide on the next step. And anyway, before you do, I think you and I need to have ourselves some fun. Faery

Land's not all doom and gloom, you know. You'll be beginning to think it's a terrible place. Cooped up here with your nose stuck in a book, you're missing out on all the wonders. Get a good night's sleep, and then tomorrow I'm taking you out on a milk hunt."

"A what?"

"Cow milk is one of Faery Land's finest delicacies. It's pretty tricky to come by, but when we can get it, we love it."

"Me too. I love milk."

"Of course. You have a faery heart, remember."

"Yes. And Lace, I truly do believe that now."

"I'm glad to hear it. Sweet dreams, Rosie. Or should I say, *Princess?*"

"Oh no, please. That I can't quite get used to yet."

Climbing into the sheets, Rosie was a little disappointed that Moss had not come to say goodnight, but her thoughts were quickly distracted by images of Guy. She reread the entry about their first kiss three more times before finally tucking the diary beneath her pillow and blowing the struggling candle out of its misery.

Although Moss and Fire both stayed behind at the Agate Abode, Rosie and Lace were evidently not going on the milk hunt alone. Early in the morning, before first light, they made their way to a dense circular clearing where crowds of other faeries had already gathered, excitedly awaiting further instructions from what seemed to be a team of leaders on a raised platform.

"They're the Elders," Lace explained to her. "The great teachers of the Council. That one there is Fluorite." She pointed to an old man with a shock of dishevelled white hair and a grey beard which reached down to his belt. Along with his gnarled staff and pointy, blue hat, decorated with golden moons and stars, he was as typically wizard looking as one could be.

"He's exceptionally wise," Lace whispered, looking upon him with ultimate respect. "He was appointed number one Head Protector of the Kingdom after your parents...well, you know, after they'd gone."

Rosie was amazed at the number of bodies crammed into the bunting-trimmed waiting area. It seemed like the whole community had come to take part.

"If this is such a big occasion, why did Moss and Fire not come?"

"Moss has things he needs to see to. Council business. And Fire…well…Fire's just Fire."

The faeries stood with long reeds, twice as tall as themselves, which seemed to have been curled into enormous drinking straws. Some also carried what looked like little buckets, but on closer observation, Rosie realized they were no more than fizzy pop bottle tops.

"Is the milk hunt usually this popular?"

"Oh yes, of course. You see, for the most part, we faeries are happy to take what we require from Mother Nature. She provides us with all the foods we need. But since humans meddle with all kinds of stuff, we don't see why we shouldn't share some of their little pleasures. Just occasionally, we indulge ourselves in a few favourites. Our two most sacred treats are milk and sugar."

"Milk and sugar lumps – my own two weaknesses. It all makes sense now. I must have carried the attachment over into my new life."

"It's a real danger though. Extraction comes at a price. Terrible accidents have happened. There have been drownings and swattings, sometimes fatal."

Rosie frowned. "So why are we even thinking about going on one of these things? I don't want to be drowned or swatted, thank you very much, and I think I can just about wait till I'm home for a glass of milk from our fridge."

Lace giggled. "Oh no, don't let me put you off. The drowning is rare. And milk hunts are fun. Come on, let's get our bucket and reed."

Streetlamps still cast a yellow glow across the roads in the human Steeple Village. Inhabitants of the local houses would still all be tucked up, oblivious in their cosy beds, as the merry band of

191

faery folk trekked in procession down the sidewalks. The troupe had brought along several extremely cute field mice, who were strapped with a spare cargo of buckets. Rosie guessed the brown mice were there to help carry the heavy load back. She loved the way faeries and animals worked together as a team and wished the human world were able to master this union a little more successfully.

"Milk hunts always involve an early start," Lace told Rosie as they walked side by side. Lace had the reed and Rosie the bucket. "We have to collect before people are awake. We watch for the milkman and his milk float coming up the lanes. The glass bottles clatter and he whistles a happy tune. What a beautiful job he has. I think if I were human, I should choose to be a milk lady."

Rosie laughed, thinking that if Lace were human she'd be far more likely to get snapped up by some top modelling agency who would fight to sell her face on every product out there.

"So in a fashion, what we're doing is stealing," Lace whispered conspiratorially, "but try not to feel too guilty about it. We always do something for the humans we take from in return – like send a little good luck magic for the day their way. We use the reeds to drain the milk from the bottles on the doorsteps before the house owners come downstairs. It's a tricky business. Like I said before, faeries have been known to fall in – and once, a faery got run over by the milk cart, and another time one got stuck to the bottom of the milkman's shoe."

"Great," said Rosie, "Now, what part of 'fun' am I not understanding here?"

The procession had stopped around the base of one of the lampposts and a funny looking faery with bright pink cheeks and long crimson robes, altogether too big for him, was frantically attempting to organize the crowd into separate groups. He stuttered as he spoke, nervously trying to project his gentle voice above a growing buzz of excitement. As he pointed teams off in different directions, he kept tripping over the cord of his trailing gown.

"Sir Rhodonite is splitting us up into assigned zones," Lace explained. "Stay with me, we're going this way."

Coincidentally or not, Rosie and Lace were ushered into the team which set off in the direction of Steeple Willows – Guy's housing estate. As they marched, Rosie became increasingly aware of the other faeries' growing interest in her presence. Many of them whispered in hushed tones behind their hands, with curious eyes turned towards her. Some unashamedly stared, quite boldly without embarrassment, not even turning away when she looked directly back at them. The old man Fluorite was among her observers. Catching his wizened glare, she smiled gracefully with a bow of her head. What she got in return was a scowl of sheer disapproval. Rosie wondered what on earth she had done to upset him so much, or if he had such a stern, unfriendly expression for everyone he met.

At the first house Lace instructed Rosie to stand back and watch while one of the younger boys flew to a milk-laden doorstep with a *Welcome* mat and carefully began to peel off the silver foil top. Once he'd achieved this, he pressed the flimsy coin down into a neat ball and tossed it to another faery youth waiting below.

"We keep the foils too, as you might have guessed," Lace said. "All the things you see in our houses which appear to be made from silvery metal or aluminium, are usually just crafted out of milk bottle tops."

"Steady there, Jasper!" The boy on the ground shouted up to his friend who balanced on the bottle rim. "Easy does it, mate." Rosie watched with baited breath as his two legs were forced wide apart on either side of the circular gap.

"Hoist up the straw, Peridot," Jasper called, and the giant reed appeared beside him to insert in the bottle neck. Using his mouth at the unsubmerged end, Jasper now sucked milk into the main body of the straw, just like you would if you were taking a long drink. But instead of letting the liquid meet his lips, he cautiously pulled out the reed with his teeth still attached to maintain the suction, until Peridot was ready. Once the bucket was in position below, Jasper released the vacuum and fresh cold milk spilt into the plastic container. He'd accomplished the task, but throughout the process he'd wobbled and swayed, his wings frantically flapping, working double time to keep himself upright. Rosie could hardly bare to watch.

"Lace, surely there must be an easier way of doing this?"

"If there was, trust me, a faery would have figured it out by now."

And as if cued by her concern, before Jasper made it down he lost his footing and slid with a loud splash into the half-empty contents of the bottle. He floundered in the thick white waves of milk, desperately thrashing his arms above the surface to stay afloat. Rosie and Lace watched in horror, completely helpless as the disaster unfolded.

"Quick, someone rescue him!"

Peridot had acted fast and in a flash the Elders, Sir Fluorite and Sir Rhodonite were also at the scene. Fluorite pointed his staff in Jasper's direction and a snapping firework display of coloured sparks shot up and then whizzed down into the milk bottle. At Jasper's level the explosives turned into a grey mist that seemed to grow supportive fingers which magically lifted the poor faery to safety. When his feet touched the ground, the phantom hands melted and Jasper collapsed in a shivering, wet heap.

"Wow, that was close," said Lace. "It could have been bad news if Fluorite had gone with another group. Come on, let's find our own doorstep and have a go for ourselves."

"What? Are you kidding? That boy just nearly drowned! He nearly died!" Rosie was running to catch Lace up. "If you think I'm doing that, you can think again. Or *you* for that matter. I will not allow you to put yourself in danger." She was shouting at her friend. She'd already dropped the bucket in defiance and was pointing her finger.

"Shhhh!" Lace had reached a familiar garden path. "This is Guy's house, isn't it? I can hear voices inside. They're awake."

Rosie froze, just like the first time she had argued with Billie and Sally about approaching his door. But so much time had passed since then. Not just months, but the knowledge of a whole other lifetime.

"I can hear Guy's voice," said Rosie. "And Helena's. That's Helena Spotswood speaking, for sure. What on earth is she doing in there with him at this time of day?"

"Maybe she stopped the night?" Lace shrugged and Rosie scowled.

"No way. Jemma Flower would never allow that. In that world, we're all still twelve years old, remember?"

"You and Guy will be thirteen in a few weeks. Teenagers."

"Big deal. Guy's mum may be cool, but she's not *that* cool. And besides, I am totally not cool with this!"

"Actually, you both being thirteen soon is a very big deal. It's the reason we're all in this predicament in the first place." Lace smiled as kindly as ever, but her eyes betrayed her inner concern.

"What? What do you mean?"

"You'll find out soon enough. I'm sure once we get back to the Agate Abode, you'll want to read the rest of that diary."

The couple's voices started up again, louder this time and far more vicious. They fought for dominance, each gaining volume over the other.

"Lace, I think they're having an argument! Can we get closer, so I can listen in?"

The two girls crept up the sandy driveway. Below the front window with its scarlet curtains, Lace took hold of Rosie's hand and flew her to the outer ledge. Jemma had recently placed a pretty box of geraniums here and the friends were able to hide among the leaves and gaze in unseen. The marble vase with its dried poppy display blocked the view slightly, but still, through the gaps Rosie could see Helena pacing angrily back and forth in the living room. Though she turned sharply in her strut, the glossy helmet of straight blonde hair never budged from her jaw line. She must have emptied an entire can of hairspray over it that morning. Her glittery make-up was immaculate as always, and even from this distance, Rosie could make out the diamond glint of her 'H' pendant, bouncing on her chest.

"She must have got here really early," Rosie said.

"She obviously had something she needed to say," Lace agreed.

"Guy, I am sick of this. It's like you don't even care how I feel." Helena was trying her best to imitate a hard-done-by tone, but on her confident lips, it just didn't have a truthful ring. "We've been going out with each other for five months now – that's almost half a year – I mean, we're practically married, and you just don't seem able to give me the kind of commitment I deserve."

"What do you want from me, Helena? I'm your boyfriend, aren't I? I spend nearly every waking moment with you. What more can I possibly do?"

"I want you to spend your birthday with me for a start. I had it all planned out. My mother's already arranged for the entire Spotswood family to come over for a buffet lunch so they can meet you. Jonathan's picking them up from the station one at a time in his new sports car. And now you tell me, you're doing something with *your* mum. What could be so special about her that she comes before me?"

"She's my mum," Guy said sadly, but already defeated. "She'll be upset if I don't spend my thirteenth birthday with her. She keeps saying what an important one it is, and she wants us to do something really special, just the two of us. You don't understand how hard things have been since my dad left, Helena. Mum gets really lonely."

Rosie realized she had tears in her eyes just listening. "She's a spoilt, hateful cow," she said. "I can't believe someone as wonderful as Guy could end up marrying her. I ought to go in there now and warn him what he's getting himself into before it's too late. I know for a fact he'll end up rottenly miserable. How I wish I weren't two inches tall and I could hit her clean in her perfect, foundation-smeared face!"

"I think I have a much better idea than that." Lace smiled, fishing out a wand from her white knee-length boot. "Have you ever heard of 'Truth Tongue'?"

"No. What's that?"

"It's a spell we faeries occasionally use to set ugly human pig-headedness back in its rightful place. It doesn't last long, but boy can it wreak havoc in the short time it does."

Rosie grinned. "You're going to put a magic spell on Helena?"

"No, not on Helena. On Guy."

"But Guy hasn't done anything wrong. I don't want you to hurt *him*!"

"It doesn't hurt. Well, only maybe Miss Spotswood's feelings. 'Truth Tongue' makes the wearer of the spell unable to speak anything but the truth – like you're solemnly swearing on a Bible in court. You know how sometimes there are things in the back of your thoughts that you're just desperate to say out loud, but common sense tells you they're extremely inappropriate and you'd be far safer to cover them over with little white lies? Well, my spell will totally eradicate that sensible type of reasoning. Guy will only be able to answer Helena with exactly what's in his mind."

Both girls laughed out loud.

"It's the greatest practical joke I've ever heard of!" Rosie cheered. "How soon can we start?"

"I've already placed it," said Lace. "Now just watch and wait."

"You're entirely selfish, Guy Flower," Helena arched her pencilled eyebrows menacingly at him, "and also completely deluded. Do you know how many boys at Steeple High School would die to have the right to call me their girlfriend? Come to think of it, forget numbers, I don't think there's a single one who wouldn't. Whereas you seem to act as if I'm some disposable object which you can easily replace."

"Helena, please…" Guy hung his head from his spot on the settee.

"Don't you dare *Helena* me! If you want to keep me, Guy, from this day forward, you're going to have to step up your game. And we can start with a ring. I want a relationship ring from you. Some form of gold and diamond eternity band which screams out to everyone that you're mine. I need people to know that you belong to me."

"Right, that does it!" Guy jumped up. "Who the hell do you think you are, Helena Spotswood? You can't just come barging into my house at six in the morning, screaming like you own the place, and worse, like you own me! I am a human being in my own right and I don't belong to you or anybody! If I want to spend my time with somebody else other than you, I am perfectly within my rights to do so. You will not dictate for me a minute longer. I'll be spending my thirteenth birthday with my mum and I will NOT be buying you a ring. People already know we're together, and if there are any who don't, then so what? Who gives a damn? Our relationship is our business, not theirs. It shouldn't have to cost hundreds of pounds to prove that!"

For a long while Helena just stood there in front of the fireplace with an expression of incredulity disfiguring her beautiful face. Rosie and Lace held their breaths among the geraniums, nervously waiting to see what would happen next.

Helena sunk to her knees on the rug and began to cry. Well, kind of cry. It was a fake, shrill sort of howl, which she'd decided to play now as her sympathy card.

"Guy, G…Guy, how could you? What are you saying? You know you don't mean any of those horrible things!"

"I've spoken nothing but the truth, Helena. You're just too self-obsessed and self-centred to see it."

Realizing the crocodile tears hadn't had their desired effect, Helena now did what she'd originally wanted to anyway. She launched herself across the room, screaming at the top of her lungs. "I wish I'd never met you, Guy Flower!"

"And where would we be now if that were true, Helena? Maybe I'd still be with Rosie Quartz. At least she understood me."

"What? That plain, shy ordinary little nobody?"

"She is not a nobody. And she's far from ordinary."

She slapped Guy hard across the cheek. He was left with a perfect red imprint of her jewellery-clad hand, a round, ring shape evident on each finger. Guy never flinched, but slowly took his seat back on the sofa, where he gently massaged the sore mark.

"Helena, I…Helena, I'm so sorry. I don't know what came over me. I don't know why I said those things. I just got so angry.

Please say you forgive me? I take it all back. I'm mad about you, you know I am, babe."

"You have some serious making up to do, mister," she snapped, "and you can start by making a promise that I never hear you mention that girl's name ever again. All talk of Rosie Quartz is strictly out of bounds, with no exception."

"Yes, Helena, of course."

"The spell's gone," said Lace, but Rosie was giggling so hard that she'd slipped to her bottom in the compost soil, almost falling off the window ledge.

"That was the funniest thing I've ever seen. Thank you Lace, thank you so much."

Lace pulled her up and dusted her down. They looked at one another and both burst into peals of laughter again.

"She really got what she deserved. Do you think they'll stay together now?"

"I don't know, Rosie, that's down to you anyway."

"He said I understood him. And he stuck up for me. Do you really think he still loves me, Lace?

"I'm sure so."

The girls left Guy's house and walked back to the road. A lot of the milk hunters had gone and they were free to wander at their own pace, albeit milkless, home to the Agate Abode in time for breakfast.

"Do you think Moss and Fire will be disappointed that we're returning without milk for them?"

"I think Moss will just be pleased to see you returning safe in one piece."

"But not Fire...?"

"Erm yes, Fire too, of course."

"You don't have to lie, Lace. I know that Fire doesn't like me. She makes it perfectly obvious."

"Don't be silly, I've told you before. That's just how Fire is. Different types of personality make the world go round. She's always been slightly more forthright than me and Moss."

"That's not it. She has something against me."

"You know, Rosie, love is a strange thing. It takes on many forms and I don't believe any of us can ever say we truly understand it. All that matters is to remember that it's far more important to love than to hate."

"Erm, right, okay."

Lace stopped and placed her hand in a sisterly gesture on Rosie's arm. They had reached the woodland and birds were singing in the trees. The music of Faery Land was playing in accompaniment with them. "Rosie, Moss really cares about you."

"I know that. You must both do to have helped me as much as you have. It's been no easy feat and I've already taken up so much of your time."

"No. No, I don't mean in that way. I mean Moss *really* cares about you. Perhaps a little more than he should. Like, in more than a dutiful-carrying-out-orders-from-the-Council type of way."

"Lace, I'm sorry, you've lost me."

"Look, I think maybe that's the reason Fire is a little testy around you. She senses the same thing I do. We know our brother too well. She's just looking out for him and only has his best interests at heart."

Rosie shook her head in puzzlement. "But Lace, Moss and I are no more connected than I am to you. We've only known each other for a few days. I like Moss a lot. As a friend. I'm sure he feels the same way too."

"I'm sure," said Lace and smiled the previous conversation away. "What will be, will be."

16

Dear Diary Part II

Dear Diary,
I've written another verse to my song. If I can finish it in time
I want the Faery Band to play it at my eighteenth birthday ball:

> *And there are times I fear we'll never make it,*
> *This dream's so real, I'm almost scared to break it.*
> *You'd be so good for me,*
> *And I'll be all you'll ever need,*
> *Let this magic bind us tight,*
> *If we only have tonight,*
> *So in the morning rub your eyes,*
> *And if it's gone, it's no surprise.*
> *But don't let life get in the way,*
> *Of what I know will be someday.*
> *Ooo, I know that one thing's true:*
> *I've always thought of you.*

I know I haven't written properly in a while. A whole week has
passed since I brought Guy through the Faery Ring and into
my world. I should have described this in precise detail, I know
I should, but the tumultuous turn of events have kept me so
busy. He was dumbfounded and terrified and cursed in denial,
as well you may expect, but also amazed and thunderstruck,
and it felt so wonderful to whisk him round the majesty of our
beautiful Kingdom. I loved the changing expressions on his face,

handsome whether a smile or a frown, pleasure or alarm. It took every effort to describe the Time Laws to him. He found this my hardest disclosure to follow and worried that Helena would be sending out a search party for him, and maybe the divorce courts. Being two inches tall he took quite well. An hour here for every second of theirs, he refused to accept.

I took him flying. This he adored. We flew above treetops with the birds flocking at our sides. We dropped low amid the bracken and passed through hordes of rabbits chasing us in the fields. He kept saying he was sure he'd wake up soon and find it'd all been a dream. I knew that feeling. I thought that revealing my true, alien identity would put him off me for good, but it seems only to have cemented our love further.

Today the sun was exceptionally hot, an enormous globular bonfire in the sky, so we lay on top of the Rainy Bridge flood tunnel. The concrete was deliciously cool, but my arms were sticky where they locked around Guy's warm skin.

"I just want to be with you forever," I said. "Three hours is never long enough."

After the visit to Faery Land I'd come clean and told him everything. He now knew all about my time limit holding the magic, so I no longer had to flee from his sight pre- shrinking, like Cinderella leaving behind her glass shoe.

He kissed my forehead. "I know, Rosie. I wish there was something we could do."

"Me too."

I thought for a long while. I watched the world blur in my sunblind focus and, suddenly, a thought popped into my head. It was so startlingly clear that I was amazed I had not considered it before.

"I'll go and see Apatite. She'll know what to do."

Excitedly, I explained to Guy that Apatite is a witch lady also known as the Fortune Teller, the wisest woman in all of Faery Land. She can see the future and the past and there is not a single spell in existence which she doesn't know or cannot perform.

She practically raised my mother as a child and the Faery Queen swears by her exceptional psychic gift of the third eye.

"Guy, how would you feel if I decided to become human… forever?"

"Why would you want to do that? Your fancy faery world is far more beautiful and carefree than mine."

"To be with you, of course."

He changed his position and shifted his weight to one elbow where he could lie on his side and look me square in the eyes.

"You would do that for me?"

"Yes. Yes I would."

Dear Diary,

Madame Apatite lives in the grounds of the Quartz Palace. She, like many of the Elders, who serve the faery King and Queen, has a staff cottage set well back in the beautiful Gardens. The Fortune Teller's house is a pretty grey stone building, decorated with a green sheet of curly ivy which kisses the outer walls below a straw thatched roof. Everyone knows which of the stone cottages is hers, even if they've never been inside, since the slanted chimney forever chugs out a multitude of billowing black smoke. These clouds drift high over Faery Land and are the result of her hard working log fire which constantly heats a cauldron bubbling her many magical spells.

In all my nearly eighteen years, I have never asked Apatite for anything before. Mainly because I would be lying to say that I didn't fear her a little – in fact fear her a lot. My mother has told me countless times that beauty and goodness have absolutely nothing to do with appearances you see on the exterior, but everything to do with what lies on the inside. Yeah? Well, try telling that to anyone meeting Guy Flower for the first time! And then to anyone who unexpectedly comes across Apatite on a dark night! For a start, she is unnaturally old. I have no idea exactly how old, but at least hundreds of years. Her hair is thin, wiry and grey, her skin is ravaged, wrinkled and dull. Of late, I suspect she is also becoming lame. She walks with a stoop and her back is twisted as though she carries a heavy weight upon her jutting shoulders. But all of this I could handle, and even feel sorry for the woman and the way aging Father Time has treated her so unfairly, but what I cannot stomach is her eyes. Her THREE eyes! She has two in their normal sockets, like me and you, but then an additional glaring ball which twists, spins and flickers in every direction from its unnatural spot in the centre of her forehead. Whenever Mother and Father force me to greet her at Council dinners or parties, I am at a loss to know where to focus and end up looking down at the ground so as not to appear rude.

Despite all this, I do know that Madame Apatite has come to Faery Land's rescue, time after time. The 'Good Witch', they call her. She brought rain when a series of long, hot summer months threatened severe drought. She halted rain mid-fall when excessively wet Augusts brought uncontrollable floods. She nurtured the failing crops and fledgling flowers which seemed never to grow and she cared for sick animals, helping injured bird wings fly again and broken squirrel legs scamper. It's even said that the Fortune Teller brought a faery back from the dead by temporarily bridging the gap between the two thin, misty veils, and reuniting him briefly with an inconsolable loved one who had never had a chance to say goodbye.

Well, today I went to ask the Good Witch if she knew a spell to make me human. I knew she has an ancient Book which contains every wise incantation passed down since the beginning of Time. This could be key to my wish.

I took Strawberry along with me for company. I feel great guilt towards the poor creature at the moment as I know I've neglected her endlessly since meeting Guy. Prior to love, she was my one trusty companion, and now she's left to hop through the Gardens alone. I hoped that riding her to Apatite's pretty cottage at the edge of the Gardens may appease her slightly.

When I got there, the arched door was already ajar. Calling out to announce my arrival, I walked in with a bright, cheery tone, more confident than I actually felt. There was just one room on the other side of the walls. This formed an all-in-one kitchen, dining, living and sleeping area. As a result, the space was packed with every kind of paraphernalia imaginable. Shelves lined each available gap. Books, bottles, boxes, and then more books, bottles and boxes jostled for space on rickety wooden supports. As expected, as her chimney always billows with black smoke, a ferocious fire was burning and a broomstick and cauldron were propped at its side. Despite the lack of room, Apatite herself was almost lost among the cluttered debris. But then I saw her, bent over the central table, working on a concoction with clawed, nimble fingers. She held a razor-sharp knife and my heart skipped a beat, but it was only slicing through the heads of lavender stems for her to measure out equally on her rusty weighing scales. She looked up from the table, but the third eye was still focused on her task, now sealing the portions into brown papery leaves.

"I know what brings you here, Rosie Quartz. I saw it in my crystal ball a whole full moon ago." Her voice was gravelly, like a heavy body being dragged across a stony track. "You come to seek my advice on matters of magic. A certain kind of magic. The most powerful I possess. Well, I will tell you now girl, it can be done. Of that I am sure. You are certainly not the first faery in folklore to request such a gift. Many hundreds upon thousands have gone before you in the history of the earth. But if you're asking whether I recommend it, if you've come to ask for my agreement and consent, then you will be disappointed to find my answer is a resounding no. Will I help you child? Absolutely not."

She looked back down at her weighing scales and continued her work, grasping a damp piece of St. John's Wort in her hands.

"Madame Apatite, I do not come to you on a whim. I did not run here in some cloudy-headed teenage fantasy as you may suspect. This is a serious matter, which I've not considered lightly. I've turned the options over in my head countless times. I want to be with Guy. It's the only way he'll leave Helena and free himself to be happy. And it's the only chance I have of us being together. I love him so much and my own life is not worth living without him at my side. I have made up my mind. I'm ready and willing to sacrifice everything I know. I want you to make me human."

"No."

"But you said you can do it."

"And I said I will not do it."

Despite myself, I stamped in temper and irritation. "Then I will keep coming back and pester and pester you every single day. You will grow so tired of seeing my face. I will knock at your door and tap at your windows until you finally see that I will never give in."

"What if I were to tell your mother and father of this? My duties are to the Faery King and Queen, and they would not be happy to know that their daughter, the Royal Princess no less, was carrying on in this way."

I hesitated. They would be outraged and lace me with a 'Fixing Spell', never letting me out of my bedroom again. "You wouldn't tell them. Your role as Fortune Teller condemns you to confidentiality. You have to keep the confidence of every faery who seeks your help."

Apatite shook her head. "You are a strong-willed young woman, Rosie Quartz. I see you have your mother's courage and determination, and will not easily be swayed. You are much like the good lady, Snow Quartz, in more ways than you could imagine. Why don't you speak to her yourself about Guy Flower. You may be surprised just how much she understands."

"She could never understand."

"She has her own past."

"With my father?" I laughed. "The joyful celebrity couple? Both of Royal blood. Both of Faery blood. A happy ending. No complications. What do they know of tragedy or desperate measures?"

The Fortune Teller's sharp blade carried on chopping but she said no more.

"I WILL be back," I said, "That, I promise you." And I slammed the cottage door hard on my way out. Strawberry, who had been waiting patiently outside, kicked her heels and trotted to keep up.

*

Dear Diary,

I have returned to the witch's cottage every day for the past seven moons. I stand and stare her down while she toils over some new ingredient or other for her latest potion. I repeat all the same frantic information over and over again: "I love Guy. My own life is not worth living without him at my side. This is the only chance I have of us being together. I have made up my mind."

Today, in cupped palms, she carried her wildflower cuttings back and forth across the room to the cauldron spitting over the fire. She shook loose any stray bits from her apron and rubbed her hands clean before starting again.

She never speaks. Just lets me rant on in desperation. I hate her. Hate her. Hate her. Why won't she listen to me? I am going back tomorrow. I'll keep going till I send her crazy and wild. Either that or I'll end up stealing her stupid Book and finding the spell out for myself.

Dear Diary,

A break-through.

Today as I waited, she began to pour a smoky blue liquid into a curved glass vial. She addressed me for the first time in over a week. It was in answer to me yelling, "You situate yourself by that rotten table each day, preparing spells and magical potions for every other faery but me! All you've done in weeks is chop lavender and stir daisies and boil tree bark and fold feathers! Why are those orders so important? What have they done to deserve your services more than I? What do I have to do to get you to create the one spell I need? I am the Princess, for Gaia's sake!"

I had never played that card before. Even as I spoke the words, I felt awful. Never in my life had I been conceited about my status and used it to belittle others. If anything, I hated my lineage for the restrictions it placed on me. I'd never felt it gave me any rights, only boundaries.

She stopped pouring and held the hot glass vial up to the light which shone in through the windows. "Rosie Quartz, you forget I am the Fortune Teller. I see all that is past and all that is yet to come. I knew from the very first moment you were born that we would have this meeting, and that eventually, though it brings me great grievance and despair, I would be forced to give in to your bold request."

She corked the bottle with a wooden stopper which made it fizz and then dropped her arm to hold it towards me. "This spell I have been taking so long to complete, working tirelessly on for many weeks…is for you."

Instantly, I was appalled at myself for the terrible things I had said.

"Oh, Madame Apatite, I…I…I can't thank you enough!"

"Please do not thank me. It may yet prove a thankless task."

Despite my previous repulsion at her odd appearance, I forgot my fears and moved to hug and kiss her. It was the witch herself, however, who stepped back and whisked the potion away from my eager, snatching hands.

"Wait!" she said. "Before we begin, there are many things we must talk of. Pull up a chair. There is a long conversation we must have."

In the same moment the fire unexplainably blew itself out and the sun passed behind a thick cloud, casting the room in cold darkness.

"Even drinking this liquid will not make the magic complete. You have many other obstacles to overcome. There will be great danger and a risk to your life. I cannot guarantee that you shall pass through all these tests safely. You must consider my severe warnings before we proceed. We are meddling with a treacherous sorcery here. Rosie, do you still wish to continue?"

"If it means I get to be human, if it means I get to be with Guy Flower, then yes. Yes with all my heart. I still want to do this."

"Very well. Then listen carefully."

Apatite reached down beneath the table and poked her crooked nose under a heavy black cloth. She hauled to the surface the largest book I had ever seen. I helped move crystals, wands and packs of tarot cards to one side as it consumed the entire desk top.

As she opened the wide, hard cover, the spine creaked as if moaning in protest at the intrusion. A thick dust powdered the air. Without physical contact, she used natural magic from her fingertips to turn the book to its required page. It fell open upon a section titled 'Faery to Human', but the rest of the words were concealed beneath cobwebs. A startled spider scuttled from what had once been a snug hiding place in the crease and ran for new cover across the table. Apatite knocked the webs away with a tap of her knuckles and began to read.

"For a Higher Realm being to step into the Lower Realm of humans and maintain this disposition with any kind of permanence, they will need the willing blessing of an existing human to bridge the gap and forge the connection for them."

"That I already have!" I shouted. "I know Guy is willing and gladly gives his blessing."

She turned another page.

"At the moment of the spell, both lives on either side of the dimensions will be terminated."

"What?"

"Both faery and human must agree to be born again as human babes in arms. They must live out their lives again as children. All memory of their previous existence will be totally erased. They shall remember nothing of their original identity."

"But then...that defeats the whole point, doesn't it? If Guy and I are born again as kids with no memories of before, we'll be none the wiser that we even knew each other. We could be born at opposite ends of the world. There's a chance our paths may never cross. If we never meet the whole thing will have been a waste of time!"

Apatite closed the book. It banged shut. "Exactly. I told you as much. This is madness. I said it was a bad idea."

I felt the water well over the brims of my eyes. A stream of complete devastation rolled down my cheeks. "But I thought you could help me. I thought you could do anything. I thought there was no spell in existence you couldn't achieve."

"Agreed. But this is where the danger begins. These parts I shall have to improvise from the recesses of my own mind. These parts are unwritten. The next treacherous steps will not be found in the pages of this Book. I will add them in my own handwriting now, but you must sign below with irreversible faery ink to say that you agree to all that I do."

I wiped at the tears and dabbed my nose with my sleeve. "Pass me the ink. Where do I sign?"

Dearest Diary,

My entries grow shaky and weak as I set upon your pages all I now know in the best and most honest way I can. Here is how it stands:

In order for the spell to work and for Guy and I to be together forever, we must have it written in our Akashic Records – the charts of fate – that we find each other out before we are thirteen years old. Before we both become teenagers. There will inevitably be obstacles placed in our way to stop this meeting. Another Helena character will undoubtedly be one of them. Even if we can fight our ways through this and still reunite, the quest is not solved. Guy must pronounce his love for me in clear spoken form before the dawn of our joint birthdays. He must actually vocalize the precise words, 'I love you', before the clock strikes the first minute of 13th April. This, Madame Apatite was keen to point out, is no easy feat from the lips of a laidback, carefree teenage boy.

"Could it not be made just a little later?" I asked her, worried. "What's wrong with it happening around the ages either of us are now?"

"Timing is beyond my control. The number thirteen is poignant to this precise spell. It is a sacred, magical number of love, passion and eternal transformation. Love before your thirteenth birthdays. Take it or leave it."

"But Madame Apatite, what happens if for whatever reason I can't make Guy say he loves me before that day? What then?"

And this Dear Diary, was the big catch.

"Rosie, nothing precious comes without a cost. This powerful magic requires something of great significance in return. Think back on all your familiar, traditional faery tales – the ones your mother read to you when you were a child – not the flouncy, sugar-coated versions watered down for weaker human ears. Think on the lessons REAL faery tales of ancient times tell. Where there is light, there is also dark. Many heroic maidens were forced to pay the ultimate price. Rosie, if the words are not spoken, the spell will be broken and you shall be transported back to your original faery form for all time. If this happens, Guy Flower will be lost to you forever."

"But in the faery tales you mention, so many of those women achieved their goals and reigned victorious. The Little Mermaid, for example. She gave up her fishtail for human legs so she could walk beside her prince…"

"And in the genuine ending, based on the true event…?"

"They got married and lived happily ever after."

"No."

"What then? What happened?"

"The Sea Witch who granted her the spell was forced to keep their initial agreement. The Little Mermaid was turned into an ocean wave and doomed to remain all time as nothing but water, crashing upon the jagged cliffs, screaming out the name of her forever-lost love."

17

Taken

A fat black crow sat high up in the shadowed branches above the Agate Abode. It had been there a very long time, but was skilled at blending into the background. Occasionally, the crow grew restless and bored, and would momentarily circle the village, displaying its impressive wingspan. Sometimes it flew to the Steeple churchyard and perched on one of the cemetery's ancient tombstones. Sometimes it soared to the war monument on the roundabout in Steeple Town and pecked at the soldier's stone gun. But it would not venture back to its home in Lock Marshland. Not just yet. Not empty clawed. The crow's name was Zombie, and his master had sent him on a task.

"Oh my goodness, I can't believe it! Just take a look at this." It was breakfast the following morning and Rosie was enjoying her usual fix of dandelion tea at the Agate's dining table, when Lace rushed in with *The Faery Times*, an expression of horror on her face.

"It happened last night. It's front page news. Just look at the headline!" Lace tossed the newspaper to Moss who dropped his cereal spoon to catch it. "It's young Peridot. He's been taken!"

Peridot and Jasper had been out late. They were walking by the woodland river when they saw the crow in the grey skies above them.

"Nasty, dirty creatures! Let's bring it down!" Jasper had fished a homemade twig catapult from out of his leafy rucksack and began to harpoon the bird with loose rocks which he scooped from the ground.

Zombie was unperturbed by the mere pinpricks he felt and swooped down like a cloak of darkness enveloping the boys. He knocked Peridot clean off his feet with a waft of his wings and while the faery lay helpless on the floor, the crow pinned him captive with his gigantic, clawed talons. He cawed at the insolent boys in a high-pitched squawk, but they were perfectly able to understand his form of communication.

"Tell me where I can find the little blonde Quartz Princess. I know she's back in Faery Land. Where is she staying?"

"We don't know what you're talking about," hissed Peridot as the air was squeezed out of his lungs under the weight of Zombie's claw. Blood dripped from the side of his mouth where he'd torn his lip as he fell. "And even if we did, we would hardly tell you. You're an evil, ugly traitor. You work for *Him.*"

The crow remained calm. He knew he was the one in control. "If you don't tell me what you know, I shall be forced to take you to the Master so you can explain your feeble cover-up to him in person."

"Do it then feather bag!"

Zombie croaked in delight. "You fool! Enjoy your flight to the Crag Mines."

"Peridot! *No!*" Jasper hollered into the air as his best friend was hoisted above him and flown off into the black night.

Brave young Peridot tried not to think of the things awaiting him at the other end of this journey, and concentrated only on what he saw below. He recognized the castle turrets and stained glass windows of Steeple High, the surrounding lush green lawns with their immaculately tended borders. He saw the identical slate roofs of the Steeple Town shops in Dark Lantern Lane, Steeple Print Newspaper Headquarters, Cobweb Attic Antiques, Calm Down Café and Ye Olde Steeple Bookstore. All had now closed for the evening, but the last Green Man bus was slithering its way down the windy lanes before retiring for the night.

*

Moss looked deathly pale, his tanned skin as white as the pages of newspaper. He had propped his thick black reading glasses on the end of his nose and was skimming the report for a second time, hoping he'd missed some important clue which would now jump out at him. Fire came to stand behind her older brother and placed her hand on his shoulder. He lovingly squeezed her fingers in recognition of her gesture.

"Moss, you don't suppose he's been taken...*there?*"

"Where else would a crow have gone? They all work for *Him* now. There are no free minded ones left in Steeple anymore. Of course poor Peridot will be there."

Lace dropped down into the armchair, her fall scattering the cushions. "Will he live? Moss, will they hurt him?"

"I don't know, Sis, it depends what He's after. I really don't know."

"Hey, what's going on here?" Rosie asked, looking from one faery to the other. "Someone let me in on this please. Where has the crow taken Peridot? Where precisely is *There* and who exactly is *Him?*"

Lace gave Moss a shooting look as if to say, *don't dare disclose more*, but fortunately for Rosie, Fire had no intention of being anything other than her usual blunt self. "He's gone to the Dark Side. To the one who murdered your parents."

"What? My parents? You mean the man who did that is still out there and free? He lives?"

"Did the Fortune Teller not tell you anything, girl?" Fire chided. "Did she never bother mentioning that he's undefeatable. Only *one* can destroy him. The only living descendant of the deceased Faery King and Queen. The bearer of the white light and true beauty within. Apparently, that's supposed to be YOU, sweet cheeks."

"Come to think of it, she did say something like that, yes. When we went to the Bearded Bark. Something about a reflection dissolving the evil in his heart. But I didn't listen much to it. I just wanted to know how to get home and why you'd brought me here in the first place."

"Well maybe that's a slight clue. Any chance you'd like to do us all a favour pretty, and single handedly save Faery Land?"

"Fire, go easy," said Moss. "Rosie, look, the man...the creature...the goblin...we speak of...is called Sulphur. And he is indeed the dark energy which killed our King and Queen."

"The name speaks for itself," Fire spat. "Look up the enchanting qualities of the rock crystal Sulphur, if you care. *'Absorbs all negative energy. Any shadows cling to it and serve it.'* He's proudly set himself up as leader of the Goblins and fancies himself Goblin King."

"Goblin? And these are different to faeries? Define Goblin."

I feel at this point in our story that I must once again step in and tell you what I know of the goblin race, since it's far more than any of the Agate siblings decided to impart to Rosie at this time. I also happen to know more about Sulphur than we will hear of here, but this is not the time to disclose that particular information. Not in this tale.

Goblins are also often referred to as Boggarts or Bogie Men. Whatever label you choose describes a faery gone bad or malicious. They are thieves, vagabonds and villains who delight in causing disaster in the human world. Where faeries inspire creative good, like poetry, music, performance and art, goblins wreak the havoc of conflict, robbery, war and disease. Goblins may have been faeries once, but their evil deeds have rendered them outsiders, rotten to the core. All hold immeasurable grudges against the Kingdom which has outcast them.

Fire continued her own account to Rosie, retelling it slowly beneath her breath for added effect, as though they were sitting round a campfire and this were her most prized ghost story. But this was no fiction. The threat Sulphur posed was as real as you or I.

"The crow will have flown Peridot to the Crag Mines. That's where they all live – if you can call it that. Fester, more like. The Crags are a filthy network of caves, caverns and long forgotten mines, running deep underground. Initially, they retreated there to mine for gold. But that has long since run out now. I hear it's always wet, the walls constantly dripping, which is what gives all goblins a damp, slimy appearance, like toads. The dirty water discolours their skin so they're always green, brown or grey. They have deformed features due to the lack of light and the fact that they so rarely come up to the surface. They send their crows and spiders to do their bidding. They cannot stand music and singing, since it is a thing of beauty and reminds them of the fun at our parties which they are no longer invited to. That's another reason they stay underground. The thick, cavern walls cut out the sound of the Faery Band."

"Right!" said Rosie. She marched to the sink in the kitchen and deposited her teacup in the soapy water. "I want to go and see this Sulphur and demand to know why he murdered my parents. If the legend says I can defeat him, then I ought to try. Someone has to go and save Peridot. Let it be me."

"Don't be stupid, you idiot," said Fire.

"NO!" Moss practically jumped out of his skin at Rosie's remark. "No one comes out of there alive. Didn't you hear? The Crag Mines are always in darkness. You can never tell whether it's night or day. It sends a faery insane. Anyone but a goblin whose eyes have grown accustomed to that eternal black would get lost down there and never find their way out again. Why do you think there are so many skeletons frozen forever amid the rocks? They are the long lost bones of dead faeries who never made it home."

Rosie felt herself wanting to cry. "You said that in bringing me here to your world I would learn things. Well, here's what I've learnt: that I do nothing but create misery and despair wherever I go. I have made such a huge mess of things. My parents were alive when I left them and the Faery Kingdom was happy. I return and it's in turmoil. And for what? I thought I was doing the right thing in following my heart – the supposed great love of my life – but even that's all gone wrong. We all know I've failed. Even in our new lives, he's still ended up with Helena. I'm never going to get him to say he loves me before our thirteenth birthdays. Let's face it. The date is only a few weeks away. The magic spell will be broken and I'll soon be back here in my old life as a faery forever. Except it won't be like my old life which I left behind, will it? My parents are gone. The Quartz Palace is gone. The Kingdom is no more. I'll have no one. And eventually my family back home in the human world will notice my absence, the seconds will catch up with them. My parents – Daniel and Debra – will notice I'm missing and it'll break their hearts. They'll think I've been kidnapped or murdered. It will kill them too. It's like I'm torturing everyone a second time round. And my best friends, Billie and Sally, I will miss them so much."

She wept now till Moss took hold of her in his arms. She felt his strong body around her. Despite her devastation, his grasp offered safety and protection.

"The spell will not be broken, Rosie. Why do you think us Agates were employed to protect you? It is our job to see to that. You are still the Royal Princess and my duty is to serve you, like I would have Smoky and Snow if they were still here. You are their daughter and I shall never let anything bad happen to you." He rocked her back and forth. "Now that you've read the diary and know the truth, I think it's time for us to send you back to your own dimension – the human world, where you now belong. I assure you that Guy will say he loves you and you'll get the happily ever after you both dreamed of."

Moss kissed the top of Rosie's forehead and smoothed her blonde hair which had become messy and matted with tears. She knew she must look horrendous, but he smiled into her eyes.

"But before you return, Rosie Quartz," sang Lace in a bright tone, "promise I get to have my last piece of sisterly fun with you? Tomorrow night there is going to be a great Faery Fancy Dress Ball. They are the grandest faery occasions you could ever imagine. We still hold them on the first day of every month in memory of the parties your parents used to throw. They usually happen in the woodland clearing, but this time, in your special honour, and with your permission of course, the Elders have decided to throw open the doors of the Quartz Palace and hold the ball of all balls right there, just like in the days of the King and Queen." Lace pulled Rosie from her brother's embrace and spun her around on the spot. "Oh, Rosie, there is more singing, dancing, music-playing, eating, drinking, fireworks, magic and merriment than your eyes will believe! Do say you'll come. You'll be proud guest of honour! Oh, what will you go as?"

"A Royal Princess, of course," said Fire.

"Why, yes! What a wonderful idea. We must find you a magnificent ball gown and tiara!" shrieked Lace.

But unlike Lace, Rosie had not missed the sarcasm in Fire's tone. It was angry and bitter and dripped with hatred.

18

The Faery Fancy Dress Ball

Late afternoon, when the sun was still up, Lace took Rosie to 'The Baths' to prepare for the highly anticipated night ahead. The Baths were at the edge of the woodland – a row of impressive waterfalls with therapeutic healing qualities, which humans thought were just springs, bubbling like a Jacuzzi from a pile of jagged boulders. But the magical whirlpool of foam which collected here was said to emphasize the most beautiful features of any faery who washed in it, as well as making them feel wonderful about themselves. It was the greatest self-esteem booster, and they were extra busy today as everyone wanted to look their very best for the party of the year.

Rosie enjoyed the calming sensation of the cool water against her bare skin. She dove below the surface. She did an underwater forwards roll and then bobbed back up and settled onto her back, where she was free to gaze up, gently kicking her ankles to stay afloat. As she saw the giant world towering high, she suddenly recognized all too well a familiar tree, and the red bricks of the side of a house. Guy's house. This was the very same spot where she'd climbed and then fallen with Sally and Billie all those months ago. She'd certainly never noticed anything magic about the water then, although having said that, the second chance encounter with Guy that day had been a contributing factor to them going out. He must have seen something vaguely beautiful about her after that brief dip in The Baths. Mud splattered, mascara running, and twigs poking out of her dripping hair, he had somehow found her attractive enough to kiss her. The recollection of that moment by the front door should have made her blush and shudder like it used to, but things had changed. It didn't affect her now. Maybe it had something to do with her memories of 'First Times' getting tangled in the retelling. Her mind had been meddled with over the past few days of reading the diary. She wasn't sure which encounter was which anymore, which event was real and which only a Fortune Teller's illusion.

"Come on, Rosie," called Lace, who was drying off on the bank, "You have to check out the outfit I've picked for you, and make sure it still fits before tonight. It's one of your Princess ones back at the Palace. I've laid it out ready on the four poster bed in your old room."

When the girls crossed the moat at the entrance to the Palace, the grounds were already crammed with workers who were rushing back and forth, checking each minute detail in final preparation for the Ball. The five Elders were there too, astutely overseeing all last minute alterations. Elaborate decorations had been hung from the Roman columns, lush feathers in silver and white. Glass lanterns floated in the air by the ceiling, and more food and drink than Rosie had ever seen in her life was stacked up in racks aboard guinea pigs and field mice. Members of the Faery Band were setting up their wooden instruments on the platform around the thrones. It was the complete opposite to the echoing, abandoned temple through which Moss had led her days before. And somewhere inside, Rosie felt a distant vision stir. She saw herself walk in the same grand hall, while her parents made arrangements for her eighteenth birthday party. She knew from the diary that it had been the last time she had seen them before she and Guy drank Apatite's potion. She also knew that the forgetting spell meant that she shouldn't remember Smoky and Snow, but more and more she did. Too may key episodes had been stirred deep down within her soul.

Up the central staircase; Rosie knew exactly where to go

this time, every turn on the long, cream-carpeted corridors. She pushed at the door to her bedroom and it felt good to be back before the large draped windows, to see the carved rocking horse, the doll's house and the music box. On the bed, as Lace had said, there lay a dress which shimmered so much, it looked alive. The material was a faint, powdery pink and the strapless, heart-shaped bodice was studded with real rose quartz pieces.

Lace helped Rosie slip it on over her head and for a moment she was lost in the gigantic folds of fabric. As it fell to her feet, her friend manoeuvred her towards the dressing table mirror. Rosie gasped. The tight waistline dropped to a 'V' and from there billowed out in multiple layers of net and voile, which sat stiff over a wire-hooped underskirt. It fitted like a glove. It was the most stunning and elegant gown she had ever had the privilege of touching.

"Not quite," said Lace when Rosie voiced her thoughts aloud. "Remember, it's only one of many you happened to have in your wardrobe. I just thought it would be the most suitable for tonight. Oh, and don't forget this!" She produced a glittering tiara, also set with rose quartz pieces and shards of blinding diamond. "I want to do your hair down and in curls. It'll really set it off. Sit on the window ledge and we'll make a start."

"What are you going to the Fancy Dress Ball as, Lace?"

"Never mind me. I'll be going back to the Agate Abode to change later. The Belle of the Ball needs to be you. When I've finished your hair, I'll leave you in peace to see to your make-up. You'll hear the Band strike up a different tune when the guests begin to arrive. That'll be your signal to come down. I'll instruct Moss to wait for you at the bottom of the stairs."

The hum of voices started to get louder and the music grew out of odd snatches of tuned violin notes into a dreamy melody. Rosie took one last look at herself in the mirror. She had hardly needed to put any make up on, since her skin radiated an already painted glow. She couldn't believe the reflection staring back was actually her own. Deep breaths. Inhale. Exhale. It was time.

At the top of the spiral staircase she stood and looked down on a sea of giddy visitors. With her first step they sensed her presence and everyone turned to look at the Royal Princess, returned home once more. She clasped the pearl banister tight to steady her nerves and descended, almost floating, lifted by the wings she no longer had. And then she saw Moss waiting midway.

His fancy dress apparel was Hawaiian: startlingly bright, garish shorts and a multi-coloured shirt illustrated with parrots and palm trees. The swirling patterns blended with the tattoos on his arms and it was hard to see where the material ended and his skin began. The shirt hung open and pink and yellow garlands hung from round his neck to cover his bare chest. Dark sunglasses were propped up on his head.

Rosie laughed out loud as she took his arm, *"Aloha!"*

"You look beautiful," he said.

"You don't look so bad yourself," she replied.

They made their way through the crowds and persistent camera flashes, forced to stop in various poses for countless pictures.

"You'll be plastered all over the front pages of *The Faery Times* tomorrow," smiled Moss.

"I think it's your shirt they're interested in," Rosie teased.

"Erm, no. I think it's more that you're the most stunning vision anyone has ever seen. If only Guy Flower could see you now, hey?" Embarrassed by his comment, she dropped his hand and hurried on ahead. Moss stopped, feeling daft, and went off to find his sisters in the opposite direction.

Rosie walked through the Palace, across the bridge and out into the Gardens as if in a trance. It was dusk and the moon was glorious in a velvet sky, surrounded by stars. She watched snails move slowly down the garden paths, sticky goo trails glistening helpfully to light people's way. Glow worms, too, hovered among the stalks of the flowers. Barn owls were giving romantic rides on their backs, offering panoramic views of the Palace and its breathtaking surroundings. Food and drink were now neatly displayed upon passing caterpillars, who offered various choices from the different segments of their bodies: sugar cube hors d'oeuvres, butter drenched dandelion leaves and whole polished red glacier cherries. The music had moved to an outdoor bandstand and all the guests wanted to dance. Fabulous fancy dress costumes swarmed into one, silhouettes moving in time with the rhythm.

Rosie saw Lace and Fire pushing through the crowd. Both looked amazing, striking beyond compare. Lace was dressed as a star, her head, arms and legs poking out of a spiky silver leotard and Fire was a wild red deer with antlers on a hairband and heavy fur waistcoats draping to the ground.

"You're both gorgeous," she said. "Everyone is. This is incredible. And the faces around me may be strangers, but they all seem so familiar. Like I've met them before. In fact, I think I know why. I think they remind me of Jemma Flower's ornaments, the ones on her stalls and in her house."

"Of course," Lace nodded. "Jemma once was a child too, you know."

"Jemma? You mean she's been here?"

But there was no chance for an answer because just then Rosie was whisked away by one of many people fighting for her consent to dance. Everyone wanted to turn her about the floor. Her hooped skirt spun feather light as she glided quickly from one friendly smile to another. Countless truly handsome faeries held her hands and cheekily winked their admiration. The frenzy was taking her breath away. Her heart quickened and she felt dizzy. Then all of a sudden it was Moss Agate's face in front of her own and everything seemed to stop.

"Hello again, it seems I'm the only one to have missed out now. So, before you grow tired, please may I have this dance?"

As he took hold of her waist, the music changed to a gentler tempo and they moved slowly together in unison. Amy Thyst, one of Madame Celestite's most promising young music students, stepped up to the bandstand and began to sing – strong and haunting. It made Rosie blissfully weak and she felt her body melt closer to Moss, till her head was resting on his shoulder.

For a while, neither spoke. Then Moss received a tap on the

back and spun Rosie round. Tight lipped and sour faced, Sir Fluorite towered above them both with his staff held firmly in his hand. He had not come in fancy dress and wore the same billowing blue cloak and pointed hat that he always did.

"I trust you are enjoying the party, Miss Quartz?" he said, but with no genuine interest in his voice.

"Erm, yes, I'm having a great time, thank you."

"And young Mister Agate seems to be ensuring you a comfortable visit to Faery Land."

"Yes. Absolutely. I owe him and his sisters so much for the way they've looked after me."

"Well, that was their assigned role. They're merely carrying out their Council duties." He drew his robes tighter around him and scratched a shallow hollow in the ground with the bottom of his heavy staff. "I will leave you both to enjoy the rest of your night. But remember, Rosie, your journey here was not for frivolous fun. Our sole purpose is to remind you that you still have a job to do, and you must make haste back to your own world now to ensure it is carried out."

"Yes, yes, Sir, I know that."

Rosie hung her head as he disappeared from view, feeling like a small child who had been told off. "Am I in trouble?" she asked Moss. "Are the Council not happy with me?"

"No, that's not it at all," Moss reassured, pulling her back into the dance. "The Elders may not agree with your actions of long ago, but right now their only chief concern, Rosie, is your safety. And your happiness, of course. They have a responsibility in their capacity as Royal Guardians to ensure that your wishes are upheld. Fluorite wants the spell to work and he's worried that we're cutting it fine, that's all."

"He has a funny way of showing it."

"He's the oldest, shrewdest Elder in the Land. He's seen things you or I could never begin to imagine. That's just his way."

"But what if the spell doesn't work out, and I am forced to come back here for good? What will that mean for the Land? What will Fluorite think then?"

"I'm afraid it has to do with Sulphur. Fluorite's worried that the longer you spend here, the more chance there is of Sulphur finding out you're around. Some people are speculating that the crow which took Peridot may already have been searching for information. I think Fluorite's concern is that Sulphur is bound to see you as a threat, and may seek to finish off what he started with your parents."

Rosie shuddered. She felt an unexplainable darkness creep over her heart and hugged Moss tighter. "Am I safe?" she said.

Moss smiled. "With me, yes. Well after all, that *is* my assigned role. I'm merely carrying out my Council duties."

Rosie chuckled at his imitation of Fluorite's words. "By the way, I forgot to say, you can really dance!" she said.

"We're hardly moving," he protested. "This is just swaying."

"Well, it's nice, whatever it is."

"Thanks."

She readjusted her arms around the back of his neck and pressed her warm flushed face against his, so they were cheek to cheek. Easily, they dropped back into a content mutual silence.

Dandelion seeds are a precious commodity in Faery Land and only blown on special occasions and poignant celebrations. It seemed someone had deemed tonight worthy of them, for suddenly a cloud of fluffy, white umbrellas went sailing into the air. They hovered for a second while people cheered and then spiralled back down, showering the dance floor. Rosie and Moss broke their dance once more and laughed, fully coated in what looked like a thick snow.

One of the caterpillar waiters toddled past and Moss swiped two goblets.

"Ooo thanks, I was ready for a drink." Thinking only of her thirst, Rosie tipped the golden contents down her throat. Instantly, she was spluttering and struggling to breathe. The hot liquid had blown her mind and burnt the back of her mouth. Moss grinned in amusement. "What is that?" Rosie screeched, just about regaining her balance.

"Honey and nectar mixture. We call it 'Hectar'. Collected

from rare flowers. The bumblebees make it for us. It's a form of faery wine."

"So it's alcoholic?"

"Immensely so."

"It's good. Pass me another."

They both started to laugh again, and this time Rosie found she couldn't stop. Moss had to move her away from the dance floor and take her for a calming walk around the Gardens. They shook dandelion seeds from their clothes as they went. Moss abandoned his shirt altogether.

A temporary Wishing Well had been created for decoration in one of the fountains. It was the one with the statue of the mermaid.

"Here," said Moss, handing Rosie one of the stray dandelion seeds. "These are more precious to us than coins. You can use it to make a wish."

Rosie hung over the side of the stone sculpture and eyed the various nick-nacks people had already thrown in. "Well, I guess I have to say the obvious, don't I?"

"Which is?"

She sighed wistfully. "Which is...to end up with the love of my life." She placed the seed on her flat outstretched palm and blew it into the water. It didn't do much. Just grew saturated and clumped on the surface.

"Maybe I should have used something heavier. How about you?"

"Me?"

"Yes, go on, Moss, now it's your turn."

Moss took his own ball of fluff and copied the action.

"Well what was it? What did you wish for?"

He shrugged. "The same."

"The same!" Rosie laughed aloud. "Moss Agate, no way. For real? You don't strike me as the kind of boy who'd want to be all romantic and loved up."

"Don't I?" He looked disappointed.

"No, not at all."

Moss was embarrassed again. "Why? What makes you say that?"

She flexed her non-existent muscles playfully. "You're so macho and manly, brave and courageous. A gallant knight of the Council. I can't imagine you turning gooey for some silly, needy girl."

"OK, I'll change my wish just for you then. Wishing Well, I wish for a shiny red human sports car and the latest human mobile phone, please. There. Does that make you feel any better?"

"Much better." She kissed him on the cheek. And then hiccupped and tripped.

"Rosie, are you okay?"

"I'm great. Can I get some more wine?"

He shook his head. "Perhaps not."

"Hmm. You know, to be honest, Moss, I think I've had enough attention for one night. I don't know if I want to go back into the Palace. It's beautiful and everything but it's getting too much for me and I'm tired."

Moss appeared to think for a while. "Come on, I know a quiet spot we can sneak off to and watch the fireworks. They'll be setting them off at midnight."

He took her hand and dragged her along. Rosie felt everything whizz and blur around her. She wasn't quite sure if they flew or not, but on arrival was convinced that they must have since they seemed to have come so far. They were out of the Kingdom circumference and back in the woodland. Before them stood a huge, rusty watering can. It was large, even by human standards, and appeared to have been abandoned for a very long time. Around it were clumps of tall yellow dandelions.

"No one will find us here. This is my most favourite place in the whole world. I've created it all myself – well, with a little help from human manufacturers and great Mother Nature. It's my private gym hang out. Rosie, welcome to 'The Can'."

As he said the word 'gym' she began to see what he meant. Moss had cleverly fashioned the old watering can to form his own workout fitness centre. Round the broad loop of the handle there ran a track similar to a running machine. The exerciser could apparently circle around this upside down, like a hamster on its wheel – well, if you were a faery and had your wings to keep you suspended mid-air. The spout was set horizontal to be used as monkey bars which Moss obviously swung from often, judging by his muscles. Tacked onto a sharp nail was a wooden sign. Moss pointed it out to Rosie now. The messy letters read, 'DO NOT DISTURB!'

"When my sisters are doing my head in, I escape here and put up this sign. They know intrusion is only allowed in the most serious of emergencies."

"This is so cool!"

"Yeah, come on, let me help you up. These dandelion heads make the comfiest couch you could imagine. I love to lie on them and it's the most perfect view for staring at the sky. We'll see the fireworks soon. The Elders will set them off at midnight as that's the most sacred faery time. We call it 'The Bewitching Hour'."

Moss flew to the highest dandelion and then reached down to hoist Rosie up. No sooner had their backs hit the soft golden petals than an almighty bang roared and cracked, shaking their bed like the heavens were opening. Next, a bouquet of shimmering stars rained down to earth…

Rosie watched in awe. It was the most splendid firework display she'd ever seen. Pinks, purples, blues, silvers and greens raced in rocket trails across the clear sky. Blossoming roses grew and then burst, shattering like coloured glass into the night. But the most impressive tricks of all were the gunpowder shapes which magically morphed into pictures of animals. A hare hopping through a field. A bee collecting nectar from a flower. A unicorn sipping water from a tranquil lake. And a ferocious dragon breathing fire from a crooked mountain top. All lived for several seconds and then collapsed into themselves, fading away.

"Wow! We don't have fireworks like this back home."

"Sir Rhodonite does them. He's brilliant at stuff like that. The secret has been passed down through his family for generations."

"Wicked!"

As they continued to stare, Moss stretched his arm round the back of Rosie's head. Instinctively, she snuggled down into the groove of his chest. They held this position till the show came to an end.

"It's turning a little cold," Rosie said.

Moss wrapped his other arm around her and she was able to study his many tattoos. Some were spiders and intricately patterned webs. Some were hearts cracked down the middle looking like they were broken. There were daisies and bands of green leaves, zigzag lightning bolts, and a cloud which puthered rain in the shape of stars. Finally, Rosie spotted an arched rainbow and two swords crossed at the blades.

"What do they all mean?"

He strained his neck to see what she referred to. "Ah, my tattoos? They mean lots of things. Symbols. Ancient secrets. Faery magic and folklore."

"I can't find any girl's names printed on here though!"

"Ha, ha, ha! No. No girl's names. Not yet."

Rosie traced the many different shapes with her fingers. At some point she must have fallen to sleep.

Fresh, dew-filled morning air prized open her eyes and as she stirred, Rosie remembered being in Moss's arms – the warmth of his embrace and the mystery surrounding him. She reached out with a happy smile, but her fingers grasped at nothing. He had gone and she lay on the dandelion alone. Rubbing the sleep out of her eyes, she pulled herself up to sit and survey the dishevelled creases of her stunning gown. She heard breathless grunts and saw Moss doing chin-ups on the bar of his gym. He dropped to the ground when he saw her and dusted himself off.

"Sleeping Beauty!" he greeted her. "Good morning."

"Morning. Did we stay here all night?"

He ignored her question. "Great news! Peridot has been found. He's home, safe and alive. He was discovered sprawled by the river bank this morning, badly bruised and a little shaken up – the crow must have dropped him back from a great height – but other than that, the newspapers say he's fine."

"Oh, thank heavens! That's wonderful."

"Yes. He didn't make the front page though." He handed up a copy, which showed her own smiling face. "You did!"

19

Jam Jars

Billie Featherstone had the rainbow strap of her shiny, red electric guitar slung over her shoulder. Sally Nuttall had two wooden drumsticks poking out of her back pocket. Both girls kicked at the doorstep as they rang Rosie's doorbell. Debra Quartz answered, eventually and looked surprised to see them.

"Hey, girls, where's Rosie?"

Billie and Sally glanced at one another, confused.

"That's kind of why we called, Mrs Quartz. We wanted to know if she's coming out?"

Debra opened the door wider and stepped out to survey her garden. "Where on earth is she then? I just went into her bedroom to ask if she wanted any breakfast, but she wasn't there. I presumed she'd got up extra early and gone off with you two somewhere."

"Not us, Mrs Quartz. To be honest, we haven't seen or heard from her properly in a few weeks, not out of school anyway. We were beginning to think maybe we'd done something wrong."

"I'm sure that's not the case. You know she thinks the world of you two. Perhaps she's nipped up to the shop. If you catch her, will you tell her I'm doing a Full English if she wants one?"

As they trudged uphill to the Steeple Village shop and post office, Rosie's two best friends began to speculate.

"Do you think she's been acting strange recently?"

"Definitely I do. It's like we said before, she hardly ever wants to hang out with us anymore, and even when she has done she seems weird and distracted. If you trace it back, I'm sure she's been like this since around Christmas."

Sally shrugged. "Maybe it's still to do with Guy. She's never really gotten over what happened with him. That dude really screwed her up."

"First love. It's always the hardest. She'll forget about it in time." Billie lectured like she had a wealth of experience on the matter. "But I do have some hot gossip for her. I heard off Des that Guy and evil Helena are not quite as loved up as they used to be. People have heard them rowing! And Deano even says that he's seen Spotswood taking Jack Baxter for a spin in her brother's newest sports car. And they had their dinner together in the canteen yesterday lunchtime."

"I just hope Rosie's okay. It's not the same without her."

Moss had his reading glasses on at the dining table, which usually meant he had business on his mind. He had an appointment with the Council later and they'd want to be filled in on any recent progress.

"We need to find out the location of the latest faery ring. It won't be at the bottom of your garden anymore, Rosie. They change all the time so we're protected against unwanted intruders."

"Who changes them?" she asked between sips of dandelion tea.

Lace answered. "Friends of ours. Amber, Opal and Ruby. They live in stone cracks behind the ivy of the Steeple post office."

"Lace, Fire, maybe you can take Rosie out there to visit them today? Then that's one job we can tick off the list."

Rosie looked at Moss intently, registering what he'd just said. "And then what, once we know where it is?"

"Then it's time for you to go back home."

Rosie wasn't sure how this made her feel. On the one hand she'd really started to miss her parents and friends, the familiar comforts of her Steeple Chase bedroom. On the other hand she'd now made new friends, friends who felt like family, and she'd established new familiar surroundings right here, which would equally be a wrench to leave behind. Her head hurt when she had thoughts like this. Nothing made sense.

It was a bright, warm morning in both worlds when they all arrived. Rosie had visited the Steeple post office more times than she could possibly count, but never before had she seen it in the way she did now. The outer stone walls were vast, no longer quaint, and the shop front seemed large enough to be a whole world unto itself. Occasionally, there were gaps in the sprawling ivy and beyond this, neat holes carved out amid the crumbling rock. This place was home to literally hundreds of faeries – like a grand faery housing estate. Betty Strudel's shop was swarming with little people. Rosie saw them now poking their heads out of their leaf trimmed doors and windows. They flew across the facet, calling out joyfully, exiting and entering from one another's doorsteps. How had she never noticed all this happening before? Had she really walked around so blind? And how did Mrs Betty Strudel actually live among this, ignorant of its secret beauty?

A pretty faery girl dressed in a yellow skirt, like the drooping head of a daffodil, floated down to them.

"Lace, Fire, it's so great to see you." She bowed down before Rosie in a curtsey. "And you, Your Royal Highness, we are honoured to make your acquaintance. My friends and I tried to speak with you at the party the other night but every time we tried one of the boys swept you away to dance. You looked very beautiful."

Rosie smiled shyly, her cheeks pink. "Thank you."

"Amber, you too look divine as ever." Lace embraced her. "We've come to ask you about the faery rings. As you know, we need one for Rosie's safe transfer back home within the next few days."

"Yes, sure, I'm already onto it. We've arranged for one in the most perfect location of all – Jemma Flower's garden! That way, if Guy happens to be home, you can call on him right away."

It still mystified Rosie that everyone here openly knew

about the situation between her and Guy and discussed it as commonplace knowledge. Back at home, her feelings for him had been top secret to anyone but Bill and Sal.

At that very moment two blissfully familiar human faces appeared by the red postbox at the bottom of the path. Although the tops of their shoes now came above her head, Rosie could never have mistaken her two best friends. Billie and Sally were making their way to the village shop. A warm smile spread across her face at the sight of them and despite herself Rosie began to wave excitedly and call out happy hellos. Her faery companions laughed at her futile display.

"They can't hear you," said Amber. "Gosh, when I think about the number of times the poor Agate family were trying to do that to you."

Rosie dropped her arms, deflated as she watched them disappear inside, the proverbial bell tinkling as the door swung to. "Yes, I know. It's just that I've missed them. I wish I could speak to them, if only just for a minute." She hung her head. "If the spell goes wrong I may never get the chance again."

"Well, if I remember rightly you used to be pretty darn good at changing your size. Why don't you give it a go now? See if you've still got the old faery magic in you." Amber winked encouragingly, a cheeky glint in her yellow eyes.

Rosie looked across at Lace to gage her opinion of this crazy suggestion. Lace shrugged. It seemed she had no major reservations.

Hesitantly, Rosie gazed down at the simple white cotton dress she was wearing. She guessed from reading her old diary that the garment would stretch with her. Although it wasn't the typical kind of thing Billie and Sally were used to seeing her in, it was at least not so odd that they'd think her insane. And of course anything was preferable to appearing in the post office naked. She took several deep breaths to steady herself, enormously conscious of the faery eyes all glued to her, waiting to see what would happen. Rosie concentrated hard on the soles of her bare feet and she began to imagine what it would be like for her legs to grow taller and taller until her toes were much further behind. As she did so it seemed that this unlikely concept really had begun to happen, and as she visualized the walls of the shop drawing level with her once more, they did indeed do so and the great feat was no longer in her mind.

Billie and Sally were perusing the chocolate bar aisle, but stopped in surprise when Rosie bounded energetically through the door.

"We just called on you. Where have you been?"

This question made Rosie laugh out loud. "I think it's more a case of where *haven't* I been? Oh, girls, I don't know where to start with all the things I have to tell you."

"Yeah, well, whatever." Billie rolled her eyes and Sally turned back to the sweets she was buying. It was clear that both of them had every intention of holding grudges.

"Bill, Sal, it feels so good to see you."

"To see us? Rosie, you haven't been interested in seeing us for months. Our band has virtually fallen apart because of you. You've given our music zero consideration for ages. For all you care, we've even been thinking of breaking it up. Sal and I might join with Des and Deano instead."

"What? No! Don't be ridiculous. We're a girl band, and in fact you couldn't be more wrong about me. I've been having some great ideas for the band. I've even written a whole new song. A complete one. I'm talking chorus and verses and no blank gaps left to fill. Oh, girls, I've got so much to share with you. You just wouldn't believe where I've been. And I've made some wonderful new friends. Amazing people. You would just love them."

"Rosie, when have you had time to meet friends? You haven't even been leaving the house."

"One of them is called Lace. And she's the coolest chick I know. She totally rocks!"

Billie scowled and scrunched up her face. "Lace, ha? Nice name."

"Yes, isn't it just? And she is so nice and kind and you'd get on so well with her. In fact, she'd be a brilliant addition to the band. She's so astoundingly pretty."

"Anyone'd think this mystery Lace girl means more to you than we do," Sally whispered under her breath as she turned a shiny wrapper round in her hands. But Rosie had heard her.

"No! No way, girls! That's impossible. You mean more to me than anything. And over the past week I've really started to realize that. Friends, *real* friends, are a sacred treasure and should never be taken for granted. True friends are so precious, far more important than a passing boy who could turn out to be nothing but a phase. Friends are always there through thick and thin. A boy may turn your head but also break your heart and a bona fide friend would never do that. Billie, Sally, I've missed you so much. You've been the greatest friends a girl could ever wish for and I don't know what I'd have done without you. I love you both and I want to say thank you for just being the wonderful people you are."

At this Rosie rushed forward and flung her arms around the pair of them, pulling them tight into a smothering bear hug.

After a moment of lung crushing through which none of them were able to draw a breath, the pack broke down and Billie and Sally were left with dazed expressions on their faces.

"She's crazy," Billie said.

"Yep, she's gone totally mad," Sally agreed.

"And by the way," said Billie, "What the bloody hell are you wearing?"

Before Rosie could explain, a flash of white drew her attention to the shop counter. The cat Spooky came prowling from behind it, padding softly but ominously on his sharp-clawed feet. Rosie instantly flapped her hands and screamed at the top of her voice. Her friends shot round to see the cause of such commotion.

"It's only that daft cat."

"For heaven's sake, Rosie, have you not got over that yet?"

But when Billie and Sally looked back around, Rosie had gone. One minute she'd been there and then the next she had disappeared, as though into thin air.

The truth of the matter was that she had quite suddenly and dramatically lost her size. She wasn't sure whether it was the unexpected scare that had broken her concentration or just the timing that had run out on her at a totally inopportune moment. Either way she was now two inches tall on the immense shop floor and Spooky towered in the distance – a giant furry monster. His ears pricked at the diminishing echo of her scream and then he pinned them back tight against his head in ultimate mission position. His eyes creased to tiger-like slits and he sat back on his haunches, ready to pounce.

Rosie screamed again in her tinier voice and opted for her automatic reaction to run. This however turned out to be the worse choice she could possibly have made, since the flicker of movement merely showed the cat where she was heading. Spooky let out a low feline growl and then gave chase in a canter.

"Rosie, Rosie, over here!" Amber's voice came from beneath a bottom shelf stacked with tinned vegetables. Rosie saw the yellow faery desperately beckoning her over with two other girls peeking out in panic by her side. Rosie guessed they were Ruby and Opal from the bright red and milky iridescent gowns. She ran full pelt towards them, knowing that her life really did depend on it, and on cue a memory danced through her brain of a summer's day in the Buttercup Fields with a runaway cow in hot pursuit. She wondered if Billie and Sally were anywhere near, knowing what was happening to her right now. Were they aware she was re-enacting that day they often joked about, right at this moment, down at their feet? Cat. Cow. It was all the same. Somehow she always managed to get tangled into these ludicrous situations. Except she still quite liked cows, whereas cats had always been the bane of her life. And now, that life was about to be ended by one...

Her foot hit a crack in the tiles and she tripped. Her heart did a somersault as her body followed suit and she fell with a thump, hitting her chin hard on the surface. Ignoring the pain, she quickly flipped herself over to judge Spooky's distance and how long she had left, but it was too late. The cat was above her, and if a cat were capable of grinning an evil, victorious smile it was doing so now as it pinned her tiny torso down with its foot. Spooky licked his lips and bared his sharp teeth terrifyingly close to her. Rosie could smell the horrible meat he had eaten for lunch hanging on his breath. *This is it*, she thought, *I'm about to be desert*. Everyone had always laughed at her cat phobia, except the faeries of course, but now even her human friends would see why.

Spooky was about to lap her up into his mouth with his slobbery, overhanging tongue, but something hit him square on the head. He turned in the direction it had come from, perturbed at the distraction. Another. Then another. They were bright, hard boiled sweets – 'Yorkshire Mixtures' and 'Rhubarb and Custards'. Lace and Fire were perched on the 'Pick and Mix' shelves by two tubs with their lids off, launching the contents right at the cat. Their aim was flawless. In anger, Spooky clean forgot about Rosie and now set off in the opposite direction, after his new prey.

Grabbing the opportunity to pick herself back up, Rosie bolted undercover to Amber, Opal and Ruby. They hugged her in relief, but their pleasure was short lived as they watched the cat career after their other friends. He had leapt onto a stool the optimum height to reach up to the sweet shelves.

"Use your wings!" Amber shouted. "Fly, Agates, fly!"

"It's all my fault," Rosie cried. "Now Lace and Fire are in danger because of me!"

He swiped at them with his paw but the sisters kicked their heels together and lifted themselves up into the air, leaving Spooky in an awkward hind legs dance. Mewing mardily while boxing his claws at nothing, the racket drew Mrs Betty Strudel from the side door which led to her living quarters. She looked cross to be disturbed from whatever she'd been watching on TV.

"What is it Spooky? What are you getting yourself so worked up about? I know we have customers, I'm going to see to them in a moment." She looked at the frustrated cat. "Wait a minute, I know what it is. It's those blasted faeries again isn't it?"

Rosie froze and turned to her companions in shock.

"She...she...knows about us?"

"Oh yeah," Amber sighed, "She knows alright."

The overweight shopkeeper struggled as she reached down below the counter and triumphantly drew out a blue plastic wasp swatter. She whacked it across the palm of her hand as if to emphasize the ferocity her apparatus was capable of.

"We've lost many friends this way."

"You mean she's killed them?" Rosie looked at the other faerie's faces in horror. "But, that doesn't make sense. Then why has she never told anyone else? Why has she never shown anyone a specimen? She could be world famous by now, not to mention filthy rich!"

Opal spoke in a sad whisper. "The dead bodies, Spooky usually gets to...although we have been able to steal away some poor souls in the past for a proper burial. Luckily up to now though – touch wood –, we've always managed to rescue the ones she gets alive. Simply telling people with an empty jam jar in her hand has never been quite enough solid evidence for old Betty. The authorities think she's mad."

Rosie was bewildered, but she had no chance to dwell on it as a pair of brown wrinkled stockings came storming down the aisle as Betty swung the wasp swatter to and fro like a psychopathic pendulum. Other faeries from the ivy wall estate had entered to check on their friends and it seemed that the old woman was encased in a shroud of fluttering spritely beings. She roared her displeasure, waving faster and scratching manically at her ears and throat as though she'd been plagued by mosquitoes.

"Get out! Get out you wretched creatures! I'll boil you all in a soup one day, you just see if I don't! Either that or I'll give you to my granddaughter to play with, and then you really will be sorry!"

Despite the danger it entailed, many of the faeries did enjoy taunting Mrs Betty Strudel. They just couldn't resist the opportunity to dangle themselves right before her very eyes and then zip themselves away before she had a chance to strike.

Amber, Opal and Ruby took the opportunity to fly over and check Lace and Fire were okay.

"Let's get out of here," they said. "I think we've had enough excitement for one day."

But although Rosie Quartz may have been a faery once, she was not, in reality, a faery now. The magic might have given her back a small portion of her powers, as growing to meet Sally and Billie had shown, but it had not given her everything. It had not given her wings.

While the other faeries gathered safely above human height at the shop roof, their quivering propellers keeping them aloft, Betty Strudel spied one tiny creature cowering on the ground beneath the shelf of tinned veg. With her face set in a determined frown, she dropped the wasp swatter and reached down to claim her prize.

Rosie was completely helpless as the bloated pink fingers closed tight around her waist.

"Ooo, I say, you're a disabled one! No wings, I declare! But you're still one of them though! You're no insect, missy. No butterfly or grasshopper I ever saw went and had itself such a pretty dress!"

With her free hand, Betty pinched at one of Rosie's ankles. She had her swinging upside down by one fragile foot. Rosie kicked with her other leg and thrashed her fists in pointless retort. Her stomach lurched as the floor disappeared below her and the shop walls spun as she was lifted to the counter.

"Let me go! Let me go!"

Betty did just that, but as Rosie's bottom hit the wooden surface, a prison of rounded glass came down beside her and she realized she was captured in an empty, upside down jam jar.

Rosie jumped to her feet and banged her palms against the glass, but her jail didn't budge. Every word she shouted was muffled and eaten up in the close confinement. She was trapped. Hopelessly defeated, she slunk against the sides, her back sliding down the slippery sphere.

She caught sight of Billie and Sally still in the shop and with one last surge of optimism she screamed and waved to get their attention. The girls didn't bat an eyelid. They were still glued to the spot where they'd watched the entire outrageous display.

"Did you hear her say 'faeries'? It was clearly just a swarm of bluebottles or something. That woman's loopy!"

"Never mind her, what about Rosie? I can't believe she just went off like that, after all she'd just said! She knew we'd been looking for her and we haven't seen her properly in ages. Then she just vanishes without even saying goodbye."

"And all those things she was telling us, it was totally weird!"

"About the Lace girl, yes."

"And the mushy stuff…"

"I thought she'd lost it before, but this is worse than we thought."

The pair shook their heads and turned to leave. The bell above the door tinkled its normal tune and then there was silence.

Mrs Betty Strudel had taken Spooky into the house by the scruff of his neck to try and calm him down. Rosie looked up as best she could through the magnified glass to see where the other faeries had gone. But there was no one left in sight. She was alone. She thought about what Opal had said. No live faery had ever been caught long enough for Betty to prove it to anyone else. Now it looked like she was going to be the first exception to the rule.

20

In Search of Sulphur

The Council were holding their meeting in the woodland clearing. The afternoon band were playing their shift as gently as possible, to compliment rather than disturb the deep thinking that was going on. Moss stood straight in the eye line of the Elders, confidently trying to answer every question they fired at him. He was just explaining how his sisters had taken Rosie to meet the ring distributors today, when Lace and Amber ran breathless through the border of wild flowers.

"Quick, you all have to come right now!"

Sir Fluorite ruffled his bushy, grey eyebrows at the rude interruption of Council matters. He banged his staff on the ground before aiming it angrily at the girls. "What in the good name of Lady Gaia do you think you are doing barging in like this? You know you are forbidden at an Elder gathering unless previously requested."

Lace stopped in her tracks and flung out her arm to stop her friend from skidding further ahead. "I know, wise Fluorite," she said apologetically, "please forgive our ungraceful intrusion, but there's an emergency! It's Rosie! She's in trouble!"

Amber added, distressed, "Betty Strudel has taken her prisoner in a jam jar. She's trapped and can't get out. We were too late to save her."

Madame Sodalite clapped her hands to her mouth and Sir Rhodonite began to stutter incoherent questions in panic. Fluorite on the other hand just continued to look furious.

"See what's happened now!" he thundered. "Ever since she returned to Faery Land that girl has done nothing but cause disruption and danger. We need to get her home to her own world as soon as possible. She's wreaking havoc. And you're just as much to blame, Moss Agate."

Moss had already turned in the direction of the rescue, ready to rush to Rosie's aid, but Sir Fluorite's words drew him back.

"It is quite apparent to all of us that you've fallen in love with the girl – an absolutely ludicrous situation, which is quite beyond your remit. You were entrusted with doing what's best for Rosie and all of the Faery Kingdom, not furthering your own feelings. The way you've been acting towards her was not part of your job description and I'm appalled at your behaviour."

Moss hung his head in shame. "I know. I'm sorry. It won't happen again, Sir Fluorite. As soon as we have Rosie safely back from the post office, I'll escort her myself to the faery ring and ensure she gets to Guy Flower in one piece. Then I'll never mention her name again. I promise."

Rosie Quartz felt scared and alone. Countless times she had tried to free herself, but without the momentum of a run up to the glass, there was no way she could overturn the jar on her own. She felt her eyes begin to smart and against her better wishes she started to cry. Her deep sobs were so loud that at first she didn't hear her name whispered repeatedly from the other side of the counter. It was only when she caught sight of the orange glow of hair by the till drawer that she realized she hadn't been deserted after all. Fire Agate had been crouched in hiding all the time. Quickly, Rosie sniffed up her tears through her nose and smiled at the welcome sight of the faery girl.

"Fire, oh, Fire, it's you! Thank goodness."

"I wouldn't be thanking anyone just yet, if I were you. You're still stuck in that thing, and there's no telling how easy it's gunna be to get you out. For all we know you're as good as on your way to the Natural History Museum with a display pin through your belly button and the back of some ornate frame crushing your butt cheeks."

Rosie sighed. "Fire, I just need some help tipping this jar over. I can't get a swing at it on my own. I thought everyone had gone. I'm so glad to see you. How come you're still here?"

"Well, someone had to wait, didn't they? Anything could've happened. You're just lucky the old bat left you on the counter." Fire was still by the till, a good meter away, but now she stood and leaned one casual arm over the lip of the drawer.

"Do you think we can do it, Fire? Do you think you can get me out?"

Fire studied her fingernails as though the careful maintenance of them were the most important chore in the world right now. "Depends..."

"On what?"

"Depends whether I want to or not."

There was a long pause while Rosie thought about what she had said. Both girls looked down at the counter floor in silence, until all of a sudden Rosie surprised Fire by bursting into laughter.

"Oh Fire, I know you're having me on!"

"Am I?" Fire wrinkled her face in genuine astonishment.

"Of course you are. You go around acting as though you don't like me, and I've never understood why. You give me evil looks and make sarcastic comments and give me the cold shoulder. But deep down, I know it's just a front. I reckon you're actually quite fond of me. I'll bet we could be the best of friends, you and I. For a start, you wouldn't be here now if you didn't care."

Fire ran her fingers through her spiky orange hair at least a dozen times. For the first time since Rosie had met her, the faery looked legitimately at a loss as to what to say. When she finally found the words she stammered her response.

"I...I...already told you. Somebody...one of us...had to stay with you. It was quite obvious that you weren't going to get out of there on your own."

"Exactly. And that person was *you*. You of *all* people, Fire Agate. Why not Lace? She'd be the obvious choice. Or even

Amber who I've only just met – even she's a more likely candidate than *you*. You hid behind that till while the others went to get help, because you were worried about me. You decided you were going to help me yourself."

Even as she made her speech, Rosie did have the terrible feeling that maybe she was entirely wrong and Fire had not had any of these inclinations at all. There was, of course, the chance that she'd stayed by the till purely in fear of being spotted and that she positively hated Rosie's guts. But it was worth a shot.

"Look missy," Fire now shot at her, hands on hips, "let's get one thing straight. You and I will never be the best of friends. I am not secretly fond of you and I was not worried about you. You're right about only one thing and that's that yes – I did decide to stay and rescue you. But not because I like you. Not because you ever have the slightest chance of me ever liking you. I'm getting you out for one reason only. And that's 'cos it's the right thing to do…That and 'cos Moss would kill me if I didn't. So I'm doing it for him too."

This was not the great reconciliation Rosie had hoped for, but for now, it would have to do. It was at least one step closer to freedom.

Fire spat on the palms of her hands, rubbed them together and then lifted each leg in turn to smear the saliva onto the bottoms of her brown sandals. She took a deep, lung-packing breath, and then sprinted at the speed of light across the counter, barging into the side of the glass with her bare shoulder. *Smack!* The jar tottered slightly, rocking on its base, but nothing more. Not enough for Rosie to nip under in time.

"Try again, try again!" said Rosie. "This time I'll push it from the inside too."

It ended up taking three attempts of the same routine before the impact got the better of the prison and the jar came right over, clean above Rosie's head. It rolled off the counter and smashed into pieces on the hard tiles below.

"Quick, before Strudel hears and comes out into the shop," Fire shouted, reaching out a hand.

Rosie grabbed it and the pair of them swooped up into the air, carried to the open window by Fire's capable wings.

"Thanks," said Rosie, not bothering to look down or behind. "Thanks so much for saving me. I really owe you one."

Fire's face was set in a sullen frown. "Yeah, well, like I said, I did it for Moss. Not you".

The girls had walked through the woodland in uncomfortable silence for a long while. They were heading to the Council clearing, since that's where Fire presumed the rest of her family would be. Every time Rosie had tried to make polite or appreciative conversation, the faery had either snapped harsh one-word answers or completely ignored her altogether. Hence the unpleasant atmosphere as they travelled.

"How come you don't fly everywhere?" Rosie asked, trying once again to break the strain. "I'd never walk a step if I had wings."

"You don't have wings."

"I know that, but I mean *if* I did. And presumably *once* I did. I know that the faeries my age, my *human* age, are not allowed to fly out of school hours till they're fully graduated, but why don't the over-sixteens just soar around to their heart's content?"

"Do you catch a bus every single place you go?"

"No. Moss said that about the sparrows, but..."

"Well then."

Rosie struggled to see the connection but pressed the matter no more. Instead she thought of something else to discuss.

"Fire, how come the..."

"For Gaia's sake!" Fire stopped in her tracks and spun on Rosie with venom in her eyes. "Do you never shut up? When will you get the message that I don't want to talk to you? The sooner you're through that toadstool ring the better. And then you can leave us all alone. Stay away and don't come back. And while we're on the subject, let me make something else perfectly clear. Stay away from my brother – as in well away."

"What? Moss? What on earth do you mean?" Rosie began to

feel the dreaded wet pinpricks at the corners of her lashes.

"Moss is a typical faery male. He's a flirt and a player. Nothing more. He doesn't care about you. He's doing his job, that's all. In fact, like me, he probably can't wait for you to clear off so he can get back to his own life. We do all have our own lives you know, not that you'd care!"

Rosie tried to fight it, but the knife was too sharp. Fire's onslaught had pierced her straight in the heart. She burst into tears for the second time today. But the faery girl hadn't finished.

"There's no wonder the Faery King and Queen met such a horrid end. They were distraught after you so selfishly left and their minds were a million miles away from the safety of the Kingdom. They were miserable, weak and vulnerable – a perfect opportunity for Sulphur to strike. Fluorite still blames Sulphur's actions on you."

Rosie was hysterical now and her words came out as gut-wrenching sobs. "What do you know about Sulphur and my parents, Fire? Was it my fault? Was it? No one will tell me what truly happened and I need to know before I go back home. Tell me. Tell me!"

Fire faced her with no shame. "Everything's your fault, Rosie Quartz. Everything."

Rosie let out one last devastated cry and then ran in the opposite direction from where they'd been heading. Fire saw her tear through the weeds and leap over stones, crashing into nature's obstacles but still gaining speed as she went.

Once out of sight, Rosie drew level with a large jutting rock and flung herself down at its side to hide in the shadow it provided. Ignorant of her camouflage, Fire flew on ahead.

"Rosie! Rosie, where are you going? Wait! Come back! Rosie, I'm sorry. I didn't mean it. I shouldn't have said those things. I don't know what I was thinking. It was all rubbish. Rosie, wait, come back, please!"

But Fire realised her call was wasted and she had lost track of the girl. She dropped to the grass with her head in her hands. She felt terrible. How could she have been so stupid? And what unbearable consequences would she have to face when she was forced to recount her deceitful words to Moss?

Of one thing she was sure, Rosie Quartz had had enough. She was fed up with being seen as a burden, or worse still, a charity case. Either way it seemed her presence in this miniature world was a disaster and while she walked among them, she would inevitably cause trouble for the Agates. She emerged from the shadows and picked up a determined stride. Her tears subsided, and her devastation morphed from upset to red-hot anger. When all was said and done, she was the human being here and therefore she should be the one in control. Humans were the superior race of the planet, weren't they? And the majority of the human population didn't even believe in faeries. So how had she come to let one of these supposed imaginary creatures hurt her feelings so much? Fire shouldn't upset her. Sulphur shouldn't scare her. Lace shouldn't calm her. And Moss shouldn't excite her. Moss, oh, Moss. She didn't even want to think about him right now.

Her mind was made up. There were things she had to do and she had to do them alone. It was time to end this once and for all. But Rosie, with years of human etiquette instilled by her parents, could not just disappear without leaving a note. Mumbling aloud exactly how she would word it, she picked her way down the path to the Agate Abode.

She'd not considered how she would play this if they were home, but lucky for her, the tree stump and all three of its birdhouses were empty. The climb up to the porch was long and hard without faery wings, and several times she stumbled, cutting her shins on the bark. Once in the dining hall, she stood still a long while, breathing in the lavender smell. She glanced at the organized kitchen on the right and the assortment of armchairs on the left. She drank in the titles in the bookcase and the magnificent carved table where they'd sat to eat breakfast every morning. All of these simple things she had come to love. And all of these things she must now leave behind.

She went up to Moss's room and got her old clothes out of the wardrobe. The white t-shirt and grey knitted cardigan, the pink trainers and white cotton shorts. She left the pretty dress she'd borrowed folded neatly by the pillow on the bed. Back in the main house she reached into a drawer and pulled out a leaf pad and charcoal to write with. There were candles and matches in there also, so she stuffed these in the back pockets of her shorts and hoped they'd serve her later.

Dear Lace and Moss, (she wondered whether to add Fire's name and then decided against it)
as we all know, I don't have long until the date of my human thirteenth birthday. You have done your jobs well in ensuring I know what it is I must do. I know where the faery ring lies and I'm more than capable of finding my own way back to Guy to determine whether the spell shall be sealed or broken. Things will be as they must be, but I thank you sincerely for all the help and kindness you have showed me so far. I promise I will do my upmost to put things right and try and make up for any past grievances I've caused. Before I leave there is one last thing I intend to do. I hope it can, in some small way, resolve the harm I brought the Faery Kingdom and alleviate the tragedy I inflicted upon your King and Queen. Please do not come looking for me. Please do not follow. I do this for you. I do it for the Elders. And I do it in the name of my parents.

Rosie scrawled her signature with a kiss, and then set off to find Sulphur.

21

Michael Depth

Rosie could not whistle, but she decided to give it a try. Her effort resembled something more like a grass snake hissing or a silly parent blowing a raspberry to a baby. It definitely didn't have the same effect as when Moss had done it. She tried placing her fingers in her mouth as he had done, but to no avail. No thunderous paws echoed through the Woods. In the end, she took her chances and plunged for the simpler option. She cleared her lungs and shouted at the top of her voice. "STRAWBERRY! STRAWBERRY!"

And just like that, she was there. Rosie beamed with joy and threw her arms around the rabbit.

"You came baby, you came."

Her furry friend nuzzled her gently and she reached up to scratch her nose.

"I have a favour to ask you, Strawberry. Remember when we rode like the wind through the woodland on that amazing ride? I'll never forget it. You were so fantastic. Well, I want us to do that again. I need you to take me somewhere now. I need you to take me to the Crag Mines."

Strawberry's lop ears defied their natural law of gravity and stood up alert. It was clear she was exceptionally uneasy about this. Rosie felt her hesitance.

"I really need you to do this one thing for me girl. What about all those carrots and tummy rubs I gave you so often, back in the day? Well, let's just say, this is my pay back."

Slowly the rabbit lowered herself to a position from where Rosie could step on a nearby stone and edge herself onto the soft back.

"Come on then, let's do this."

Rosie hardly ever went to Lock Marshland, even as an adventurous schoolgirl with Billie and Sally, so to head there now as a faery was daunting, to say the least. It was in the middle of nowhere and once you reached the nowhere, there was nothing much of anything to see. Lock Marshland was known as a farming area, but it was dull, uncultivated and barren. It was hardly surprising that the home of the goblins should be set in this dreary, distant cousin of Steeple. It could have been purely psychological, but Rosie was sure that as they neared its border the sky grew darker and the air turned colder. Strawberry slowed and with each step now seemed to quiver against her will. Rosie patted her neck in reassurance.

A filthy road sign set at their level swayed ominously ahead of them. Two boards of rotten wood swayed on rusty chains from a post. They squeaked eerily in the breeze. One had an arrow pointing left that read, 'PATH OF WICKEDNESS'. One had an arrow pointing right that read 'PATH OF RIGHTEOUSNESS'. Both Rosie and her pet knew which way they'd like to be heading, but if they were still intent on reaching the Crag Mines, it was the other path they must take.

In the spindly, silhouetted trees above them, flocks of jet-black crows sat watching their every move. Their heads seemed to turn three hundred and sixty degrees so as not to miss an inch as the girl and the rabbit made their way up the jagged hill.

Rosie steered Strawberry in and out of low hanging branches with mean, crooked fingers which reached out to grab them. Occasionally, dark shapes appeared beside them, and Rosie realized the hill was also home to a swarm of black rats. She'd never particularly minded rats, but these squirmed and scuttled aggressively, and like the crows, she supposed they were one of the few creatures happy to give up their souls to the dark side by working for Sulphur.

At the peak of the hill, a pile of unevenly stacked stones spilled out across the worn grass. To a human, it could have been no more than a messy, untended garden rockery. To Rosie, it loomed menacingly high like a mountain. At the base was a hole which served as an entrance – the mouth of a tunnel which wound deep underground to a series of secret caves. Rosie knew they must finally have reached the Crag Mines.

She jumped down and tried to show Strawberry a confident smile which meant she'd be okay. Her pet couldn't squeeze past here and nor would she want her to. "Wait at the bottom of the hill, girl. All being well, I'll see you really soon. But if by any chance you sense I've been too long then you must return to Steeple. Above all else, do not put yourself in danger. If you feel threatened at any time, then run! Don't wait around for me, is that clear?"

Rosie had begun to understand that she could have said all this telepathically to the animal and there was no need to speak her words out loud, but she still hadn't quite got total faery faith just yet. Regardless, Strawberry understood and cautiously picked her way back down the slope.

As Rosie entered the passage she remembered Moss saying that anyone but a goblin would get lost in here and never find their way out again. It was so dark that there were no means of telling whether it was night or day and she quickly forgot the fresh air she'd breathed outside just moments ago. She felt for the candles and matchsticks in her back pocket. It took several attempts to strike the match against the potholed surface. When she succeeded and the caves came dancing to life in an orange glow, she wished she had left the place dark. The walls were bubbled like brain cells and the further the path wound down, the faster dirty streams of water coursed through the grooves like blood through veins. Too late to suppress the natural scream which escaped her, Rosie clasped her hands over her mouth to quash its echo. She was surrounded by an endless multitude of skulls and skeleton bones. Hollow faces with deep, empty eyes and cracked, splintered ribcages layered the surfaces in odd arrangements so they were no longer quite the bodies of the people they had once been. With shaky fingers, she carried the candle at arms length and tried to look beyond the devastating reminder of the poor souls who had joined her parents as Sulphur's conquests.

The tunnel dropped suddenly, and Rosie swayed to keep balance. Silvery stalactites and stalagmites now shimmered above and beside her and despite her fear she found herself pausing at their strange beauty. She held her candle nearer to the walls and saw the surface was smoother. Carved pictures had been ground into the rock here, ones like the images in Daniel Quartz's Aboriginal history books. The rough scrapings showed black beings as stick men in various throws of fighting, mining and war. It was the story of the goblin's banishment from the Faery Kingdom and their subsequent plight.

Rosie heard footsteps. There was someone behind her. She spun round and the noise stopped. Cautiously, she carried on. But there it was again. Definitely behind her. In the recess of shadow where her candle wouldn't reach.

"Who's there?" her voice echoed loud, bouncing back at her from all sides.

Then she registered just a pinprick of light ahead, but it grew to two large saucer shapes blinking on and off inquisitively. These were joined by another pair. Then another. She looked back and saw there were now literally hundreds of these glowing circles, suspended in mid air. They were eyes. Big yellow eyes crowding around her and watching her in the dark. Rosie gasped in horror and dropped the candle as suddenly she was swarmed. Sharp, pinching fingers scratched at her arms and legs. She had no time to react or retaliate. They lifted her clean off the ground and she was tossed onto a ragged stretcher, barely held together with old sack and sticks. There was a sickly, pungent smell and Rosie fought the urge to vomit as her waist was coiled tight to the stretcher with spiky cord.

They began to move. Whatever *they* were, they set off at a frantic pace with her tied, defenceless above them. "Stop! Wait! Please! What's going on? My name's Rosie Quartz and I've come to see Sulphur." Although the string cut into her skin, she twisted her body to sneak a glance at her kidnappers. Through the dark she began to see that they were black, brown, green and grey. Their charred skin looked mud-splattered and infected. Their ears, noses, chins and elbows were pointed and unnaturally long. Each had revolting deformities which set them quite apart from the next – forked tails, webbed feet, blistered cheeks, razor teeth, drooling gums, sprouting horns, missing limbs…They were the ugliest and evilest things she had ever seen and every last one of them looked perfectly capable of murdering her right then and there on the spot. She screamed a bloodcurdling sound as the severity of her bleak situation sunk in. She had been captured by goblins.

The largest one at the head of the stretcher turned at her outburst and slapped her strikingly hard across the face. Rosie blacked out.

She came to in an enormous open cavern. Immense crystals glimmered in the rock surface. The army of goblins had gone and she was no longer tied to the uncomfortable stretcher. She flexed fingers sore from the struggle and rubbed her back which felt tender and twisted. Her face smarted from the slap, but she was still in one piece. The floor was hard and cold but no restrictions held her in place. She was free to stand and acknowledge the grand, high-backed chair turned away from her at the opposite end of the space. A figure sat in this chair. She could hear its steady breathing even from here. She could see the outline of a pair of arms resting on the elaborate golden sides of the throne and a pair of immaculately polished black shoes tapped up and down on the ground. But she couldn't see a face. The faceless man began to speak.

"What a lovely surprise that you decided to pay me a call." A pause. "You know I sent my head crow, Zombie, out to search for you. He bore an invitation which requested you visit for supper. Any time, at your convenience. Turns out you saved him the trouble." He laughed. "To what do we owe this unexpected pleasure, Miss Rosie Quartz?"

The voice was nothing like she had expected. It was much younger, full of youth and enthusiasm. It was somehow almost… normal!

What had she wanted Sulphur to sound like? Gruff? Angry? Monstrous? Well if the goblins she'd seen were anything to go by, he would certainly look like a monster. She shuddered, remembering their awfulness, and mentally prepared herself to be terrified when the leader of these creatures turned round. She tried to stay calm. She would refuse to let him see how much his face frightened her.

Slowly, he rose to his feet. The chair moaned beneath him and his shoes clicked as he walked round into the light. Rosie held her breath and squeezed her eyes tight shut. She planned on reopening them just a little at a time. As she did so she had an extraordinary shock. The man standing in front of her was… GORGEOUS. He was jaw-droppingly handsome. He spelled out style from every stitch of his chicly tailored couture. He oozed good looks from every pore of his being. Rosie choked on her mammoth mistake. How skewed could one's preconceptions be? Had she come to the wrong place? He took a chivalrous bow.

"Welcome. I'm the one they call Sulphur."

He had glossy, black hair swept across his forehead in a thick quiff, and piercing blue eyes which twinkled mischievously in a perfect olive complexion. He wore a full black tailcoat suit with a bright yellow waistcoat and matching cravat. A fresh yellow rose poked out of his top buttonhole and a silk scarf hung open round his neck, also in a garish bright yellow. He looked dazzlingly cheerful and wealthy.

Rosie remembered seeing Guy Flower for the first time and the effect he'd had on her. Unbelievably, the evil creature who had murdered her parents and cast relentless fear over Faery Land, was now provoking a similar reaction. She was lost for words. How could this be possible? She guessed from his boyish good looks, and masculine frame that he was around nineteen or twenty years old. Just a little older than her faery age. And he was one of the most beautiful things she had ever seen in her life.

It was like being hypnotized and trying to fight it. In her mind she argued with herself to stay focused. She had to remember why she was here. She had come for answers and she'd come for revenge. This man had killed and she had to know why.

But he was the one doing the talking.

"If you don't mind me saying, you are very beautiful."

Rosie felt her cheeks flush at the compliment.

"Just like your mother. Ah, Snow Quartz. You remind me of her. I was so very fond of your mother, you know."

Rosie found her voice at his impertinent mention of the Faery Queen.

"Fond of her? You *murdered* her!"

He laughed again. A rich, velvet sound. "Is that what they're telling you? Back in the winged world?"

Rosie had noticed that the goblins, including Sulphur, did not have wings. "So you're saying you didn't?"

"No. Not exactly."

His carefree approach to the serious matter infuriated her. "You either did or you didn't."

"Okay, okay, so I did. But she deserved it."

The cruel retort hit her like a blow to the stomach. "You demon! How dare you!"

"You have no idea what she did to me!" Sulphur raised his own tone for the first time. "What your parents put me through! You haven't the slightest clue about anything. You're nothing but a pathetic little child."

The perfect vision had lost its charm and Rosie ran at him, bearing her fists and pounding his chest with all her might. Sulphur shouted indecipherable words of magic and the spell shot her back with a slam against the wall. Winded, she dropped to her knees. Sulphur returned to his calm and collected, almost bemused conversation.

"You know, I said they call me Sulphur, but that isn't my real name. My real name is Michael. Michael Depth. I've not been down here for so long that I've forgotten my roots, my true identity, my past. My history and origins are still very important to me. I once was a man, a human just like you."

"You could never be a man. You're nothing but a monster and always will be."

He raised his eyebrows in mock offence. "Shame to end our little tête-à-tête on such a bad note. You do realize don't you, that I have no option now but to kill you? Apparently, a legend has it that you're the only one with the power to defeat me and for that reason I'm afraid I mustn't put myself at risk. However harmless you may seem, I have to dispose of you while I have the chance."

Rosie focused once again on why she was here, why she had come. She knew the things Sulphur – Michael – whoever – was saying only too well. The power. The something unique inside which she alone possessed. Part of her royal bloodline. The white light. How it was supposed to reflect and shatter evil. She concentrated hard on the area around his heart, narrowing her eyes in determination. She imagined Sulphur exploding into a million pieces under her stare. But nothing happened.

"You foolish girl! Did you honestly think you were going to walk in here, kill me and then walk out again as simply as that? Was that your grand plan? What are they teaching these young people at Steeple High School these days?"

Rosie flinched at the mention of her school. How did this underground goblin know so much about her in both of the worlds she straddled? He unnerved and intimidated her. And, infuriatingly, fascinated her.

Michael Depth produced a knife from his inside pocket. The blade could have sliced a falling sheet of silk and the metal twinkled like the crystals in the cavern. He made his way over to the frightened girl and came to stand behind her. Gently he wound one arm around her waist and rested his hand on her stomach. The other held the knife tilted at her throat. Softly he whispered in her ear.

"While I'm behind you, your magic won't work. Our battle must take place eye to eye." He traced the knife across her white skin. It tickled. "What a waste. You are so pretty. So like your mother."

Last thoughts and final wishes flashed through her head. What a mess she'd made of things yet again. In a crazy bid to avenge parents she couldn't even remember having met, she had jeopardized her chances of ever seeing her human parents again. Daniel and Debra Quartz had been her world, her everything, prior to life shrinking and turning upside down. Now she had no chance of saying goodbye. There was no chance of ever getting Guy back. No chance of saying how sorry she was to Lace and Fire and Moss. Fire had been right. They had all wasted their time on her. She was useless. A hopeless case.

Sulphur angled the blade and the knife sliced down across her delicate throat. Hot blood trickled from collarbone to breast. She experienced no pain. In fact, the exact opposite, she felt a warm calmness consume her. She grew weak and faint in Sulphur's arms and slipped from his grasp to the floor.

So this was how it felt to die – though her heavy eyelids hung on a little while longer to take in every last detail of the scene. Her final image was of someone else appearing at the entrance to the cavern. Moss…Moss Agate…wonderful, perfect, heroic Moss. This was surely just hallucination. A mirage in the throes of death. Wishful thinking of what she most desired at this moment. But wait – no. There was a struggle. A fight between him and Sulphur. Other male faeries rushed in now, too. They joined the resistance and held Sulphur to the wall. The Elders were there – Fluorite, Hematite, Rhodonite – the goblin army were upon them but flying sparks of magic somehow kept them at bay.

Moss…Moss above her…looking down at her. He held her head in his hands. She smiled. He was the last beautiful image she saw as her vision blurred and her eyes slipped out of focus.

She faded away.

22

The Return?

In and out. In and out of dreams. Dreams of darkness and evil. A pain beyond imagining burning in the chest. Tossing and turning. Coughing, spluttering. Snatches of distant melody and song...

And there are times I fear we'll never make it,
This dream's so real, I'm almost scared to break it...

Kicking and screaming. Throwing off covers. Rosie woke with a start at the Agate Abode.

She was in Moss's bed. She had a damp cloth tied to her head and one pressed at her neck. A crowd of faeries surrounded her. Some were unfamiliar faces. Others she knew only too well – the Elders, Amber, Opal and Ruby, Peridot and Jasper. And then Fire, Lace and Moss. They all applauded her first moment of consciousness.

Lace ran to her side, knocking other bodies out of the way. Gently, she perched on the edge of the bed and held her hand. "Don't rush to wake, Rosie, you're still very weak. You need to take it easy."

"Lace, what happened?"

Fire stepped forward and cut in. "You're lucky to be alive girl!" But there was none of the usual malice in her tone. In fact, she too came and sat at the opposite side of the bed, and even took Rosie's other hand.

Rosie yawned and found herself drifting back to sleep.

*

Later that evening she was able to prop herself up on a pile of cushions and sip the dandelion tea which Lace had left her on the bedside table. The room was quiet. Her horde of visitors was gone.

Moss tapped on the doorframe before entering. "Hey, how are you feeling?"

"Hey. Loads better, thanks."

There followed an uncomfortable silence before Rosie finally spoke again.

"Moss, I don't know what to say. If it hadn't been for you... You saved my life. I don't know how I can ever repay you...But in the process I risked yours and everyone else's. I was so stupid, so thoughtless and careless. People could have been killed. I'm so, so sorry."

"All that matters is that you're alright. Rosie, I thought we'd lost you..."

He leant over and the pair of them embraced.

"Moss, what happened to Sulphur? Where is he now?"

"Same place he always is. The Elders' strength and magic could only sustain him for so long, but at least it was enough to get you out of there."

Rosie looked away, out of the window. So it was all for nothing. She'd risked her own life and that of the other faeries for absolutely nothing. Sulphur still walked free. She shook her head, unable to believe it.

"Moss, he was nothing like I expected...Sulphur. He was..."

"I know."

This answer seemed to be enough.

"Why did you come after me? I told you in the letter not to."

"Are you kidding? Knowing how unsafe it was? Do you honestly think I was going to listen to you? And Strawberry came back to tell us you were in danger."

"Strawberry! Is she okay?"

"Strawberry's just fine. She's a tough old rabbit. You can see her later. I know she'll be desperate to check up on you."

"Was anyone else hurt?"

"Nothing that can't be healed. We've put Barberry Juice on your neck wound. It's doing okay. Your strength seems to be back up, though it's taken time. Wherever possible, the Elders have tried to manipulate the passage of the clock and mould it to suit our requirements, but there's only so much even they can do. You've been out of action for months."

"What?" This triggered Rosie's hazy memory. "Months? Moss, the thirteenth of April! What date is it? Have I run out of time?" She clapped her hands to her mouth.

"No, Rosie, you're not too late. It's still the morning you left. You've been gone only an hour. Amber still has the faery ring in Jemma's garden. You can still get to Guy in plenty of time. All you have to do is tell him you love him and I'm sure he'll say the same thing too. It's all salvable. But if I were you I'd go now, before you think about getting yourself into any further scrapes."

Rosie peeled the sheets back from her body and her heart was beating faster. "Moss, before I do go, there are some things I need to know." Shakily, she got to her feet. "Before I went in search of Sulphur, Fire and I, we had a row, an argument. She said some things…"

"Rosie, please don't dwell on that." Moss offered a hand to steady her uncertain steps. "You know what Fire's like. She told me what she said. I know it may be hard to believe, but she really didn't mean them."

"I don't blame her, Moss. I know that since I came here all I've caused is trouble. She said Fluorite blames me for the King and Queen's death."

"Fluorite is the wisest, most ancient faery in all of the Land. Do you seriously think a man of that stature would be petty enough to hold such childish grudges?"

"No, I guess not."

"No. Fire said those things to provoke a reaction from you. But she got more than she bargained for, and that's her fault. She means well really, you know. She just has her own unique *little ways*. She takes some getting to know. She's been through a lot, as a little girl. There's a lot of history there that plays its part.

Maybe I'll get the chance to tell you about it someday."

"Maybe. I'd like that. And, Moss, one last thing. Fire, she said…she said that you were just doing your job by caring for me and that you'd be glad when I'd gone home so you could get on with your own life…"

"Rosie…"

"Is that true, Moss?"

"What do you think?"

"I'd like to think it was just another one of Fire's *little ways*."

"Well then you'd be right. Rosie, I can't begin to tell you how much we'll all miss you when you're gone. It's been a pleasure getting to know you. Lace will be inconsolable. She's come to think of you as a second sister. All of Faery Land have loved having you here. But most of all…most of all…*I* will miss you beyond imagining."

"Oh stop it! I'm no good at goodbyes."

"Well shut up, we best not do one then. Except with Lace. She'll go mental if you leave without telling her. She'll need hugging at least a thousand tearful times. You better not deny her that, she'll never forgive you."

Rosie lay face down in the sweet-smelling, freshly-mown grass. Beside her was a grey wheelie bin with a number seventeen on it. This everyday, human object did not tower over her like a mountain on the skyline. It was completely in proportion to her own body. She was back to her regular size. This was Guy's garden and she saw the tiny circle of toadstools, quite indiscernible among un-mown clumps of weeds at the hard to reach edges. She remembered her last brief encounter with this bin when she and Jemma had first met – the day of Doris's tragic end. That all seemed so long ago now.

Rosie flipped herself over and for a moment just enjoyed lying on her back, basking in the sunshine, listening to the birds. The world seemed at peace. As if on cue, Guy came out of the front door, spotted her strange position and presence, and ran to her side. Before she had a chance to register what was happening, he had leant over her and was pouring his heart out.

"Rosie, I'm so happy to see you. You can't believe what an amazing coincidence this is. I was just thinking about you!"

Coincidence or not, he seemed to have totally accepted the bizarreness of her having somehow just turned up on his lawn. As if by magic!

"I've been thinking a lot recently, and I've made some huge realizations. Helena Spotswood is not the one for me. I've missed you, Rosie. There's no one else like you. You're all I can ever think about. I miss your smile, your warmth, your friendliness and your crazy sense of humour. You're fun and you laugh a lot. We were brilliant together. I don't know what I was thinking when things ended between us. All I know is I'm going to break up with Helena. And if there was any chance that you could ever forgive me and take me back and want to be with me again... well, that would be wonderful. I think I love you. Well, I know I do. I love you, Rosie." Guy pressed his lips down upon her own and kissed her.

Rosie was too shocked to respond. The sensations ringing through her body were not purely emotional but also physical – a tingling like pins and needles began in her cheeks and travelled through her blood right to the tips of her toes. She was sure she saw jumping sparks of white light in the grass blades around them. She felt warm and floaty, like she was levitating inches above the ground. It was a heavenly feeling, cocooned in total satisfaction like a rounded conclusion.

Guy took her wistful smile as an invitation to steal another kiss.

"You know, I always thought it was strange how we both shared the same birth date. I've never met an April the thirteenther before, let alone one the exact same age as me. In a way, I always found it a bit creepy, like maybe it really was destiny for us to be together or something, you know like your weird friend said. But joking apart, maybe there is something written in the stars for us. And maybe we could still have that big joint party we talked of!"

Rosie sat up straight. "Guy, wait, rewind, before all that, a bit back. You just said you loved me."

"Yeah, yeah, I did. I know it might sound a bit extreme. I know we're only young, but I really do mean it, Rosie. Why else can I not get you out of my mind? You mean the world to me. I do love you."

She stayed deathly still for a long time and allowed the words just to pour over her like she'd taken a shower in them. She'd done it. She'd achieved it. Madame Apatite's spell had worked. The Fortune Teller would be proud. But…There was a but…and it changed everything…

"Guy, that's wonderful. It's so nice and it's so flattering to hear you say. After all, you're so perfectly handsome and charming, the most good looking boy – and grown man for that matter – that I've ever, ever met. Any girl would fall over themselves to have you, just like I did. But the only thing is…the problem is… I don't love you."

She stood up, leaving him dazed on the grass. "You see, I love someone else. I love someone else very much indeed. And in fact, I need to get back to him right now."

Guy could only stare in silent, stunned shock as she began to pace determinedly to the edge of the garden and the faery ring.

"See ya', Guy. And thank you. Thank you for all the valuable life lessons you've taught me."

He couldn't be sure, but Guy Flower was convinced that Rosie Quartz then just vanished straight into thin air, right before his eyes. He rubbed his floppy yellow fringe out of the way to double check. Yep, she'd gone.

"Rosie Quartz. What a girl! Only she could just have gone and done something like that!"

She knew exactly where she was heading. She remembered the route, but she didn't run. She wanted to savour every moment of her walk to the Can.

Moss was stretched out on the dandelion. She stood beneath his private gym and observed him. He was staring into empty space. He looked lost, sad and alone. She'd never once considered him vulnerable, but everyone has their moments, she supposed. She thought she'd been inconspicuous but his astute faery ears had heard someone approach.

"Go away, Sis. You know not to be here."

"Moss, it's me, Rosie."

"Rosie? Oh no! What in the name of Lady Gaia happened? The spell! Did it not work? You still have more time you know, it's not too late. We'll work it out. I'll take you to the Fortune Teller. She'll sort it. She has to. There's got to be another way!"

"Moss, Moss, calm down. The spell worked just fine. He said the words and I felt the magic. I could have remained my human self forever and things could have carried on just like they were before."

"Well, that's great. But then…Why?…What are you doing here now? At your faery size? I don't understand."

"Moss, I didn't say the words back. I didn't tell Guy I loved him too. In fact I did the exact opposite and told him that I now know I don't love him at all. I think that pretty much went and rendered the spell completely redundant."

"Rosie, what were you thinking? What have you done? What happens now?"

"Just shut up, will you? I don't have a clue what happens now. We'll just have to wait and see. A little faith goes a long way. Especially in Faery Land. And anyway, Moss Agate, something is telling me, that this is not the moment for words. Are you going to give me a hand up there, or what?"

Moss had been peering down at her anxiously all the while from the dandelion and Rosie had a strained neck from calling up. Slowly his frown creased into an all-consuming smile.

"I don't think I need to, Rosie. Look…You have wings!"

Rosie glanced over her shoulder and was startled to see two vast pillars of fluorescent white light, vibrating in luscious splendour behind her. She gasped, wondering how and when it could have happened without her noticing, but it felt fantastic, and now she found she need only focus her intentions and the wings would do their work. Gently they lifted her feet off the ground and she came to rest beside Moss on the soft dandelion bed.

She wrapped her arms around his neck and he pulled her tight into his chest for a passionate kiss. The two became one and as their kiss lengthened and intensified, Moss reached out a hand to feel for the wooden sign. He spun it round so the words were clear to any potential visitor: DO NOT DISTURB!

The End

*If you have enjoyed reading about Rosie Quartz and her
friends, you can learn more about their stories
and adventures in future Faery Tales.*

*Find out what happens next in Book 2
The Faery Tale of Amy Thyst.*

Lightning Source UK Ltd.
Milton Keynes UK
UKOW03f1132110614

233212UK00002B/32/P